The Last City of Light

The Mistwalker Chronicles, Volume 2

Keller Marie

Published by Keller Marie, 2022.

THE LAST CITY OF LIGHT

First edition. September 1, 2022.

Copyright © 2022 Keller Marie.

ISBN: 979-8201089153

Written by Keller Marie.

Table of Contents

I dedicate this book to my aunt, Irene, for she always believed in my, even when nobody else did. I just wish I could have done more for her in the end.

"When I first found myself in these lands, there was nothing but darkness and despair. I was sure I was going to die, but then I was saved by the Illume. I still struggled, but their hopefulness in the survival of the Last City helped me to continue. Bhaskara; I have never seen anything like the city before, and the first time I saw the Last City it took my breath away. It's a spectacular sight, and I only wish I could have seen what the rest of the Illume cities looked like in comparison."

~ *Molly, Inducted Illume of Amshu*

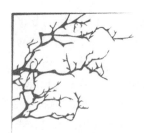

1

R ourke could feel his heart pounding in his chest, and he hadn't even actually made it to the city yet. Next to him, Sammy was all smiles; his hair, though a tangled mess, was pulled by the breeze that came up off the lake surrounding Bhaskara. Hesitantly, Rourke pulled his hood off, enjoying the fact he didn't have to wear it as they walked toward the city. "This is incredible. The entire valley is lit up! You didn't tell me that the cities looked like this." Sammy was babbling next to Rourke. "Your little stone can do *that*?"

"No, it's too small." Rourke shook his head, eyes trained on the city ahead of them. Before them, the crater opened, a large hole in what was once the mountain top. The hills — fields full of swaying purple-gray grass — all sloped gently down toward the center where they met the lake edge, a large body of water that served as another layer of protection from the Wolves. Rourke was sure that when the city was built, protection hadn't been one of the concerns, but it also partly explained why Bhaskara hadn't been attacked and destroyed like the rest of the cities. In the center of the lake, with only one long bridge to connect it to the surrounding land, sat the actual city of Bhaskara.

Rourke had never seen a city from the angle he saw Bhaskara now; from high above. It was something almost small and below him, but quickly growing larger as he walked down the hillside toward the bridge. The city was huge, glowing brightly from the middle of the lake, with a slight curve that reminded Rourke of a fish. Tall towers functioned as lookouts across the length of the island and dark roads crisscrossed the entire city. One road, darker and wider than most, must have been the market street, but from Rourke's vantage point it looked more like a horrible scar against the white light of the city. On the far side of the island, Rourke could see what looked like a patch of purple; more than likely the Sanctuary of Bhaskara.

Near what looked like the front of the city was the bridge that they were walking toward. Rourke could see the large city archway and was able to see the banners that were flying across it. Rourke's breath caught in his chest as he gripped tightly to the straps of his backpack. He wondered if the banner of Olin would be flying; hung as a way of remembrance for those who hadn't made it out of the destruction of the cities. Perhaps the banners of Amshu and all the other destroyed cities would be there, too.

Luna jumped through the grass, before she flopped over onto her side and rolled around. Next to Rourke, Sammy chuckled. "She's loving the grass, Rourke."

Rourke nodded in answer, watching the young shadow cat as she got up to chase bugs in the long grass. On the far side of the lake, Rourke spotted a large herd of umbra, grazing and ignoring everything around them. Things seemed peaceful here on the outskirts of the city, and Rourke hoped that remained true.

As they drew closer to the city, Rourke noticed two people standing by the edge of the bridge. Sammy must have spotted them, too, as he moved to Rourke's side after having wandered a little as he played with Luna. Sammy practically leaned against Rourke as they moved. "Who are they," he asked quietly.

"No idea," Rourke replied as he looked back to the bridge. "They could be part of the Illuminari that Aetius talked about."

"A city guard of sorts, that makes complete sense." Sammy stepped away from Rourke, and he felt lost without Sammy's touch. Reaching out, Rourke took Sammy's hand, holding tightly as they drew close to the bridge.

"You should call Luna to us," Rourke suggested. His heart was beating madly in his chest. The nervousness he felt at the lip of the crater was coming back with each step closer that they took toward the city.

"Luna," Sammy called. The shadow cat instantly turned back for them, trotting up to walk by their side. "Good girl," Sammy praised, reaching down to scratch behind her ears.

"The light shines upon you," one of the two guards called to them when they finally drew close enough, and Rourke felt his breath hitch as the reality of arriving began to fully set in. The forward arch of the bridge loomed overhead and gave off the appearance as if it were watching Sammy and Rourke's approach.

Rourke didn't answer right away, but after a moment of tripping over his words, he managed the reply. "And guide your steps," he said weakly, unsure of himself. Overhead, hanging from the archway, the many city banners of Bhaskara, Amshu, Olin, and so many others fluttered in the breeze. The largest and central banner must have been the one for Bhaskara; a black banner with a white argi embroidered onto it, open mouth showing many serrated teeth with powerful jaws.

Next to him, Sammy squeezed his hand. "I'm right here," Sammy murmured to Rourke. "What's the worst that can happen?"

Before Rourke had a chance to answer, one of the guards gasped. The marks on his cheeks scrunched with how large his smile was. "You're a Warden," he almost yelled, and Rourke turned to glare at Sammy.

Sammy frowned at Rourke and rolled his eyes. "Okay, sorry, I guess that can happen."

"Quiet," the second guard scolded. Rourke turned his attention to him. He was a little shorter than Rourke was, and his marks were dark, thick lines under his eyes and down his cheeks, as well as one down the middle of his forehead toward the bridge of his nose. At his side was a sword, one that Rourke instantly recognized as that of a Guardian, even if he hadn't seen any other styles besides his or Aetius' before. The white sheath of the weapon was a giveaway. "That's not how you speak to a Warden," the man finished.

Next to the guard was an argi — the same mighty animal as on the banner — a massive beast that had broad shoulders and a strong back, thick tree trunk-like legs, and clawed paws bigger than Rourke's hand that were able to easily carry the heavy weight of the animal. Rourke had only seen an argi once when he was little, but it was just as big as he remembered, maybe even bigger. The massive animal stood from where it had been dozing on the bridge, and the Guardian placed a gentle hand on the beast's head. "It's all right, Isik," he said calmly to the argi.

Rourke slowed to a stop just before the edge of the bridge. Luna was growling from where she had pressed herself against Sammy's leg. Sammy let go of Rourke's hand to crouch down to talk to her in an attempt to calm the shadow cat.

The demeanor of the two guards was strikingly different. The one who had the argi was much calmer than the other man, who seemed barely able to stand in place. Rourke felt dread twist in his gut. Even here it seemed, Illume of his position couldn't move about in peace, seemingly more coveted than the other Illume around them. "Welcome to Bhaskara, the Last City of Light. I'm Lor," the guard with the argi started. "And this Zohar. I'm sure you are tired from your journey. Come, I'll escort you to our city hall. I assume the shadow cat is trained."

"Her name's Luna," Sammy started with a nod. Standing, he gestured to himself then Rourke as he spoke. "I'm Sammy, and this is Rourke." Without even hesitating, Sammy stepped onto the bridge, leaving Rourke and Luna standing in the grass. Lor had turned slightly to listen to Sammy talk, eyes moving from Sammy to Rourke and back again. Zohar seemed far more interested in Rourke, watching every move that he made. It only made Rourke more nervous, and he hesitated.

He wasn't even in the city, and Rourke was already worried about how his position was going to affect him. Zohar's eyes remained on Rourke, and he felt himself take a step back, a sudden fear of moving forward welling in his chest. Rourke closed his eyes, trying to calm his racing heart, and realized his breathing was becoming short and fast. He could hear a ringing in his ears, and he felt hot and dizzy. "Sammy," he mumbled, unsure if he was even speaking out loud or not. Rourke staggered back a pace, feeling like the heavy weight of his backpack on his shoulders was trying to pull him to the ground.

"Rourke." Rourke heard Sammy say his name and felt hands press against his cheeks. "It's all right," Sammy started, voice low. "Just breathe. Take a deep breath, Rourke. Open your eyes and look at me."

Rourke raised his hands to grab Sammy by the arms. He tried to take a deep breath, but he seemed unable to do so. Sammy ran a hand through Rourke's hair before he tugged Rourke's hood back up over his head. His voice was low and calm as he spoke. "It's okay; I'm right here. Take a deep breath. You can do this."

Carefully, Rourke opened his eyes. Sammy *was* right there, close enough that if Rourke leaned forward just a little bit, their foreheads could touch. Mindlessly, he did so, feeling better the moment he did. His heart was still racing, and Rourke still felt hot, but he managed to inhale and exhale a deep, shaky breath. "I'm sorry."

"For what," Sammy asked, keeping one hand in Rourke's hair, fingers idly running through the short strands. "You haven't done anything wrong."

Rourke closed his eyes again. He felt like he should have been stronger than this; he'd hunted umbra and killed Wolves yet going back to his own people terrified him. "I shouldn't feel this way about being here."

Sammy chuckled lowly as he pressed a kiss to Rourke's forehead. "That's not true at all, but I can understand where you are coming from. You are safe here. *We* are safe here. You've done what you set out to do. You have made it here, guiding us along the way. Now let me guide you." Sammy took Rourke's hand in his own, cupping Rourke's cheek with his other hand. "Just stay with me, Rourke, and we will do this together. It's all we have done since that day you saved me."

Rourke frowned, grumbling under his breath as he spoke. "You sound ridiculous when you talk like that."

Sammy stifled a laugh. "You haven't stopped me yet. Come on. You ready?"

Rourke took a deep breath and pulled away from Sammy, but he didn't let go of his hand. He looked up at the arch that marked the entrance to Bhaskara along the bridge, and finally to a second, larger arch that was the true entrance to the city on the other side of the bridge. "I think so, yes," he said, hesitating for just a moment. "If you're with me."

"Who sounds ridiculous now," Sammy teased, bumping shoulders with Rourke. "They can't hurt you, and they can't take me away from you."

"I know," Rourke whispered. "I'm just nervous. I haven't been in a city since before the Wolves attacked. I stayed in the Sanctuary."

"I thought you said you lived in Olin," Sammy asked quietly as the two fell into step behind Lor. Lor stayed close, but also gave them their space, something Rourke was much more thankful for than he first thought he would have been. Next to Lor, the argi lumbered on quietly, much to Luna's hatred of the idea.

Rourke looked over his shoulder to see Zohar watching them as they walked away. He seemed upset, and Rourke couldn't help but think it had everything to do with the fact that Lor had been the one to take them to city hall. Moving his attention from Zohar, Rourke turned to Sammy as he tugged his hood a little farther down his forehead. "I did. Olin's Sanctuary was like a small and separate little town outside the city."

"That's because it was the first one." Lor turned slightly to face them. "Sorry, for intruding on your conversation. You won't find such a luxury here. The Sanctuary is built right into the city, Warden."

"Don't call me that." Frowning at Lor, Rourke took a deep breath. "My name is Rourke."

Lor tipped his head in a small nod. "I was just trying to maintain the respect you deserve, but if that's what you wish, I won't call you that. My committed, Alina, doesn't like to be called 'Warden,' either." Lor paused, a small smile tugging at the corners of his mouth as he clearly remembered something. "Though she doesn't have the same amount of hatred for it as you seem to have."

"Thank you," Rourke murmured, bobbing his head in a nod.

They fell silent after that as they walked across the bridge. Rourke kept a hold of Sammy's hand, grip tight as Lor led them under the second arch and toward city hall. When they arrived at the steps, he made his leave, and hoped to see them again once they undoubtedly arrived at the Sanctuary.

The sounds of the city were loud and overwhelming to Rourke. Every noise seemed to echo off the surrounding buildings, and it only caused Rourke to begin to regret coming into the city to begin with. Searching for something to distract himself, Rourke looked up the steps toward city hall, eyes drifting over the banners that hung from the roof. Next to him, Sammy watched Lor leave, the argi by his side. "He seemed nice," Sammy commented, turning back to Rourke.

Rourke shrugged, turning away from the banner of Olin to look at Sammy. He was looking at Rourke, a soft and worried expression on his face. "What," Rourke asked.

"Are you okay? I know this is a lot for you. It must bring back a lot of memories."

Rourke took a deep breath and sighed as he turned back to the banners. "You see the white banner on the far left? The one with the haldis?"

"You still haven't explained to me what a haldis is, Rourke." Sammy pointed. "I assume you mean the one right next to the purple banner that has the same symbol as my backpack?"

"Yes." Rourke nodded. "That's the banner of Amshu, which was near Olin. The one to the left, the white one is the banner of Olin. The banner of my home. The symbol in the middle is a haldis. You'll see them at the Sanctuary, I hope."

"What's the Sanctuary?"

Rourke started up the steps before he turned back to face Sammy. "You'll see," he started, the smallest hint of a smile playing at the corners of his mouth. "It's where the haldis live, and where the Order resides."

"Is that where they are going to send you — send us — to this Sanctuary? Simply because you are a Warden?"

"I thought I asked you not to call me that."

"I wasn't calling you a Warden, I meant it in a general sense. I guess I mean —" Sammy paused as they walked up the steps, taking a deep breath when they reached the top and started walking across a cobblestone yard toward the large wooden doors. "I guess I just mean, whoever is in charge won't give you the option of asking where you want to go. They will see that you are a Warden and assume you want to go to the Sanctuary."

Rourke sighed, resting his hand on the handle of one of the two doors. He was nervous, was growing more and more nervous with each step that he took. He knew Sammy spoke the truth, and he hated to think that his wants and requests would go unheard simply because of his position in their culture. Rourke also knew there probably would be no use trying to argue, either. He was getting a headache and the bright light of the city was already becoming too much for him to bear.

"The light hurts my eyes," he murmured to Sammy in a way of explanation, although Rourke was sure it would only confuse his committed even more. With another deep breath, Rourke pulled open the door to city hall, ushering Sammy and Luna inside before he followed behind them.

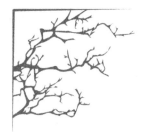

2

Sammy had never seen anything like this building before. While it somehow resembled the city hall of his home — large open spaces where voices echoed — it was also vastly different. Dark stone and wood made up most of the building with smaller pieces of bhasvah set here and there to give the interior light. High and thin windows let in light from outside, reminding Sammy of the sun filtering through panes of glass, but he knew it was just the light of the stone from outside the walls of city hall.

As the door closed behind them, Sammy noticed a board with several pieces of rough paper pinned to it. Everything was written in a language he didn't understand with an elegant ink. He turned to ask Rourke, but Sammy found Rourke crouched on the floor with Luna in between his legs as he scratched her chest. Concern twisted in his chest, but he pressed on nonetheless. "Can you read these," Sammy asked as he pointed toward the board. Rourke looked at him, but Sammy was unable to figure out what the expression on his face meant. "It's an honest question, Rourke, because I can't read this."

"I can, a little," Rourke started, keeping his fingers buried in Luna's thick fur. "But I haven't tried since before Olin fell. I can remember not really liking having to go to lessons."

"So, you probably can't read this stuff then?" Sammy waved a hand toward the board and sighed heavily. Running his hand through his hair, he looked around. "All right. I guess I just figured Lor would be a bit more helpful than he was. Kind of a jerk move to just leave us here and not give us any direction on where to go or what to do." Walking over to Rourke, Sammy reached out to scratch behind one of Luna's ears. "Are you okay?"

"No, I'm still nervous. I have a headache and my eyes hurt." Reaching up, Rourke rubbed his forehead with the back of his hand.

Sammy frowned. "You said that. I wonder if it's a combination from the stress and being in the light after being in the darkness for so long. So, like a tension headache."

"Just hurts," Rourke mumbled as he moved to rub his temples.

"I know." Sammy leaned down and pressed a kiss to Rourke's cheek. "I'll see if I can maybe find someone to help us. Keep an eye on Luna."

"She's going to want to go with you."

"I know, that's why I asked you to keep an eye on her, Rourke. She is going to try to follow me." Sammy spoke as he moved, half turning as he stepped away from Rourke. They were right, Luna tried to follow Sammy, but Rourke wrapped his arms around her chest and spoke to her, quieting her down as Sammy walked down the open entryway.

There were several closed doors, but Sammy had no idea where any of them led and had no way to tell either since he couldn't read the carved stone plaques that he assumed served as directions and location identifiers. He was almost to the end of the hall when a young woman came down a set of large stairs that opened onto the first floor. "May the light shine upon you," she started, gasping in shock at seeing Sammy.

"And, um," Sammy started, blushing in embarrassment because he couldn't remember the rest of the greeting he had heard Rourke, Molly, and Aetius use. It took Sammy a moment to collect his thoughts, distracted as he was by the thin marks that traveled down the length of her nose. "Can you help us?"

"Us," the young woman asked. She looked past Sammy as he pointed back to where Rourke and Luna still sat. "Oh! Yes, of course, you must be refugees! My name's Aila. I'd be more than happy to help you. If you would follow me, I can bring you to Siraj; he's in charge of entering new refugees into the books of Bhaskara."

"Oh, okay, that would be great. Thank you." Sammy turned to look at Rourke, smiling at him as he stood and started walking toward Sammy. Luna trotted ahead, pushing her head between Sammy's legs as she came up to him. Aila took a step back, clearly scared of Luna, but Sammy reached down to pet her, reassuring Aila that Luna wouldn't hurt her.

Rourke walked up to Sammy's side but remained quiet as he reached for Sammy's hand. With a curt nod, Aila motioned across the hall, and slipped past Sammy, Rourke, and Luna. She opened the last door in the hall that Sammy had barely even realized was there. It opened into a low and broad hallway that was much darker than the main hall, but still bright with periodic bhasvah stones along the wall. "Right this way." Aila smiled, ushering them into the hall.

It was a quiet walk down the hall to another door, and Sammy got the feeling that despite Luna behaving herself and walking quietly, Aila was very scared of her. Sammy could understand why, especially if what Rourke had said about shadow cats not usually being pets was true, but Luna had been trained by them both, and was very well mannered. Sammy had no worries that Luna would do anything, but he kept an eye on her just the same.

Clearing her throat, Aila stopped at a door, her hand on the handle. "Siraj is right through this door. He should be of more assistance than I have been. Welcome to Bhaskara." With a curt nod, she pushed open the door before she turned and almost fled back down the hallway. Sammy watched her go before he turned his attention toward the room.

It was clearly an office, and Sammy found it sort of ironic that even here, in this place that was so very different from where he'd come from, of all things *offices* were still pretty much the same. He snorted back a laugh, sheepishly clearing his throat when Rourke looked over at him and was clearly not impressed with Sammy laughing. "Sorry," he muttered quietly. "I'll tell you later."

"Whatever," Rourke muttered, turning back toward the simple room. There was a desk and a couple small windows to allow for light to filter in from outside. The room wasn't very big, but big enough for Sammy, Rourke, and Luna to stand comfortably without bumping into the desk or the walls. There were two doors, each one on a different wall of the room. One of them opened just as Rourke sighed heavily and rubbed his temples again. Sammy was sure his headache was making this entire thing that much more difficult for Rourke.

An older man stepped out with black hair that was graying around his temples. Sammy could only assume that this was Siraj as he stopped short, clearly startled by Rourke and Sammy's presence in his workspace. "For the love of the light," he started, raising a hand to his chest. "You boys startled me! Ah! Forgive me; may the light shine upon you. My name's Siraj."

Rourke tipped his head in a small nod. "And guide your steps," he said easily, even though his voice was low.

Siraj hurried over to his desk and sat, flipping open a thick book that sat in the center of the desk. "Have you just arrived in the city? Usually refugees are sent to me, so that must be the case."

"Yes." Sammy nodded. "Aila brought us here."

"Ah, yes, yes. That makes sense." Siraj nodded as he continued to flip through the pages before he stopped with a small, excited gasp. "Here we are! Now, I will need your names and the city where you have come from."

Rourke took a deep breath next to Sammy, grabbed his hand and squeezed tightly. Sammy looked down at their joined hands before looking up to Rourke as he started speaking. "This is Sammy; and I'm Rourke." Rourke paused and bit his lip. Sammy could see he was nervous and waited quietly next to him, silently encouraging Rourke to continue. Rourke looked over at Sammy before turning back to Siraj. Sammy could hear the shake in Rourke's voice as he continued, "Warden of Olin."

"Warden of Olin," Siraj murmured as he wrote. Sammy could hear the scratch of the quill pen he held in his hand. "Warden of Olin," he almost yelled a second time, slamming his hands down on his desk. "You're a *Warden*?" Siraj stood, moving back toward the door he had exited from just moments before. "Why didn't you say so! Wait right there! I will get one of the Nari to take you to the Sanctuary!" Without even waiting for an answer, Siraj slammed the door and was gone.

Rourke groaned, dropped his forehead against Sammy's shoulder, and squeezed his hand tighter.

"That went well, I think." Sammy rested his cheek on top of Rourke's head.

"This is a disaster," Rourke muttered as he pulled away. While he didn't let go of Sammy's hand, Rourke did seem to close in on himself a little bit, hunching his shoulders as he pulled his hood down farther over his face.

"Your headache," Sammy asked, knowing it was more than just Rourke's headache that was bothering him. Rourke was clearly anxious over this entire ordeal. He'd told Sammy how much he hated the position he held in his culture, and even though Sammy didn't fully understand what being a Warden entailed, if Rourke wanted nothing to do with it, then Sammy was going to stand behind him. "Do you think you will be able to relax once we get to this Sanctuary? I assume there will be other people like you there, right?"

"Yeah," Rourke nodded, finally turning to look at Sammy. "I don't know what will happen, but I always felt normal in Olin. Hopefully, that will remain true here in Bhaskara."

"Well, good, then it's almost over." Smiling, Sammy leaned over and pressed his forehead against Rourke's, moving his free hand up to rest against the back of Rourke's neck. "Maybe we can get something for your headache, too."

"Maybe," Rourke murmured quietly, eyes closing as he spoke. Sammy was glad he was able to offer even a little bit of comfort to Rourke, but he wished he was able to do more.

Across the room, the door slammed open, and Siraj returned with another man following close behind. Sammy looked up, noticing the wide-eyed look the newcomer was giving Rourke, as if some celebrity was standing in front of him. "It would be an honor," the young man started, voice sounding almost whimsical as he spoke. "To escort you, Warden —"

"Rourke," Rourke interrupted.

"To the Sanctuary," the young man finished without even acknowledging Rourke's request. He bowed his head in respect. "My name is Ilo. Please, we should go."

Ilo turned toward the second door in the room, walking across the office space easily before opening the door. Light flooded into the dim room along with all the sounds and smells of a busy city. Sammy felt Rourke stiffen next to him and Sammy turned to look at him again. "You got this, Rourke. I'm right here. It's almost over."

"When I was last in a city, it didn't end well." Even though Sammy could see Rourke was nervous, clearly remembering something he wasn't talking about, he took that first step toward the door and Ilo. Sammy stayed by his side, and Luna walked calmly ahead of them, pausing to sniff Ilo's pants before she made her way outside. To Ilo's credit, he didn't react to Luna except to pale and swallow thickly in fear. Sammy couldn't help but smirk as Rourke and himself passed the guard out onto a small porch.

Siraj sat back at his desk and picked up his quill. "Forgive me, I do need more information from you. I can send someone to the

Sanctuary to collect it later though. It has been a long while since a Warden has come to the city, and I admit my excitement got the better of me. Please follow Ilo, and again: welcome to Bhaskara."

Rourke completely ignored Siraj. Sammy looked over to him, smiled in acknowledgement, and turned back to Ilo and Luna. Luna had made her way down the steps and was sitting in a narrow alley, washing her face with her paw. The sounds of a working city became very loud, and Sammy couldn't help but smile at the thought that yeah, some things would be the same here after all. It wasn't quite the same sounds he was used to; instead of cars and horns, Sammy could hear the clomping of hooves and what sounded like animal calls, but there was still the yelling of people, and that brought some sort of comfort to Sammy.

Ilo closed the door behind them and made his way down the steps. "This way, please, Warden. The Sanctuary is on the other side of the city, and it's a busy part of the cycle."

Rourke heaved a very defeated sigh, and ever so slowly made his way down the steps. Sammy followed right along with him, and when they reached Luna, she stood, walking with them behind Ilo toward the end of the small alley. Rourke stopped just before they turned onto a larger and more open street, tugging on Sammy's arm as he did. "I haven't been in a city since I was very little," he said, but Sammy got the impression that Rourke was more speaking to himself than Sammy. "I can remember being with my father, and everyone we saw wanted to stop and talk to us because we were both, well, you know."

Sammy nodded. Rourke didn't have to say the word for Sammy to know he meant being a Warden. He couldn't imagine what it would have been like for every person they saw to want to speak to them. Rourke's reaction to all of this, as well as how reluctant he was to tell anyone he was a Warden or show his hair color made a lot more sense now.

"And now you will go into a city again," Sammy replied, turning to face Rourke. Behind them, Sammy could hear the bustle of the city growing louder, and he realized he was really excited to see Rourke's culture. "I will be with you to help keep people away. I need you to show me," Sammy started, tugging on Rourke's arm. "I need you to show me this city."

"I've never been here, Sammy." Rourke frowned, but Sammy was glad to see Rourke back to his old self if only for a moment right now. "I don't know Bhaskara."

"I've never been here, either!" Sammy laughed. "Come on, Rourke! Aren't you excited to explore?"

"Not really. I told you I have a headache."

"I know. I didn't mean right now, but we will be exploring in a way as we head for the Sanctuary, right? I'm excited to see this place. It's already been more than I could have ever imagined, Rourke! I want to see more. And." Sammy closed the small gap between them and kissed Rourke firmly before he pulled away. "I want to see it with you."

Rourke turned his head away, the faintest of blushes coloring his cheeks. Sammy couldn't help but grin as he watched Rourke close his eyes, clearly flustered with Sammy, as well as everything else. After a deep breath, Rourke opened his eyes, looking at Sammy intently. "All right," Rourke started, and Sammy found he couldn't look away. The intensity of Rourke's eyes was captivating. "Let's go."

THE LAST CITY OF LIGHT

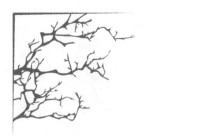

3

Ilo walked along ahead of them, giving Rourke and Sammy just enough distance to maintain a sense of privacy, but close enough so that Sammy was able to always keep his eyes on him. Not that Sammy was doing much of that; the sights of Bhaskara were wonderful, and Sammy found he was looking pretty much at everything except where it was Ilo was taking them. He kept his hand firmly grasped with Rourke's, but it didn't stop Sammy from pausing every now and again, and making Rourke have to tug on his arm to keep him moving.

The buildings were incredible. They were amazing structures built from bhasvah stone, wood, as well as a darker stone that didn't glow. A lot of them reminded Sammy of a much simpler time in his own world's history, and it almost felt like he'd been brought back in time in order to see those buildings in their best days. The roads were made of cobbled dark stone, creating definitive lines that crisscrossed the entire city.

Ilo turned a corner onto a broader road, and Sammy paused, breath catching in his throat at the sight before him. Next to him, Rourke groaned, and Sammy caught him pulling his hood a little lower over his face from the corner of his eye. "This way, please," Ilo started, looking over his shoulder to Rourke and Sammy. "Stay close, the market is very crowded right now."

"This is the market?" Sammy was in awe, excitement bubbling through him at the sounds and sights all around him. People were yelling, trying to sell their wares; food, clothing, tapestries, reagents, and anything else that Sammy could possibly think of, and he was sure there were a lot of things he couldn't think of. People were everywhere. Men, women, and children walked up and down the street, pausing to buy food, or look at fabric.

Ilo pushed on ahead, and Rourke tugged on Sammy's hand once again. "Come on," he insisted, and Sammy frowned as he turned back to Rourke.

"All right. I was just looking. This is fascinating!" Sammy laughed as he started walking. Rourke's grip on his hand was tight, and Sammy leaned over to rest his head on Rourke's shoulder. "I know you're nervous, but I'm right here with you. I just want to look, is all. This is nothing like I have ever seen before! The city is like something out of a children's story to me."

"You come from a weird place," Rourke grumbled, stopping short as someone stepped out in front of him. The young woman apologized quickly before turning away. Sammy turned to watch her go, smirking when she met up with another young woman, both turning to look over their shoulders to Sammy and Rourke. Both had long black hair and light gray eyes, the tattoos on their faces vastly more intricate than any Sammy had seen so far.

Sammy raised his hand in a small wave, chuckling when both women turned from him, whispering and giggling to one another at presumably being caught staring at them both. Rourke elbowed him in the ribs, and Sammy coughed, turning to face him. "What," he asked, rubbing at his side with his free hand. "I wasn't doing anything."

"You were flirting with them." Rourke hesitated as he spoke, turning his head forward so Sammy wouldn't see his face.

"Hm," Sammy shrugged. "I guess I was. I didn't mean anything by it." Sammy reached up and tugged the edge of Rourke's hood aside so he could see his face. Rourke was scowling, eyes searching the street ahead. He was still tense; Sammy could see it in the set of his jaw. "Does it bother you? I'm sorry, that wasn't my intention."

"I don't know," Rourke shrugged. "I'm too upset right now to give you an honest answer."

"Fair." Sammy nodded, squeezing Rourke's hand in his own and turning to find Ilo in the throng of people. "I'll stop. I didn't realize I was doing it. I'm just really excited." Leaning over, Sammy pressed a kiss to Rourke's cheek. "You're still my favorite."

"Thanks." Rourke rolled his eyes, but Sammy could see the slightest hint of a smile on his lips.

Ahead of them, Ilo stopped at an intersection, pointing toward the right side of the street as he waited for them to approach. "Not much further. The Sanctuary is just on the other side of this alleyway."

Rourke sighed, and Sammy felt the tension bleed out of him. Despite not wanting to remain in the Order, a part of Rourke had to be relieved to be returning to something he knew, even if it wasn't exactly where he had come from. The Sanctuary would be familiar to Rourke, and Sammy hoped that Rourke would be able to relax and be more like himself once again. He didn't like seeing Rourke tense, worried, and anxious. Those emotions didn't suit the swordsman one bit.

Ilo turned onto the road, which was smaller and less crowded than the loud and busy market street. The tall buildings seemed to crowd in as they towered over the alleyway, their dark stone and wooden structures the normal for the parts of the city Sammy had seen so far. There were still lots of people walking around, but there was also more space to maneuver, even with it being a smaller street. Sammy looked around, fascinated by the buildings with their tapestries to help dim some of the light. "Was your home like this," Sammy asked suddenly, turning to look at Rourke.

"The city was." Rourke looked around before he shook his head. "But the Sanctuary was not. It was built mostly out of wood. We had bhasvah structures, but I can remember my home was wood, as well as most of the other homes."

"I bet it was still beautiful."

"It was," Rourke whispered, still looking around to the different buildings. "I wish you could have seen it."

"I have you. That's enough." Sammy smiled as Rourke looked at him, a faint blush coloring his cheeks.

"This way," Ilo interrupted, pointing to his left as he turned the corner. Luna looked over her shoulder to where Rourke and Sammy were, waiting for them before she followed Ilo.

"She seems very nervous," Rourke commented, and Sammy couldn't help but agree. Luna did seem nervous and leery of her surroundings, but Sammy was also thankful that Luna was serving as a distraction to help take Rourke's mind off whatever it was he was thinking about.

Rounding the corner after Ilo and Luna, Sammy stopped. "Oh wow," he gasped in shock, looking at the wall in front of him. It was made entirely of bhasvah and taller than he was. The entire length of it was carved with intricate patterns of trees, and animals, much like the wall of the city they had stumbled across in their travels. Along the top was what appeared to be a type of climbing vine with dark blue-gray leaves. Small moths flitted around the bright yellow flowers. Farther down the road was a beautiful archway with a wooden sign hanging from it, words Sammy couldn't read carved into it and stained black with some sort of paint. From where he stood, Sammy could just barely see what appeared to be purplish colored grass on the other side of the archway opening. "Rourke, this is amazing."

"Yeah, it really is," Rourke agreed, nodding as he let go of Sammy's hand. "Come on." Sammy looked over to Rourke as he pushed his hood back and ran a hand through his hair. "You haven't seen anything yet. The haldis are incredible." Rourke had a huge smile on his face, making Sammy smile, too. Even with everything that Rourke had talked about, he seemed excited now that he was actually here.

Ilo stood by the archway to the Sanctuary, looking down at Luna from where she stood a few feet from him. She was peering inside the Sanctuary, but thankfully wasn't going inside. "I shall leave you here. I hope you find Bhaskara to your liking." With another slight bow, Ilo turned and walked away, leaving them at the doorway to the sanctuary.

Rourke crouched down, pulling Luna against him as he leaned close to her. She twisted her head to lick his face, and Rourke let her as he wrapped his arm around her tightly. "I know you understand me," he started, and Sammy watched carefully. While Rourke interacted with Luna regularly, he'd never spoken to Luna as he was speaking to her now. "We are about to step into a very sacred place. A place created specifically for the haldis. You have to behave yourself here." Standing, Rourke looked over to Sammy. "Of all the things I would want to show you within the city, to me this is the most important one."

Sammy walked over to Rourke and reached for his hand. "We can do it together, same as we have been."

"Yeah." Rourke nodded, looking through the archway into the Sanctuary. "We can."

Sammy bumped Rourke's shoulder with his own. "Whenever you're ready."

Rourke nodded as he took a deep breath. "All right." Sammy could see he was getting nervous again, and he squeezed Rourke's hand in his own. Glancing over at him, Rourke smiled, then moved, walking under the archway into the Sanctuary without hesitation. Just like everything else they had done together up until this point, Sammy walked with him.

The small patch of purple grass opened into a large field, a few houses and smaller dark stone walls littering the area. The Sanctuary seemed much calmer than the rest of the city, and Sammy could see Rourke starting to relax a little bit as they looked around. Though the sounds of the city could still be heard, they seemed muffled in the Sanctuary, almost as if they had stepped out of the city and into a completely different space. Off toward their left, two people came walking toward them, unaware of Rourke and Sammy's presence for the moment. Both had green hair, completely different shades of green from Rourke's hair, and Sammy looked over to Rourke as Rourke snorted back a laugh.

"Of course, we have different hair colors, Sammy. Not everyone has hair as dark as mine."

"I said that out loud?" Sammy felt his cheeks flush in embarrassment. "I'm sorry. I guess I just sort of assumed all Wardens would have the same color hair, just like albinos are all lacking pigment."

"I told you I'm not albino," Rourke started, pausing as the two people noticed their presence and called out to them. Rourke returned the greeting before looking over at Sammy. "And I asked you not to call me that."

"I know. I'm sorry. Again, I just meant it as a general thing, not a 'you' specific thing."

"I'm so sorry I didn't see you! I hope you haven't been standing here long. You must be refugees. I'm Alina." The young woman spoke as she approached, raising a hand to throw a thick braid of mint colored hair over her shoulder. She had thin tattoos that started under her eyes and ran along her cheeks to disappear under her chin. She wiped her hands on an apron she had tied around her waist. "And this is Isa."

The young man at her side waved a hand. "Hi."

Sammy smiled, noticing he didn't have any tattoos like Rourke, and made a mental note to ask Rourke about it later. "Nice to meet you both," Sammy nodded. "I'm Sammy, and this is Rourke." Sammy waved a hand toward Luna. "This is —"

"Luna!" Rourke scowled as she started growling. Crouching down next to her, he wrapped his arm around her again, keeping her close to his side. A large group of strange, scaled creatures was coming toward them, led by two that were several steps ahead of the others. "Shhh, it's all right," Rourke said to Luna as the first two creatures approached, walking up to Alina and Isa respectively.

Alina bent down to pick up the large one that was pawing at her skirt while Isa laughed and crouched down to scoop the small animal off its feet. The rest of the creatures swarmed around them, crowding not only Alina and Isa, but Rourke and Sammy, as well. Luna growled again, raising one paw as if to strike, but Rourke pressed her foot back to the grass.

Sammy had never seen anything like these creatures before. They were roughly the size of a cat; the largest ones were a little bigger than a happily overfed house cat and the smallest ones were the size of a young kitten. They walked on thick back legs, and looked up to everyone with dark beady eyes, small trembling ears turning to listen as they waited quietly. One of them yawned, showing a mouth full of tiny needle-like teeth and a long pink tongue that curled comically during the innocent display.

Each one was covered in thick diamond-shaped plated scales from the tip of their narrow snouts to the end of their long prehensile tails that were held off the ground. Front feet were held close to their rounded bodies with long curved claws blunted from digging through dirt. They were brownish in color but ranged from a deep chocolate to a light tan. Some even looked to have a tinge of purplish gray to them, while others seemed to have splotches of the weird color covering several of the scales. No two animals were the same color, or had the same patterns, each one unique in its own way.

Rourke had shifted to rest on his knees, and with one arm still wrapped around Luna, he reached his other hand out into the crowd of small creatures. They crowded around him, bumping into one another and making themselves shuffle back and forth on their front legs and claws. Rourke ignored them all, stretching his hand out toward a smaller one at the very back of the herd. While it seemed like it wanted to partake in the excitement, it held off, and Sammy wondered if it had something to do with what looked like a nasty injury to its shoulder. As it rose onto its back legs to sniff Rourke's fingers, Sammy could see that the scales that should have been covering the animal's shoulder were missing. He watched quietly as Rourke curled his pinkie and ring finger to brush against the side of the creature's head while it sniffed his fingers. As soon as he touched the animal, it squeaked in fear and backed away, turning and waddling off away from the rest of the group.

With a defeated sigh, Rourke dropped his arm and stood. He seemed much calmer now, a huge smile on his face as he took a step back, mindful of the animals, to stand next to Sammy. "These are haldis," Rourke explained, still smiling.

"Like Orin," Sammy asked. Rourke's smile faded, but he nodded.

"Isa, will you take the herd back to the water, please." Alina set her haldis down on the ground.

"Yeah, sure thing! Come on, everyone!" Making his way through the crowd at their feet, Isa wandered away, the large group of animals all turning and lumbering after him. "It was nice meeting you two," he called back with a wave.

"You, too," Sammy answered.

"I'm sorry about that," Alina started. "Our herd is very nosy, and always has to greet anyone who comes into the Sanctuary."

"It's all right," Rourke said, watching them move away from where they stood. "It's been so long since I have seen haldis, I —" He cut himself off. "It's fine," he said instead.

"I am sure there is much you wish to do now that you are here. But first, would you like to put your things down, maybe wash up, eat, and rest? I can show you to one of the smaller homes that are empty right now, and then let the High Warden know you are here."

Rourke nodded, reaching out to take Sammy's hand. "That would be great, thank you."

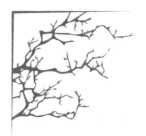

4

"Do you mind if I ask which city you are from?"

Rourke looked over to Alina as she walked next to him. Her haldis came running back across the yard and she bent to pick it up, hugging the large animal close to her chest. "Far away," Rourke started. "I'm from Olin. We are from Olin." Rourke looked over at Sammy, who was once again looking around and only half paying attention to Rourke. Rourke didn't mind, Sammy was simply mesmerized by everything around them. Rourke couldn't blame him; the Bhaskaran Sanctuary was nice for its small size.

Alina nodded. "The first city. I have been told it's a long journey. I always wanted to go there, but then..."

Rourke nodded, understanding where she was going. "It's gone now, I'm sorry."

"Don't be sorry. It's not your fault." Alina hugged her haldis a little tighter to her chest. "I'm glad you've made it to our Sanctuary, Rourke. Forgive me for asking, but I am curious as to where your haldis is, though."

"He's gone," Rourke whispered, feeling sorrow twist in his chest. "I wasn't able to save him when the city fell."

Alina gasped. "I'm so sorry. I didn't mean — I would be lost if something ever happened to Izusa." Reaching out, Alina placed a hand on Rourke's arm. "Our herd is your herd now, Rourke. I know it's not the same, and I am sure they could never replace your haldis, but please try to make our Sanctuary your new home."

"We'll see." Rourke smiled briefly, looking over to where he could see Isa and a few children playing in the water with the haldis.

Some lounged on the edge of the water in the mud or grass, while others splashed around in the shallow water with Isa and the children. He took a deep breath, remembering his own childhood when he used to do the very same thing. "I don't know how long I can stay here."

"Why would you leave?" Alina looked at Rourke and frowned. "Forgive me, it's not my place to ask. The house I was talking about is right over here." Alina pointed to a small single level wooden house near the water. It had two steps up onto a small porch and a tapestry for a door. "It's not a lot, but it's the best I can offer for the moment. I will go and speak to Ozni, he's the High Warden, if you would like."

Rourke stepped up onto the porch, followed by Luna and Sammy. "That would be excellent. Please let him know that I wish to speak to him. Thank you for all that you have done." Rourke felt a sudden want to be alone wash over him, and he very badly wanted to end this conversation with Alina so he could try to get some sleep.

Sammy walked up next to Rourke and rested his hands on the railing of the porch. "It's been so lovely to meet you, Alina," he started, all smiles like he normally was. Rourke was very appreciative of Sammy's normalcy right now, after the cycle they'd had, he needed it.

Alina smiled, shifting Izusa in her arms. "You, too, Sammy; Rourke!" She waved and turned to leave but stopped. "Oh! I almost forgot! You two must join myself and my committed for dinner later. I am sure you would love to have a home cooked meal after your travels."

"Yes, thank you." Rourke nodded, hands gripping the porch railing. He could feel himself growing more impatient with each passing moment. He knew it wasn't Alina's fault, but he could feel his headache growing worse, and the thought of being able to lay down in a real bed was very welcoming.

"Great! I will have my committed come get you later. His name's Lor. Enjoy your rest!" With that, Alina turned and walked away, leaving Rourke and Sammy on the porch to themselves.

"She said Lor," Sammy sputtered next to him.

Rourke shrugged. "Makes sense. He did say his committed was here, after all."

"I just didn't expect to meet her like that!"

Rourke chuckled. "Come on. I still have a headache. Let's get some sleep."

"I like Alina much better than Lor," Sammy grumbled as he followed Rourke into the small house. There was one large room with a square table and chairs big enough for four people. In the corner, under a window, was a bench with a stone washbowl, a pitcher for water, and a few towels stacked neatly on top. Off to the right of where Rourke stood, he could see a second doorway, a curtain tied to the side of the door allowing Rourke to see the corner of what looked like a large bed. Behind him, Sammy gasped, and Luna started sniffing around the corners as she explored. "This is cute."

"It's little," Rourke agreed, taking off his backpack and setting it on the table. As he unbuckled his sword from his waist to set on the table as well, he looked over his shoulder to Sammy, noticing a door that could be closed for more privacy.

Sammy walked past Rourke over toward the bedroom, peering in before he turned back to Rourke with a large grin on his face. "It's bigger than the cave, and the bed looks comfortable."

"That's good." Rourke nodded, only half listening to Sammy. He took his sword from his side and rested it on the table. Then he pulled out one of the chairs to sit and take off his boots. "I don't know about you, but I'm tired."

"I'm not actually. I'm really excited, and I kind of want to go explore!" Rourke could hear Sammy moving around behind him as he took off his backpack. His boots thunked across the wooden floor as Sammy came to crouch down in front of Rourke, resting his forearms on Rourke's knees. "Do you think it would be okay if I went out and looked around the city for a little while?"

"This is our home now," Rourke started. "You might as well begin to settle in." Shaking his head, he leaned down, careful of Sammy, to untie his boot. "Do what you want. I am going to sleep and see if I can't get this headache to go away."

Sammy reached up and ran a hand through Rourke's hair, pressing a kiss to his temple. "You should relax. You did it though, got through everything. Now we are here, and we can take things at your own pace."

"I hope." Rourke turned his head to look at Sammy, but this close he looked more like a blur than anything, and Rourke could feel the warmth of Sammy's skin against his cheek even though they weren't quite touching. Closing that small gap, Rourke pressed a simple kiss to Sammy's cheek, feeling the scratch of his beard, before resting his head against Sammy's shoulder. "Thank you."

Sammy twisted, dropping to his knees, and hugged Rourke even though the angle was awkward. One hand pressed against the back of Rourke's head. "You're welcome," Sammy murmured. "Though I am not sure what I did."

"Just being here; doing this with me. I'm glad you're with me." Rourke raised his arms to wrap them around Sammy's shoulders.

Sammy hugged Rourke a little tighter before he let go, pushing Rourke back to arm's length in the chair. "You get some sleep, and I am going to go explore. I won't get lost; I promise."

Rourke nodded, smirking. "You better not because I will not go out there to come get you."

"Thanks." Sammy rolled his eyes and huffed. "Some boyfriend you are." Standing, Sammy took a step back before he pulled Rourke to his feet. "I won't be gone too long, I don't think." Leaning forward, he pressed a chaste kiss to the corner of Rourke's mouth before he turned for the door. "Can I leave Luna here with you?"

"Of course." Rourke nodded, looking over his shoulder to see where Luna had gotten off to and spotted her sneaking her way into the bedroom. Looking back to Sammy, Rourke grabbed him by the arm and pulled him close, pressing their foreheads together. "Stay safe."

"I'm only going exploring. I will be fine." Sammy chuckled, raising his hands to rest on Rourke's hips. "You worry too much."

"Stay away from the umbra."

"Yes, yes." Sammy turned his head and kissed Rourke again. "I will be fine. Go to sleep. I will be back before you know it."

Rourke nodded as Sammy walked to the door, pushing the tapestry aside and reaching for the door. "Bye," Sammy said as he closed the door and left. Rourke stood for a moment, not sure what to do. Despite being on his own for as long as he had, he's grown so used to Sammy's presence that now that they were apart, even if for a little while, he felt lost. Luna walked over to the small window by the door and jumped up, mewing as she must have watched Sammy walk away.

"Come on, Luna." Rourke walked over to her, scratching behind her ears as he looked out the window. All he could see was the porch and the other small houses nearby. He could hear the haldis, Isa, and the children splashing about, but he couldn't see anything. "Let's get some sleep."

Turning, Rourke walked across the small space to the bedroom doorway, resting a hand on the frame as he called to Luna. She turned from the window, making her way over to him. The bedroom was small, the large bed taking up most of the space with a small desk and a bureau to complete the furniture. With a groan, Rourke sat on the bed, took his knife from its place at his back, set it on the small table, then laid down, throwing his arms over his head in a stretch.

Luna jumped up on the bed next to Rourke, licking his face before she laid down near him.

Twisting his head to look at her, Rourke reached out to pet her idly as he thought about what was going to happen now that he was here. He knew he didn't want to stay in the Order, but he didn't know how to approach that conversation with the High Warden other than simply saying it. His talk with Aetius about the Illuminari came to mind and Rourke took a deep breath. He trusted Aetius' opinion, and he had said the Illuminari would be a good place for Rourke to go since he didn't want to continue with the Order.

Rourke shifted on the bed, lying lengthwise and accidentally kicking Luna as he got comfortable. She huffed, he apologized, and all was forgiven as she crawled her way up to lay against his side with her head on his chest. Resting a hand on her neck, fingers sinking into the thick fur, Rourke thought about taking her collar off, but decided it was something he would have to discuss with Sammy first. With all the new sights, smells, and sounds of the city, it would be wise to leave the collar on her. "We could get you a proper collar once we settle in and get some scale coin," Rourke said to Luna, but she was already asleep.

Taking a deep breath, Rourke closed his eyes and tried to clear his mind. So much had happened so very quickly and it was all swirling about in Rourke's head. He inhaled again through his nose, holding his breath a moment before he exhaled the same way, deciding to just listen. He was in a Sanctuary again, and that meant that the haldis were close. After another deep breath, Rourke was starting to relax, feeling content to lay on the bed with Luna by his side. The haldis began to chatter, a low and constant jumbled hum in the back of his mind, the whole herd, he realized. For a fleeting moment, Rourke wondered if this was what happened to Wardens who lost their haldis before they, too, became Last Lights. He wondered if they became able to hear the entire herd over the single voice of their own companion. Just before Rourke fell asleep, he thought he heard the herd quiet down as one voice rose above the rest, but when he woke up, he didn't remember what had happened, and even the herd had fallen silent.

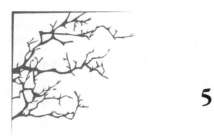

5

The city of Bhaskara was truly a wonder to behold. Sammy had to be careful as he moved about because he kept bumping into people and not paying attention to where he was going. He happened to notice a cart being pulled by two large umbra — their wide antlers helping to clear the way for them as people moved aside to let them pass. Sammy didn't think much of it as he moved, stepping into the doorway of one of the many buildings along the market street. He watched in awe as the mighty animals passed, their magnificence and grace much more splendid in the living form than that of the dead one Rourke had butchered. These two umbra, with their leather harnesses, were a light gray, not black like the wild one he'd seen, but their eyes were still red, and their fangs were still long.

"Truly an impressive creature. One of the many marvels in Bhaskara."

Sammy yelped in surprise and jumped at the new voice that spoke from behind him. He half stumbled down the single step back onto the market road. "I am so sorry," he started, raising a hand to his chest, heart beating madly. "I didn't mean to block the doorway. I was just trying to get out of the way."

"It's all right," the man said laughing. "I can tell you don't belong here."

Sammy frowned. "What gave it away? My hair? Or my skin?" So far, whenever Sammy had stopped to talk to someone about anything, Illume had commented about his hair or his pale complexion. He was beginning to realize how Rourke felt and wished he had a hooded shirt like the one Rourke wore. "Yes, I'm an Other," he scoffed, rolling his eyes.

"Yes, true, but that wasn't what I was referring to." The man waved a hand at Sammy. "Come in, come in, I have something I would like to give you. One Other to another." Laughing at his weird little joke, the man stepped deeper into the building.

Curious, Sammy followed, stepping back inside and actually looking at his surroundings. He was in a small shop full of dried herbs, spices, incense, and other such things. One wall was lined with shelves full of glass jars, their labels smudged with fingerprints. A second wall was lined with crude mirrors, ones that reminded Sammy of ancient times in his own history. The third wall had all sorts of oils, clothes, weapon scabbards, and Sammy even saw something like what Rourke had, something he had called a whetstone.

"Come, come," the man was still waving Sammy forward, and in a large case at the far back of the store, Sammy could see two shelves with knives resting on them. They sat behind a half wall counter where the man was now standing, a low hinged door still swaying quietly.

"What is this place," Sammy asked as he rested his hands on the countertop.

"A reagents store," the man answered, turning to Sammy and sitting down on a stool as he set a small box down on the countertop. "And a small blacksmith shop, of sorts. My wife rearranged the whole store so I could put some of my works on display. Started leatherworking, too."

"That's incredible!" Sammy looked over his shoulder to the wall with the leatherwork again. "Wait," he stopped, turning to the man. "You said 'your wife.'"

"Yes," the man nodded, holding out his hand. "Name's Craig."

Sammy shook Craig's hand and took a moment to really look at him. He had black hair like the Illume did, long and pulled back into a ponytail, but now that he was looking, he could see that Craig's eyes were green, and his skin, though darker than Sammy's own, was still light in comparison to the deep almond of the Illume. He couldn't help but laugh. "No shit," Sammy started. "You're the first human I have run into since arriving. Name's Sammy."

"There are a lot of us humans here in the city." Craig nodded. "We have to stick together, even as we adapt to living here. I've been here for four or five years as best I can figure from people I have spoken to. Long enough for me to accept this life, settle in, and make something of it. I met my wife in the same manner as we met. Stumbled into the store when I first saw an umbra. Although, from the looks of your reaction, you knew to get out of the way."

"Yeah, my boyfriend mentioned to be careful of them." Sammy waved a hand in the direction of what he hoped was the Sanctuary. He laughed, suddenly really excited to be talking to another person who understood him. It was like speaking with Molly, and it gave Sammy a sense of something being normal in a place that was everything but normal to him.

Craig nodded. "You two get pulled here together?"

"Ah, no." Sammy shook his head. Craig was making him feel really welcome in a city that had so far tried to shun him, and he felt some sort of comradery with him, even though they had just met. "He's Illume. Saved my life, actually. We've been traveling together for a few months or so from what I was told. We just got here; he's taking a nap in the little house we were loaned."

Craig nodded. "Couldn't wait to go exploring, could you? I was the same way. As soon as I was able to, I was out wandering around the city. I wanted to give you something, a welcoming gift of sorts. I keep several of them on hand for this exact purpose. You would be surprised how many Others come wandering into the store by chance." Craig picked up the box that he'd set down earlier. "Now, I won't have you telling me 'no' either, all right? I had to make my own, and so, I always try to help whenever I see another man who has just come to Bhaskara."

"I don't have any money, or anything." Sammy frowned. He hadn't been expecting to buy anything knowing Rourke and himself had no way of paying. He had just wanted to go exploring.

Craig held up a hand. "I'm not asking for money, nor am I asking anything for this in return. It's a gift; a way for me to say congratulations on making it through the darkness to your new home. What city did they stick you with?"

"What city? I'm from the suburbs of —"

"No, no," Craig laughed. A loud boisterous sound. "Not our cities, Illume cities. The city clerk slapped 'of Bhaskara' on me since I appeared right near the city. Most Others I talk to are from Bhaskara, I think they just label us with that as our 'home city.' Whatever that means."

"Oh." Sammy nodded, thinking back to what Rourke had told the clerk when he gave their names. "I'm from Olin, I guess. That's where Rourke is from anyway. That's my boyfriend; committed, is the word he uses."

"Olin, huh?" Craig nodded. "I had a couple shamans in here the other cycle talking about an Olin shaman. Wonder if it's the same place."

"I wouldn't know." Sammy shook his head. "It was nice meeting you, Craig, but I should get going. I want to keep exploring."

"Right. Oh, wait! I forgot! We got sidetracked. Here." Craig held out the box, and Sammy took it, carefully opening it. Inside was a beautifully hand-crafted blade with a wooden handle. "It's a straight razor," Craig explained. "Sharp, too, so be careful. Meant for shaving." Craig ran his hand over his chin, and only then did Sammy realize he didn't have any facial hair.

Sammy raised his hand to his face, running his fingers through the knots in his beard. He had just given up on the idea of ever being able to shave again. He didn't know why he didn't think about the fact that once he got to a major city, he would have access to more things than what Rourke and himself had in the darkness. Made perfect sense. Sammy grinned, closed the box, and held it tightly in his hand. "I can't take this," he started, laughing. "It must have taken so much time to make."

"Sammy, I insist." Craig leaned on the countertop. "I really do. I know what it's like to be a stranger here, and not feel like yourself. Take it, even if it just collects dust on a shelf in your home. I will feel better knowing I gave it to you. Besides, I told you, you can't tell me 'no.'"

Sammy nodded, opening the box a second time to look at the gift. "Thank you," he started. "I really do appreciate it. I know I will use it. I don't mind growing my hair out, but I can't stand the beard!"

"Agreed," Craig nodded. Placing both hands on the countertop, he stood. "All right, off you go, Sammy. Was great to meet you. Go finish exploring and get back to that boyfriend of yours. Just don't let him cut himself with that razor. And come back anytime you need it sharpened; I can do it for you."

"I will, thanks; and don't worry. He knows his way around a sharp blade. He has a sword!" Sammy waved over his shoulder and turned for the door as Craig laughed.

Holding his new gift tightly in his hand, Sammy couldn't keep the smile off his face. He had never expected to run into another human, though why he wasn't sure. He knew more than just himself had been brought here. Molly had told him such, but to encounter someone who was familiar in a sense was weird. He'd grown used to being around Rourke and his weird idiocies that now meeting another human was strange.

Laughing to himself, and once again opening the small box, he wasn't paying attention as he bumped into someone. Sammy stepped back as the young woman turned to him. "I'm so sorry," she started, gasping as she turned. "I wasn't paying att — Sammy?"

"Alina?" Sammy started laughing. "Of all the people to literally bump into, I find you! I'm sorry. I wasn't watching where I was going."

"It's all right." Alina smiled, shifting the basket she was carrying on her arm. "I'm glad you are here. I am trying to get the last few things I need for dinner, and realized I needed more than I thought."

"Do you need help? I'm just looking around. I can help." Sammy put his razor box into the pocket of his vest to free both hands. "What can I do?"

"Just walk with me." Alina smiled, looking down at her weird little pet. "Or, well, would you mind carrying the basket? Izusa wants me to pick her up."

"Yes, of course." Sammy reached for the basket as Alina bent to pick up the animal, hefting her weight in both her arms as she smiled. "Rourke said that's a haldis, right? That's their name?"

"Yes, the haldis are very important to Illume culture. They are the ones who showed the Illume the bhasvah."

"The glowing stone," Sammy asked. "Rourke has told me a little bit, but not a whole lot. We spent most of our time simply trying to survive, but that doesn't matter now. Where do you need to go?"

Alina pointed with one hand. "I need to go to the butcher to get the roast for our meal. Are you sure you are okay with taking the basket? Izusa can walk, she just doesn't like the crowds."

"I got it, don't worry." Sammy grinned. "What are you making for dinner?"

"Lor asked me to make him a roast, and this is his favorite butcher, so I wanted to start there. The man who runs the shop puts a dry rub on the meat that Lor absolutely loves." Alina moved as she spoke, weaving in and out of the crowd, pausing every so often as someone called out to her, stopped to speak to her, or wanted to pet Izusa. By the time they entered the butcher shop, both Alina and Izusa looked exhausted.

Taking a deep breath, Alina walked toward the counter. "May the light shine upon you," an older man said from behind the counter. "How may I help you, Warden?"

"And guide your steps," Alina replied casually. Sammy listened to the conversation quietly, looking around as he did. He didn't recognize a lot in the small store, but he did hear the butcher mention umbra several times. Finally, he handed Alina a roast that looked to be wrapped in paper. Thanking him, Alina turned back to Sammy and placed the roast in the basket alongside several types of what looked like vegetables, and a loaf of bread. "There," she said, adjusting Izusa in her arms. "Ready to go back home?"

"I am if you are." Sammy nodded, more than happy to follow Alina back through the market street toward the Sanctuary. They were quiet as they walked, once again needing to pause every now and again to speak to someone. "Can I ask you something," Sammy started when they turned into the smaller street headed back. There were less people in the side alley, and it made talking much easier.

"Of course, what is it?"

Sammy hesitated. Rourke would more than likely be upset with Sammy if he knew Sammy was talking about him, but Sammy didn't think Rourke would want to talk to him about this. While Rourke clearly had a level of respect for the haldis that surprised Sammy, Rourke still seemed adamant about leaving, and the little bit of information that Rourke had told Sammy about his life before the fall of Olin hadn't been very helpful. "How important is Izusa to you?"

Alina seemed to understand where Sammy was going with his question. "What did Rourke tell you about his haldis, if anything."

"That he died, and that he was more than a pet. He blames himself for his death." Sammy did feel bad about talking about Rourke, and about something so personal without him around, but Sammy also felt that he would never get Rourke to open up and talk about why the haldis were so important.

Alina was quiet for a moment before she took a deep breath. "Rourke said you are from Olin."

"Yes, I guess. I don't know. That's his home."

"Olin," Alina started, her voice low. She hugged Izusa a little tighter to her chest. "Olin is the first city, the beginning of our culture as we know it now. It's where the haldis first showed our ancestors the light, and it was where the Order of the Watchers was created."

The two stepped around the corner and before them the Sanctuary wall loomed over them. Alina walked over to it and pressed her hand against one of the carvings on the wall. It was a pictograph carving of a tree with what appeared to be several Illume and haldis standing underneath the high branches. In the open space between the top of the Illumes' heads and the lowest branches was what appeared to be a glowing stone. "This carving represents that exchange. Our people used to be nomadic, moving through the darkness in order to survive. The city of Amshu kept those traditions alive until even they fell to the darkness."

Alina took a deep breath and turned to Sammy. "Rourke didn't tell you this?"

"Rourke, well," Sammy paused. He tightened his grip on the basket. "Rourke's not sure what he wants to do now that we are here."

Alina nodded and pointed to another carving farther down the wall. The carving showed several haldis surrounded by what appeared to be bhasvah stone. "The haldis are the keepers of the light. Seeing our struggles in the darkness, they approached us, guiding us to the bhasvah, and giving us a new way to see through the darkness. In return for this great gift, the Illume built the haldis a safe haven, the first Sanctuary. Several men and women were put in charge of the protection of the haldis, their Guardians, and watched over them with their swords at their sides."

Alina moved as she spoke, pointing out different carvings in the wall as she did. Sammy listened quietly, looking at the pictures. He was excited to learn about Rourke's culture but saddened that he didn't get to learn it from Rourke.

"As a way to pay tribute to the haldis, and better connect with them, the Guardians created a mixture of ground haldis scale — they shed their scales regularly — bhasvah dust from mining the stone, and water. Together they drank it, sealing their fates to a life of protection and servitude to the haldis."

Alina came to the doorway of the Sanctuary, smiling as she watched the large herd of haldis milling about in the grass. Izusa squirmed to get down, and Alina put her down, watching as the haldis waddled her way off to join the others. "One of the Illume Guardians was with child when they took their oath. When her daughter was born, she had dark green hair. The young girl's connection to the haldis was stronger than anything anyone had seen before, as if she, herself, was a haldis. She seemed to connect with the haldis better than other Illume, almost as if she could understand what the animals were saying, and when she was still very small, one of the haldis chose to walk by her side. As she grew, and as more Guardians joined the Order, more children with green hair were born. They became the first Wardens, and it soon became tradition for all committed partners who were with child to drink this tribute to the haldis in hopes of their child being blessed with green hair as well."

"So, you can talk to the haldis?"

"Sort of." Alina smiled and raised a hand to the back of her neck. "It's a feeling. I know Izusa is always there. And I usually know what she wants or needs from that feeling. The High Warden says that the darker the hair, the stronger the connection. I can only imagine what Rourke must be going through after having lost his haldis, and then seeing our herd here. He must be so overwhelmed and sad being near them."

Sammy watched the herd for a moment. "And everyone does that? Drinks that tribute when they are expecting a child? Is that the only way a Warden is born?"

Alina took a deep breath, running a hand down the length of her braid. Sammy looked over to her, noticing the loose wisps of green hair that caught the light breeze. "I hope Lor and I will be able to conduct that sacred ceremony at some point. We've talked about it, but so far nothing."

"I'm sorry," Sammy murmured quietly. He hadn't expected to get something so personal from Alina. The information about Rourke's history and how he came to be a Warden was a lot to take in, let alone the fact Alina and Lor were talking about having kids. "I didn't mean for —"

Alina smiled. "Don't be sorry, Sammy, it's just not meant to be right now. It will happen, I can feel it! Just not right now. Come on, I want you to help me start dinner!"

"I wouldn't want to impose on you, Alina. I was happy to help you out at the market."

"Nonsense!" Looping her arm in his, Alina tugged on Sammy's arm. "I insist! Lor is hardly ever home to help me cook, and I could use the company."

Sammy chuckled, letting Alina tug him along toward her home. It was a nice large house with a wraparound porch and two floors. "All right, if you say so."

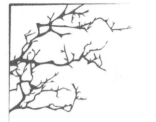

6

Rourke woke to the sound of footsteps on wood. Sitting up, he half turned, and reached for his knife on the table when he caught Sammy entering the bedroom from the corner of his eye. With a deep breath, Rourke fell back to the bed, rubbing his hands over his face. "I almost attacked you."

"Sorry." Sammy sat down on the edge of the bed. "I didn't even think about the fact I could wake you up. I didn't mean to startle you."

"It's all right." Rourke dropped his hands, scrunching his nose in disgust when Luna licked the side of his face. Pushing her away with one hand, Rourke reached out to Sammy with the other. "How did exploring go?"

"Good!" Sammy grinned at Rourke, turning on the bed to face him. Rourke looked up at Sammy, finally taking a better look at him. His hair was wet and pulled back, tied with what appeared to be a hair stick, and his beard was gone. "I ran into another human, another Other —" Sammy paused to laugh. "He gave me a straight razor to shave with. I feel like a damned person again! And Alina let me take a bath in their little bathroom."

Rourke reached up, running his fingertips along the curve of Sammy's jaw. He'd grown used to seeing Sammy with all the facial hair, but he liked the way he looked now, too. "I didn't realize your hair was getting that long. Where did you get the hair stick?"

"You know what that is?" Sammy turned his head to the side slightly, showing Rourke the small bun he had with wild strands of damp hair sticking out in places. As Sammy turned back to look at Rourke, a strand came loose and fell into Sammy's eyes.

Mindlessly, Rourke reached up and pushed the damp hair behind Sammy's ear. "Yeah, my sister used to have some. Not that she used them often, she kept her hair loose."

Sammy nodded; his voice quiet. "Dinner is going to be ready soon. Alina asked me to come get you, and to see if you wanted to take a quick bath before we ate."

"Yeah, I would like that." Sitting up again, Rourke ran a hand through his hair and turned to sit on the edge of the bed next to Sammy. "Did you find anything interesting in the city? Or just this — razor, you said?"

"Yeah." Sammy nodded and pulled a small box from his vest, handing it to Rourke. Opening it, Rourke saw a strange looking knife, the wooden handle still dark from water and a testament to Sammy using it. "I saw a living umbra, and I ran into Alina and helped her get what she needed for dinner! Then I came back and helped her for a little before I took a bath and came to get you. She's really nice, Rourke. I really like her."

"That's great." Leaning over, Rourke pressed a kiss to Sammy's cheek, the sensation completely different without all the hair. "I'm glad you are fitting in."

"Well, I wouldn't say 'fitting in.' I still stick out rather easily. Hair and all." Sammy waved a hand to indicate his person. "But Alina is willing to talk to me, and I can't say 'no' to spending time with her. She's just so easy to talk to."

"That's good!" Rourke laughed as he stood up. He felt a little better after some sleep, but he still knew it would take a while for him to get used to being in the light again. He was glad that Sammy was enjoying himself. He'd been a little worried that Sammy would find the city a boring place like Rourke did. While he was excited to be here, Rourke also knew that excitement would wear off quickly and he would hate having to be caged in. He took a deep breath as he reached for his knife. "This is our home now," he said, unsure if he was talking to Sammy or himself.

"Yeah," Sammy agreed, standing up and pulling Rourke into a hug. Caught off guard by the action, it took Rourke a moment to return the affection, but finally he wrapped his arms around Sammy's waist and rested his head against Sammy's shoulder. "I'm glad I get to discover it with you, Rourke."

"Me, too," Rourke breathed out, closing his eyes. He heard Luna stand on the bed before he felt her bump her head into his side. Looking over at her, he reached out and scrubbed his hand between her ears. "We should try and find a real collar for her if you are going to keep one on her."

"Do you think so?" Sammy pulled away, turning to Luna and raising both hands to the shadow cat's cheeks. "Do you think you are going to need a collar, Luna? No, I don't think so!"

Rourke rolled his eyes as Sammy continued to coo at Luna, pitching his voice and showering the shadow cat with affection. "I think it may be a good idea if we are in the city. Shadow cats usually don't become pets."

"Yet people walk around with fucking bears — argi, sorry. Alina said that Lor has had Isik since he was a cub!"

"You two talked about a lot." Rourke walked out of the bedroom into the small front room to the table where he had left his backpack and sword.

Sammy followed along with Luna on his heels. "Yeah, we did," he started. "She also told me about the origins of the Order, and why your hair is green."

Rourke hesitated before he reached for his sword. He gripped the white scabbard tightly in his hand as he looked up to Sammy, meeting his eyes. "She did," he asked. Rourke knew that Sammy would learn about his history at some point, he just didn't think it would be this soon.

"Well," Sammy looked away. "I asked her about the haldis, and the connection there." Pulling out a chair, Sammy sat at the table. "You didn't tell me Olin was the city where your culture first began, Rourke."

"It doesn't matter anymore," Rourke replied with a shrug. He could feel himself getting annoyed already and tried to swallow down the feeling. Twisting, he wrapped his sword belt around his hips. "Olin is gone."

"I know why you don't think you can stay here," Sammy murmured, and Rourke felt the building anger in his shoulders melt away. Sammy rested his hands on the table, finally meeting Rourke's eyes. Rourke could see sorrow, concern, and resolution swirling in the depths of Sammy's eyes. Rourke felt himself swallow thickly under his committed's gaze.

"Yeah," Rourke asked, voice just as quiet as Sammy had been. He hadn't thought he'd ever be able to explain to Sammy why he couldn't stay in the Sanctuary, why he couldn't be around the haldis, and why he had decided long ago to leave the Order when he got to the Last City.

"And I get it, I think. Alina explained it to me." Sammy raised his hand to the back of his neck. "She said that you can feel the haldis speaking to you, your own and others. Shit, it must be overwhelming for you."

Rourke looked away, raising a hand to his neck. It had been quiet since they arrived here; that low hum of a herd escaping him. "No." Rourke shook his head. "I haven't heard them. Even this herd knows I failed to protect the Olin herd."

Sammy stood from his chair and walked over to Rourke. "That's not true. You didn't fail. That's not where I was going with this." Sammy reached out, resting his hands on Rourke's shoulders. "I just wanted you to know that even though I don't fully understand that connection, I think I get where you are coming from. You don't want to be here, and I will stand behind you on this. Besides." Sammy smirked, running a hand through Rourke's hair and pressing a kiss to his forehead. "Alina said: the darker the hair, the stronger the connection. And your hair is really dark."

Rourke frowned, but he didn't pull away. "I was surprised at how light Alina and that kid's hair is, honestly. I have never seen hair that light before. Everyone had darker hair in Olin."

"Probably because the connection was stronger there. You're special, Rourke, even if you don't want to be."

"I still failed though."

"Stop saying that. It was a long time ago. Stop beating yourself up over it. Start anew here, and if that means walking away from the Order, then that's what we do, right?" Rourke nodded, but he didn't speak, and Sammy grinned. "Okay, good. Now, let's get you to Alina's so you can have a bath because now that I am clean, I can smell how gross you really are."

ଓ

A bath had been just what Rourke had needed, even if in the end it had been cut short by Sammy coming to get him for dinner. They had brought their little bit of clothing with them after Sammy had explained that Alina offered to wash them. Sammy had apparently only agreed if he got to help so he could learn to do it himself. Rourke had started to laugh, but stopped, thinking that if that was the type of thing Sammy needed to do in order to help himself settle into living in Bhaskara, who was Rourke to stop him.

While Rourke didn't get the cleanest of clothing when he got out of the bath, the clothing he had brought with him was cleaner than what he had been wearing. Honestly, Rourke was just happy to take a real bath, he didn't mind putting dirty clothes back on knowing his skin and hair were clean.

The small bathhouse was located behind the main house, almost as if added on as an afterthought to the building. Closing the door back into the hallway behind him, Rourke walked into the living room of Alina's house behind Sammy just as Lor was walking in the front door. The large argi — Isik, Sammy said his name was — plodded his way across the open space to lay down in a corner of the room on a rug by a quiet fireplace. Luna growled from where she had curled up on the couch and Sammy instantly moved to her side, comforting her, and trying to calm her down.

Lor chuckled from his place by the door. "Isik won't hurt him," he said calmly. "Welcome to my home."

"Is that him? I want to see the shadow cat!" A second voice that sounded almost the same as Lor's, but was much more energetic, spoke from behind the door before Lor was pushed aside and a second man appeared in the house. Rourke took a step back in shock when the man looked up, his face the same as Lor. "Oh, wow! He's purple! I'm Lao! You must be Rourke! I can tell from the hair. Lor said you arrived during an earlier phase."

Lor huffed as he rolled his eyes. "Forgive my brother —"

"Twin brother."

"Yes, twin brother. He was very excited when I saw him at the barracks and told him you had a shadow cat for a pet. I am sorry. He can be quite the handful." As he spoke, Lor took the sword he had from his side and set it in a rack on the wall. Rourke watched, a memory of his sister doing the same to the sword he had forcing itself to the surface of his mind.

"Am not." Lao turned toward Sammy as he spotted him on the couch next to Luna. "Oh! And you must be Sammy. Um... how do you do?" Rourke watched as Lao stood up straight and reached his right hand out to Sammy, who was grinning at Lao, even with one arm still around Luna.

"Yeah! How did you know?" Sammy reached out and took Lao's hand. "You're the first person I have met that knows how to shake hands."

"I talk to the Others a lot. Your culture is interesting, if not complicated! I really enjoy talking about it." Lao turned to Rourke as he spoke and bobbed his head in a small nod. "It's nice to meet you as well, Rourke."

"You, too, Lao." Rourke nodded, gripping his sword hilt a little tighter. "Lor, thank you for letting us into your home. Sammy and Alina seem to be becoming fast friends."

"I heard my name!" Alina appeared from the kitchen, walking over to Lor and reaching out for him. Lor wrapped an arm around Alina's waist and leaned over to kiss her. "Welcome home. Dinner is ready."

"Can't wait." Lor grinned and turned for the kitchen and dining area of the house. "Let's continue this conversation while we eat. Alina is a great cook! I have been waiting all cycle for this meal!"

"Stop." Alina pushed away from Lor, but Rourke didn't miss the blush that rose over her cheeks at the praise from her committed. He could also see how Lao and Lor could be twins, even with their vast differences. There were similarities in how they walked as they all followed Alina toward the kitchen, talking as she went. "Sammy helped actually. I ran into him while I was out."

"Ah, well, thank you to you, too, Sammy. It's always great to hear Alina had someone to talk to." Lor turned toward Rourke. "I'm sorry I had to leave you the way I did earlier. I couldn't leave Zohar at the bridge by himself for too long. I really do wish I could have brought you to the Sanctuary myself. How are you settling in?"

"Well, I guess." Rourke nodded, moving to the chair across from Lor that he motioned to at the table. "I haven't done much since our arrival. I had a headache. Sammy says it was more than likely from the light of the city."

"It makes sense." Sammy cut into the conversation as he sat next to Rourke. Across from them, Alina sat down next to Lor, and Lao sat at the end of the table. "You've been in the darkness for so long that I'm sure your eyes have gotten used to it, and then to suddenly be surrounded by light again? It would be like walking into a dark room and just flicking on a light switch and blinding yourself."

Lao laughed, his voice echoing around the open room. "Your speech is really weird, Sammy."

"Yeah, it really is." Rourke frowned as he looked over to Sammy. "I have no idea what you are talking about."

Sammy groaned and leaned back in his chair. He was quiet for a moment before he took a deep breath. "I guess I am just saying: it's not surprising your eyes are going to need time to adjust to the light again."

As Sammy spoke everyone began to serve food, passing around dishes to one another as well as pouring drinks. After swatting Lao's hands from the roast, Lor began to carve it so everyone could take what they wanted. Rourke couldn't remember when he'd last sat down at a real table to eat with others, but something in the back of his head told him it hadn't ended very well.

"Sammy's right," Lao started as he picked up his fork to snag one of the pieces of the roast from the serving platter. He motioned with his hand for Sammy's plate, and Sammy eagerly lifted it for Lao to give him a slice of the roast. "It will take a little bit for you to adapt. You aren't the first person to say that the adjustment took a toll on their minds and bodies when first arriving."

Rourke nodded as Lao served him. It was weird, yet nice to feel welcomed so openly. Lor, Alina, and even Lao, had accepted them without question, inviting them into their home. Alina paused as she offered a bowl full of vegetables to Sammy, looking down to the floor. "No, Izusa, you can't sit in my lap during dinner."

"You don't eat with her?" The words were out of Rourke's mouth before he realized what he had said, and he ducked his head in embarrassment when everyone turned to look at him. "Sorry," he muttered. "I just always ate with mine, but I was little."

"Oh, she does." Lor smirked from his place beside her. "Just she's trying to be polite because we have company."

"Yeah, because I am company!" Lao laughed as he picked up the pitcher of water from the table.

"I didn't mean you, Lao." Lor rolled his eyes. "I meant Rourke and Sammy."

"Don't let us stop you from what you normally do." Sammy looked over to Alina with a smile. "Besides, I like Izusa. She's cute."

"Rourke?" Alina looked over at Rourke, and he could hear the unasked question in how she said his name. Did he mind if she had Izusa in her lap at the table?

Rourke shook his head. Despite not having his own haldis, being around them again was comforting in a way. Painful, but still comforting. "It's your home, Alina."

"I was just trying —" Cutting herself off, Alina leaned over, picked the haldis up off the floor and settled Izusa into her lap. They all fell into silence for a moment before Alina cleared her throat and handed Izusa a small piece of bread before returning to her own meal. "Before I left for the market and ran into Sammy, I went over to speak with High Warden Ozni."

"Oh?" Lor turned to her slightly as he motioned to the table. "This is amazing, Alina. Completely worth the wait I had to go through this cycle."

"Thank you." Alina smiled, turning to Sammy. "I think we did a good job, Sammy."

"Yeah, this is great. Much better than the food I get from the barracks." Lao grinned. Rourke was quickly discovering the differences between the two brothers. "I mean, don't get me wrong, the food is good, but nothing beats Alina's cooking!"

Rourke listened quietly to the conversation around him. He kept his attention on his food, wanting to eat before he knew the conversation would return to the reason why Alina had spoken to the High Warden. Everyone's voices sort of blended together into one as they babbled back and forth at one another. The High Warden would want to see him, rightly so, but Rourke knew that he wouldn't be able to remain here. He had decided long ago to put this part of his life behind him, and he couldn't change his mind now; wouldn't let himself change his mind now.

Next to Rourke, Sammy bumped his knee under the table, smiling at him as Rourke looked over at him. "Do you like it?"

"Yeah," Rourke replied with a nod. He suddenly felt like an outsider to the small group, even though he knew that wasn't the case at all. He had just spent so much of his life by himself that now sitting here with others felt weird to him. He knew it shouldn't have, but part of him simply wanted to return to the small lodgings Alina had loaned them and forget this had happened.

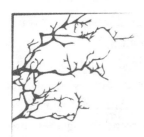

7

Alina dragged the conversation back to the High Warden after everyone had praised her and Sammy for a job well done with dinner. "High Warden Ozni said that he wouldn't be able to meet with you during the next cycle as he has to spend it with the city council, but the following cycle, he can meet you whenever you are ready."

Rourke nodded as he swallowed a bite of food. He wasn't very hungry suddenly, and that urge to return to Sammy and his temporary lodgings twisted sharply in his chest. "That's actually good," he made himself say. "It will give us a cycle to rest and decide what it is I want to say."

"I thought you knew already." Sammy looked over at him, reaching out his hand under the table to rest on Rourke's knee.

Rourke glanced down at Sammy's hand before looking at him and nodding. "I have an idea, yes, but I haven't ever thought about what I am actually going to say yet."

Sammy nodded but remained quiet. He squeezed Rourke's knee before returning to his food. Across the table Alina looked concerned as she tried to keep Izusa from climbing onto the table. The haldis had her front feet on the edge of the table, occasionally grabbing bits of food off Alina's plate. "Sammy mentioned that you weren't sure what you wanted to do now that you are here. Forgive me, Rourke, but what could you possibly do if you don't stay here to tend to the haldis?"

"I've never heard of a Warden not taking care of the herd." Lor picked up his glass and took a drink. "I noticed you didn't have a haldis, but I didn't think it was wise to ask about it."

"He was killed when Olin fell." Rourke sighed. He knew this was going to come up, but it was still difficult to talk about. "I've been without a haldis for so long at this point I'm not sure what I would do with one."

"Doesn't it hurt," Lao asked. Everyone looked over at him, and he ducked his head as he stabbed a piece of meat with his fork. "I just mean, you are connected. Doesn't your haldis' death hurt you physically somehow?"

Alina gasped. "Lao, you don't ask things like that! The connection between someone and their haldis is very personal."

"I'm sorry! I never learned that! I had no interest in being a Guardian when we were little." Lao looked over at Alina and frowned. "I knew this wasn't the life I wanted, even when little. It's why I joined the Illuminari as soon as I could."

"You joined the Illuminari," Rourke asked, and Lao nodded. Taking a deep breath, Rourke decided to answer Lao's question before asking more about the Illuminari. "I don't think his death hurt me physically. I don't really remember a lot from when the city fell. I just know he's gone. I can't feel him." Rourke raised a hand to the back of his neck. "I haven't been able to feel him since I was little."

"So, you plan to leave the Sanctuary," Lor asked, leaning back in his chair and crossing his arms. Rourke didn't get the feeling Lor was judging him, he felt more like Lor was already thinking of different things Rourke could possibly do if he wasn't going to stay.

"I plan to leave the Order entirely. There is nothing for me here now. This isn't my Sanctuary, and I can't offer anything of my own. I know that being from Olin is supposed to mean something, but it doesn't. I'm not any different than the rest of you."

"Your knowledge of Olin would be more than helpful, Rourke." Alina shifted Izusa in her lap. "I have never met anyone from so far away, and the few Wardens that have made it to Bhaskara were from closer cities. You're the first Warden from Olin."

"There was that one Amshu Guardian. What was his name?"

"Aetius, Lor. His name was Aetius." Lao shook his head. "You're so bad with names."

"I remembered Rourke and Sammy." Lor shrugged. "But yes, Aetius. Very few from the Order have made it through the darkness. So, anything you can bring is worth knowing, Rourke."

"We know Aetius!" Sammy spoke up. "We met him and Molly out in the darkness. Rourke said he —" Sammy cut himself off as he looked over at Rourke. "Aetius said to leave the Order, didn't he, Rourke?" Sammy's voice was quiet as he asked his question.

Rourke nodded. "Yes. I do — we do know Aetius. I have known Aetius and Molly since I was little. Lysha, too; she's my cousin, and a shaman. I owe them my life if I am going to be honest about everything. When we met them in the woods near the city, Aetius told me about the Illuminari. He said he thought that would be the best place for me given what I have done since the darkness fell." Rourke took a deep breath and rested his hand on the table. "I don't expect you to understand when I say: I just can't do this. I can't be here among the haldis with how I feel, and it has always been my plan to leave the Order once I arrived at the Last City."

"Well, that settles it then!" Lao slammed both his hands onto the table, startling everyone in the room. "You tell Ozni — who is a horrible person, by the way —"

"He is not," Alina interrupted, frowning at Lao. "He's always nice to me. I'm sure he will be fine with Rourke."

"Alina, I love you, but you have never seen him at the barracks or city hall. He is a horrible person." Lao looked over at her before turning back to Rourke. "You tell him you want out and I will introduce you to Asha!"

Rourke felt a hurt twist in his chest. He hadn't heard his sister's name spoken out loud unless by himself for what seemed like forever. "W-who is Asha," he asked hesitantly, trying to convince himself that this wasn't his sister. He knew his sister was dead. Lysha would have no reason to lie to him, and his sister would have never come to Bhaskara without him.

"Asha is the person in charge of the Illuminari. She helped to found it, now that I think about it. It was right after we first heard of the Wolves attacking other cities and Others began to appear." Lor set his glass down.

"Asha is — well, it isn't important. Asha is the person in charge of the Illuminari. I'm sure she would be more than excited to have you two join her ranks of Nari." Lao took another bite of his food.

"Nari," Sammy asked.

"Nari is what the Illuminari are called. Just like Warden or Guardian. Lao is a Nari, and I am both a Nari and Guardian." Lor pointed toward where his sword hung on the wall in the other room. "While I paid attention to our lessons when little, I joined the Illuminari with Lao when we got our marks. Lao was assigned to outskirt patrols, and I was assigned to city patrols. That's how I met Alina and Izusa." Reaching out, Lor ran his hand along the back of Izusa's head where her scales were small. The haldis turned and half jumped at Lor causing both him and Alina to try to catch her before Lor took her and settled her into his lap. "Well, I should say I met Izusa, who I found wandering down the street, and I had to return her to the Sanctuary."

"She had been acting strangely now that I think back on it. I think she knew we were supposed to meet." Alina took advantage of her free lap to eat some of her dinner. "She's always been very fond of you."

Lor hummed in agreement as he shifted his attention to the haldis. "I wouldn't worry too much about the meeting with Ozni, but Lao is right. Be leery of him and know what you want to say when you go to his home. Do not let him twist your words or your thoughts. He's very good at getting what he wants by talking circles around another."

"I really don't think it's nice to talk about the High Warden like that," Alina scolded. "Lao, you are known to cause arguments."

"There is nothing wrong with wanting to have a bit of a discussion on the inclusion of Others and the Inducted Illume." Lao crossed his arms over his chest. "I will continue to have those 'arguments' as you call them until it happens."

Alina turned to Lor. "And, Lor. You have never gotten along with High Warden Ozni since we decided to commit to one another."

"You do remember how he told me I 'wasn't good enough for you,' right? Who is he to decide who you commit to? Isn't it our choice?"

"This guy sounds like a real winner," Sammy grumbled under his breath, and even though Rourke didn't understand his words, he understood Sammy's tone of voice. Ozni didn't seem like a very nice person and Rourke wasn't looking forward to their meeting at all.

"He told me he thought you were Lao," Alina retorted.

"That's offensive," Lao scoffed.

"We look nothing alike," Lor snapped.

"Yeah, I got all the looks," Lao added in unhelpfully.

"You're twins! Of course, you look the same. Even your marks are the same!" Alina threw her hands in the air before she took a deep breath and turned to Rourke and Sammy. "I hope you don't pass judgment on High Warden Ozni until you meet him, Rourke. I'm sure he will be open to listening to you."

Lor and Lao both snorted back a sarcastic laugh and muttered under their breaths, once again proving that despite their differences, they truly were twins. "Let's change the topic, shall we?" Lor spoke up, looking over at Rourke and Sammy. "I must know: why a shadow cat? He seems quite tame."

"She. Her name is Luna, she's a girl." Sammy corrected Lor and Lor bobbed his head in apology. "And I don't know. I found her in a tree when she was little, and Rourke said I could keep her."

"I told you 'no' if I remember the conversation correctly." Rourke turned to look at Sammy, thinking back to that cycle out in the woods with a very tiny and hungry shadow cat cub. "She seemed to quickly attach herself to you though."

"She did. We've been training her as we traveled here. She's very well behaved." Sammy turned in his chair to see if he could spot her in the living room. "What about you, Lor? You own an argi. It looks a lot like what I know as a bear, and those are not pets."

"Bear," Lor questioned.

"Oh, I have heard that word before! A lot of the Others in the barracks say it about our argi. Apparently, a bear is a wild animal, much like the shadow cat, and really isn't much of a pet." Lao grinned as Sammy agreed with him, and Rourke just shook his head. He felt tired suddenly, overwhelmed and ready to sleep again. He stifled a yawn and reached out to take a drink.

"The differences in our cultures never ceases to amaze me," Lor commented as he picked up Izusa and handed her back to Alina. "I feel we are finished with dinner. Let's get the table cleared and move into the living room."

"Sounds like a good idea." Sammy stood to help Lor start clearing the table and Rourke moved to stand as well, but Sammy rested a hand on his shoulder. "You sit, I can do this. Relax a little bit."

"Are you sure," Rourke asked, looking up to Sammy.

Sammy smiled and nodded. "Yeah, I got this. You look tired anyway."

"Yeah, I still am."

"You two don't have to stay." Alina stood from the table, Izusa in her arms. "Sammy, you helped me cook, and I have Lor and Lao to help me clean up! If you are tired, please don't feel like you need to stay. Go get some rest. I'm sure you could use it after your long journey here."

"Ah, Alina I wouldn't want —"

"Thank you," Rourke interrupted Sammy as he stood. "I'm sorry to just leave like this, but I think a good rest will do both Sammy and I some good."

"But..." Sammy trailed off as their eyes met, and Rourke hoped his growing discomfort was clear to Sammy. It wasn't that Rourke didn't like Lor, Alina, and Lao, he just wanted to be alone now that everything was beginning to settle down a little bit. Sammy sighed. "All right. At least let me bring our plates to the kitchen."

"Leave them, Sammy, I insist. I am sure we will do this again. I really enjoyed your company and talking with you!" Bending over, Alina set Izusa on the ground and the haldis scurried off toward the kitchen where Rourke could see and hear Lor and Lao talking.

"Yeah, I really enjoyed hanging out with you, too! All right." Sammy let Alina take the plates he was holding from him. "Okay. Night, Lor; Lao."

"Night," Lao called back. "Are you leaving?"

"Yeah, Rourke's tired." Sammy nodded. Rourke turned from the conversation to go find Luna, glad to see she was curled up asleep on the couch. Isik hadn't moved from his spot by the fireplace, and Rourke hoped that maybe the two animals would be able to get along. At the least, they seemed to be able to be in the same space together. "You ready," Sammy asked, appearing by Rourke's side. "Everyone says to sleep well, and that they will see us in the next cycle. Whatever that means."

"Okay." Rourke nodded.

Luna woke up at the sound of Sammy's voice, and with a stretch, climbed down off the couch. Together, they exited Alina and Lor's home, and as soon as they closed the front door behind themselves, Sammy took Rourke's hand. Looking up into the sky, Sammy sighed heavily. "This is going to throw me off. I feel like it should be nighttime, what with us just having dinner and all, but it's still light out. I miss the stars."

"What are stars," Rourke asked, looking around the Sanctuary as they walked back toward their small lodging. Everything was calm and quiet, even most of the herd seemed to have settled down for some sleep leaving just a few splashing about in the pond.

"Stars are — well, stars are kind of like the moon. They come out at night, but they are tiny little specs in the sky, and they sort of twinkle."

"Twinkle?" Rourke raised an eyebrow as he looked over at Sammy.

"Yeah. Twinkle, twinkle little star? No? Ah, well. I just miss the stars." Sammy shrugged and the two fell quiet as they crossed the yard. Rourke didn't feel a need to answer Sammy, and Sammy didn't seem to be looking for a reply from Rourke. It was a comfortable silence, one they had spent a fair amount of their travels in. It had become welcoming in a way, as well, without a need for either of them to feel as if they should be filling the silence. They could rest, and though they were with one another, they could be alone, also, which Rourke very much appreciated.

Just as they were nearing their lodging, Rourke noticed something move from the corner of his eye, and he turned to see the small, injured haldis he'd tried to touch during their arrival waddling its way across the yard. The haldis was headed away from the rest of the herd, and Rourke frowned as he watched it disappear around the corner of one of the other small lodges. "Remind me to ask Alina about that haldis."

"What haldis?" Sammy turned and looked over his shoulder back the way they had just come.

"The little one that looks injured. I'm worried it's seriously hurt." Rourke looked over at Sammy before stepping up onto the porch. He stood by the railing to see if he could spot the animal again, but the small haldis was gone. Something felt off to Rourke about its actions, and he really was concerned for the small animal's wellbeing. Luna slinked past Rourke, sniffing at the door and waiting to be let inside.

"Oh, okay." Sammy nodded and let go of Rourke's hand to open the door. "I can ask her tomorrow. Maybe we can catch it or something so you can take a closer look?"

"No." Rourke shook his head as he followed Sammy inside. "I don't want to scare it any more than it already seems to be. It's not even with the rest of the herd, wandering around by itself. That's why I'm concerned."

"You're adorable." Sammy leaned over and pressed a kiss to Rourke's cheek as he closed the door behind them. "Let's get some sleep and we can talk about it in the morning."

8

The cycle of rest hadn't helped much, and Rourke found himself wide awake much earlier than he needed — or wanted — to be. He wasn't even supposed to meet with Ozni until the beginning of the second phase, but Rourke was already worried about what was going to happen. Unable to clear his mind, what he wanted to say kept swirling around in his head. Next to him, Sammy was still asleep, and Rourke rolled over onto his side to face his committed in hopes that he'd be able to fall back to sleep. Pulling his umbra hide a little tighter around his shoulders, Rourke tried to settle down, and took a deep breath as he closed his eyes.

"You done," Sammy asked, voice slurred.

Rourke inhaled sharply. "I thought you were asleep." Moving his hand, Rourke tried to find Sammy's hand in the mess of pelts, blankets, and the quiet of the room.

"Your moving woke me up. Are you okay?" Sammy sat up on his elbow, pushing his bangs from his eyes. In the near darkness, Rourke could see Sammy yawn, and he turned his head so he could look at him better. "Want to talk about it?"

"Not much to talk about. I'm worried about meeting with Ozni; that Lor and Lao's warning has more weight to it than Alina's words."

"You worry too much." Sammy leaned down and pressed a kiss to Rourke's forehead as he ran a hand through his hair. "I'm sure it will be fine. What's the worst he can do, tell you no?"

"Yes." Rourke frowned. "That is exactly what he can do."

"Oh," Sammy replied quietly as he laid back down. Taking a deep breath, Sammy shifted his shoulders against the bed a little. "Well,

I guess I hadn't thought it would come to that. I am sure he will be fine with it. Why wouldn't he be? All you have to do is explain your reasoning and I am sure the High Warden will let you go free." Sammy raised a hand into the air as he spoke, dropping it back to his side as he finished.

Rourke wasn't so sure, but he didn't comment as he moved closer to Sammy. He cuddled up against him, rested his head on Sammy's shoulder, and wrapped his arm around his waist. In turn, Sammy wrapped his arms around Rourke, and pulled him a little closer. "Don't stress too much. You've made up your mind anyway, haven't you? Even if he tells you no, you're still going to leave, right? Go talk to Asha about the Illuminari?"

Rourke nodded against Sammy's shoulder. "Yes, but I would rather leave on good terms with Ozni."

"I can understand that." Sammy was quiet a moment before he asked, "Do you want to get up, or do you want to stay here?"

"I am pretty comfortable, but I know I won't get any more sleep either. Might as well get up." Rourke moved to sit up, and Sammy reluctantly let him go. "I'm kind of hungry, too."

Sammy perked right up at the mention of food. "I brought some of the bread Alina and I made yesterday, and she gave me some of the li'kai berry jam she made. It's really good!" Climbing out of the bed, Sammy pushed through the curtain that served as a door to their room into the front room. He was still talking, even though Rourke wasn't really listening to what Sammy was saying. It was nice to hear his voice, and to feel how calm Sammy was about everything that was going on. Rourke couldn't explain why he was so anxious, heart still beating madly in his chest, but he was glad Sammy seemed at home in the city and was there.

"One or two?"

"What," Rourke asked with a chuckle as he looked to the door to see Sammy lifting the curtain out of the way so they could speak. "One or two what?"

"Pieces of toast. Well, bread. Whatever. How hungry are you?"

"Oh." Rourke moved to the edge of the bed and stood. Stretching, he groaned and yawned. "Two, I guess."

With a curt nod, Sammy disappeared, and Rourke followed Sammy into the front room after he picked up a shirt. The cycle before had also been filled with washing their clothing, as well as going through all their meager belongings. "I really wish you hadn't gotten rid of my sweatpants," Sammy started as he picked up two plates. Turning, he stopped short, eyes going wide as he inhaled sharply. Rourke watched Sammy for a moment before he realized Sammy was probably looking at his scars, and he raised a hand to press against his stomach. "I wasn't," Sammy started, clearing his throat and walking over to set the plates down on the table. "I wasn't looking at your scars," he said quietly.

Rourke shrugged as he pulled his chair out, reaching for one of the apples in the bowl on the table. "It's okay." Taking a bite, Rourke realized Sammy was a bit too focused on his food, and he reached out to touch Sammy's arm. "What's wrong?"

"Nothing." Sammy shook his head. "I was just — I was just looking at you — all of you — was all. You caught me off guard. Sorry." Taking a bite of his bread, Sammy finally looked over to Rourke. "I'm just so used to only partly seeing you because of the darkness that sometimes I forget what you really look like, and then you go and do something like this, and it just takes my breath away."

"Do what," Rourke asked. He took another bite of his apple and raised an eyebrow at Sammy. "All I did was come out here."

"Yeah, that's all you had to do." Sammy smiled, one corner of his mouth lifting faintly. "Wandering out here without a shirt on." Taking a deep breath, he sighed. "You just look good, Rourke."

Rourke felt his cheeks heat up as he shifted uncomfortably and looked down at the table. "Oh," he managed, with a nod. He knew Sammy was flirting with him; he'd begun to be able to pick up on Sammy's tone of voice easily, but it always caught him off guard when Sammy would say something to him. "Um, thanks."

Sammy chuckled as he reached out and rested his hand on Rourke's arm. "Let's eat, and maybe go spar? Don't we have some time to kill before we meet the High Warden?"

"Kill? I don't plan on killing any —"

"What? No! It's an expression. Shit, Rourke. That's not what I meant! Um, how can I explain this? Oh! After we eat, we still have to wait to go see him, right? There will be a time gap?"

"I think, yes." Rourke narrowed his eyes at Sammy. He was beginning to understand that when Sammy referred to 'time' he meant the phases of the cycle, but it was still very confusing. "We can't meet Ozni until later in the cycle."

"So, we will have a chance to spar a little after we eat? If you're up for it, that is."

Rourke took a bite of his apple, speaking around the food in his mouth. "I am always willing to teach you, Sammy."

"Okay; good." Sammy nodded. "Eat your bread."

"I will. I'm having my apple first." Rourke grinned as Sammy nodded, and the two fell into a content silence while they ate. After finishing and cleaning up, Rourke pulled his shirt on, and the two of them went out into the yard to spar and wait for when they needed to go meet with Ozni.

They hadn't been out in the yard very long before Isa arrived, a large portion of the herd of haldis following along behind him. With a bright smile, he waved, raising his hand over his head as he called out to Sammy and Rourke. Luna growled from where she had been resting on the porch, and Sammy walked over to sit with her while the haldis passed by them to the pond. Rourke watched them from where he was still sitting in the grass, more than content to revel in the moment of peace that always seemed to follow the haldis.

"Father says he's ready to speak with you." Isa walked over to Rourke. "Why are you sitting on the ground?"

"Sammy and I were sparring. I'm still trying to teach him how to defend himself."

"From what," Isa asked. "Aren't we safe here? Father says we are safe in the city."

Rourke shifted, resting his hands on his knees. At the edge of the pond, the younger haldis were playing in the mud while the older and larger ones waded out into the shallow water. Rourke had yet to spot the small one with the injured shoulder. "Yeah, but you can never be too careful. I'm sure most people thought they were safe in their homes, too, and look what happened."

Isa nodded solemnly as he watched the herd play in the pond. He took a deep breath, kneeling as his haldis lumbered toward them coated in mud. "Alina told me what happened to your haldis. I'm sorry."

Rourke shrugged as Isa picked up the large male, not even caring that he was going to get covered in mud. Rourke couldn't help but smile. Isa reminded Rourke of himself when he was little. "Thank you, but it was long ago. I wouldn't say I am over his death, but I am working on overcoming the grief I feel."

"Is that why you want to talk to Father? I overheard Lor and Lao mention you wanted to leave. Is it because you lost your haldis?"

"Isa, who is your father," Sammy asked from the steps. Rourke looked over to him to see Luna had tried to climb into his lap, half lying on Sammy as she sat on the steps with him. He had his head turned awkwardly to the side as she tried to lick his face.

"The High Warden," Isa said quietly. "He asked me to come get you."

Rourke looked up to Isa from where he sat. Isa seemed like a good kid, still young and naïve, but he had a good heart, and cared greatly about the haldis. Besides Alina, Isa was the one who Rourke had seen tending to the herd.

"I know my father isn't the nicest person." Isa hugged his haldis a little tighter to his chest. "But please don't blame him. He's under a lot of pressure from the council to keep the Order running perfectly, even with everything that has happened. You may be the first Warden to openly say you want to leave, but you aren't the first who wants to leave, and Father knows that."

"Don't worry, Isa." Sammy pushed Luna off his lap and stood. Rourke stood also, walking back toward the small lodging as Sammy kept talking. "We don't plan on making waves. I think it is Rourke's plan to leave, yes, but I don't think he plans to cause a lot of trouble."

"No," Rourke paused to answer before he stepped inside to get his boots and retrieve his sword. "But I won't stop anyone from wanting to leave the Order, either. I understand what it's like to feel caged in and not doing what you are meant to do."

"Not helping, Rourke," Sammy called after him, but Rourke didn't even bother to reply. He had a lot on his mind still about meeting with Ozni, and finding out that Isa was not only his son, but was probably harboring some of the same unease of being in the Sanctuary as Rourke did, was jarring. Rourke knew it was possible, but he didn't think it would be likely, and he certainly hadn't expected to find anyone who felt the same way he did.

Walking into the bedroom, Rourke picked up his sword — no, his sister's sword, his Guardian's sword — and simply held it in his hands. He had no right to wield this, even less right to use it as a weapon, yet that's what he had done, and he'd made an entire life out of doing just that. He'd always been defiant, Asha would tell him that regularly, but he'd never thought about what his defiance could mean outside of his own actions until now. Holding his sword a little tighter, he took a deep breath, and exhaled slowly. He couldn't turn from this path he had chosen; wouldn't do it, but he wasn't leaving the Order to make a statement either. For him, this was personal, although Rourke wondered if Isa's want to leave the Order was personal, also.

"What are you thinking about?" Sammy startled Rourke, and he turned to face Sammy wide eyed. Sammy laughed. "Wow, you must have really been deep in thought for me to scare you. Or am I just getting that good?"

"No, I was thinking about what Isa just said."

"Yeah?" Sammy looked back over his shoulder. "He said he would go tell the High Warden that we would be there in a sec."

Rourke rolled his eyes at Sammy's words and moved to strap his sword to his side. "Do you think Isa would leave?"

"I don't know." Sammy shrugged. "He's still young Alina said. He talks a lot about what he will do when he's High Warden, and how he will change the Sanctuary for the better."

Rourke felt memories tug at his mind. "I used to say something like that, too, and look at what I am about to do. I see a lot of my younger self in Isa, not going to lie, Sammy."

"Before the Wolves came you wanted to be High Warden?" Sammy laughed. "I don't believe it."

"Yeah, well, I did. And I am worried I may have just inadvertently told Isa to leave the order."

"Naw, I wouldn't worry about it. He doesn't even have the weird tattoos, yet. He's not old enough to make any decisions on his own, right?"

"I don't have my marks either, Sammy." Rourke frowned as he pushed past Sammy out into the kitchen area. "Come on."

"Wait." Sammy grabbed Rourke's arm. "Please don't get upset, that's not what I meant. Your situation is different. You grew up out there —" Sammy pointed off toward the darkness surrounding the city. "It's not your fault you don't have your marks. Isa *is* still a child. I know, and everyone we have spoken to, knows you are an adult. Cut the crap."

Rourke huffed, meeting Sammy's eyes. They stared at one another quietly for a moment before Rourke sighed. "You're right. I'm sorry. I am just worried about speaking with Ozni, and what it could mean for both of us."

Sammy raised his hand to press against Rourke's cheek. "I am sure it will be fine. You worry too much. You can do this, and I will be right there with you."

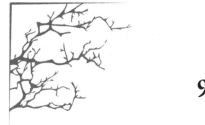

9

Ozni's office was large, and it matched not only the rest of the house, but Ozni's ego as well. Isa had been sitting on the porch playing with his haldis, but as soon as he opened the door for Rourke and Sammy, he left, saying he needed to go help with the nesting haldis. From where they had been standing on the porch, Rourke could see several nesting houses for the haldis, and wasn't surprised when Isa ran off in that direction.

Rourke and Sammy had barely closed the door behind themselves when a woman — Rourke and Sammy could only assume it was Ozni's wife and Isa's mother — stepped into the hall, a Guardian sword much like Lor's strapped to her back. She didn't speak but led them the rest of the way down the hall before opening the door to Ozni's office.

The middle-aged man was sitting behind a wide desk with papers strewn about. In one corner was a pitcher with several dirty glasses and an empty plate. On the floor, curled up on a pillow was a very overweight haldis, part of an uneaten cookie clutched in its claws. Rourke had heard the expression that haldis take after their owners, but never had he seen two that seemed to resemble one another so perfectly.

It was hard to tell if Ozni was smiling or not with his chubby cheeks, but it didn't stop him from motioning both Rourke and Sammy closer to his desk. With a wave of his hand, he motioned for them to sit in the high-armed chairs opposite his desk as he tried to clear his workspace of crumbs with the other hand. His eyes seemed dark and small, sunken into his pudgy face, and his greasy hair — that had already gone white at the temples — didn't help to add anything in his favor. "Welcome, welcome," he started, finally deciding he'd wiped enough crumbs off the desk and into his lap. "Welcome to Bhaskara."

"Um, thanks." Rourke took his sword from his side and sat in one of the two chairs while Sammy sat in the other, pulling Luna between his feet. Something about Ozni's house didn't sit right with Rourke, and he felt naked without the rest of his things, which besides his sword, he had left back in their lodging. Sammy, having not seen a reason to bring it, hadn't even brought his knife.

"I am very glad you are here. I was very excited to learn of your arrival!" Ozni grinned, his double chin moving as he spoke. "What did you say your name was again?"

"It's Rourke," Rourke started as he turned slightly toward Sammy. "And this is Sammy."

"Of Olin, yes? Very good!" Ozni spoke over Rourke, reaching out to pluck an ink quill from another cup on the desk. He searched through his papers for a moment before locating a book, and Ozni flipped it open as he scribbled down what Rourke could only assume was his name onto a blank page. "Yes, very, very good. The Sanctuary could use one of your caliber, Rourke."

"My caliber," Rourke asked, looking over at Sammy. Sammy shrugged, keeping his hands buried in Luna's fur.

"Why, yes, of course! A Warden of your background could be of much use to our humble Sanctuary, indeed."

"You mean because I am from Olin." Rourke figured this would come up, most people he spoke to seemed overly excited to meet someone from the first city. Even Alina had been excited to learn of Rourke's origin. "That's actually what I —"

"Yes, exactly! To learn from a Warden of Olin! What teachings can you offer myself, and the others, of course," Ozni added as an afterthought. "I am sure you have met my son, Isa. He would be a great protégé, if I do say so myself. Teach him all that you know so that he can carry on with my legacy after I pass on the mantle of High Warden to him. He will make a most excellent leader with your council to help guide him."

Rourke hesitated, afraid that once he started talking Ozni would simply interrupt him again. "That's not why I am here. I need to speak to you about something very important."

"Why? What could be more important than the Order and the haldis?" Ozni gasped in what Rourke could clearly see was exaggerated shock and pressed one of his fat hands to his chest. "What did they teach you at the Sanctuary of Olin?"

Rourke shrugged. "Don't remember most of it, but I assume the same things that are taught here. Reading, writing, care of the haldis —"

"Yes, good! Start there. The haldis of your Sanctuary must be very — wait." Ozni stopped, leaning forward over the desk as far as his body would allow as he searched for what Rourke could only assume was his missing haldis. Ozni's greedy eyes narrowed into slits. "Where *is* your haldis, Rourke of Olin?"

Rourke inhaled sharply as Sammy gasped in shock. He knew the question of what had happened to Orin would be brought up, but he never thought that the High Warden of all people would ask that question in such an accusing tone. Next to him, Rourke heard Sammy repeat what Alina had said to Lao at dinner: "You don't just ask someone that!"

Rourke tried very hard to keep the smile off his face. Sammy was adapting to life with not only him, but Bhaskara so very quickly, and honestly Rourke couldn't have been prouder — or happier — to have Sammy by his side. Reaching out, he placed his hand on Sammy's arm. "It's okay. I knew it was going to come up."

Ozni sputtered at Sammy's words, and finally seemed to notice him sitting in the room as he fell back into his chair. "An *Other*? You're an Other?"

"So, I have been told," Sammy muttered quietly. Between his legs, Luna shifted on her front feet, growing anxious at the shift of emotions in the room.

"Why are you in the company of an Other, Rourke?" Ozni turned his attention back to Rourke, his want for clarification clear in his eyes.

Rourke really didn't know what to say, so he settled with the truth of the matter. "Sammy is my committed. We —"

"Committed? *Committed*? You? *To an Other*? Of all things! This is unacceptable! You're a Warden, your bloodlines are better than this; better than committing to an outsider."

"Hey!" Sammy stood from his chair. Between his feet, Luna stood as well, clearly scared by Sammy's sudden outburst.

"That's not fair." Rourke stood also. He could see the anger on Sammy's face, a few wisps of loose hair falling into his eyes with his movements. Rourke was just as upset at Ozni's words as Sammy was. "It's my choice to commit to whom I want! You can't make that choice for me."

"That's where you are wrong. I am the High Warden; I run this Sanctuary, and I expect it to be run in a very specific way."

"You're out of line, Ozni," Rourke growled in anger. "I have never met a High Warden as selfish and arrogant as you!"

"You can't just decide peoples' lives for them!" Sammy threw his arms in the air. "What kind of leader does that?"

"Well," Ozni started, still very taken aback by Sammy's presence in the room. "This just cannot be! Neda! Neda, come here! Quickly!"

Rourke turned as the door to the room opened, and Neda — the woman who had escorted Rourke and Sammy in — stepped into the room. "What is it, Ozni," she asked, her voice hard and cold. Rourke found it very unbelievable that Isa was the son of these two. He was nothing like either of them from what he had seen so far.

"Will you please show this disrespectful ruffian out of our home?" Ozni pointed at Sammy. "I am trying to have a civil conversation with Rourke, and this Other is bothersome."

"Me," Sammy balked. "I'm the one being bothersome?"

Neda took a step toward Sammy and Rourke stepped between them, raising his arm defensively against Sammy's back. "He stays, or we both go."

Neda faltered, looking between Rourke and Sammy to Ozni. Rourke looked over his shoulder to the fat man, but he didn't have to wait to see what he was going to do. Ozni stood from his chair, pushing his great bulk up with his hands. His haldis scurried over to him behind the desk, startled awake, and cowering with fear. Rourke could see that same fear in Ozni's eyes, even though he was trying to hide it. "I have never been spoken to this way before," Ozni started, and Rourke could hear the shake in his voice. He was sure Sammy could, too. "Not even by my own son!"

"Feel bad for Isa," Sammy grumbled under his breath, looking over his shoulder to Neda. She hadn't moved from her spot several paces away. Tense silence filled the air for several heartbeats before Ozni cleared his throat.

"Very well, he stays. But!" Ozni bent over to pick up his haldis before sitting down in his chair. "So does Neda, and one more word out of you, and you will leave."

Sammy inhaled to speak, but Rourke grabbed his arm. Sammy looked at him, and Rourke hoped his message was clear as they locked eyes. *Just a little longer,* he was trying to convey. *Just give me until I can tell him I am leaving.*

Sammy sighed in defeat and sat down, pulling Luna back so she was sitting once more. Rourke didn't move until after Neda had walked by him to stand by Ozni's desk, and when he sat back down, he picked up his sword, resting it across his knees. Ozni once again cleared his throat and tried a happy smile. "Now, where were we? Ah, yes, what happened to your haldis?"

"And why do you carry the sword of a Guardian," Neda added in.

Rourke tightened his grip around his weapon, trying to remain calm. His heart was racing, but no longer out of worry. Now his heart was beating madly in his chest in anger, and he wanted nothing more than to leave, and not come back. Rourke took a deep breath to explain what had happened to Orin, Asha, and the fall of Olin, but stopped, and decided to start over. "I came to tell you one thing, as a courtesy of you being the High Warden." The word still tasted bitter on his tongue, but Rourke pushed himself to say it, pointedly ignoring the look Sammy gave him when he did. "And what I wanted to say was that I am leaving; the Sanctuary, the Order, all of it. My role in the Order died when Olin fell. There is nothing for me here any longer."

Ozni sputtered, trying to think of something to say as Neda gasped. Rourke looked over to Sammy and stood as Ozni regained his ability to speak. "*Leave the Order*? Preposterous! No one has ever left the Order! You're a *Warden*! It's your duty to serve the haldis in this Sanctuary!"

"No." Rourke shook his head, returning his sword to his side as he did. "It was my duty to serve the Sanctuary of Olin, which no longer exists. I am not required to tend to the haldis here."

"You're a disgrace," Neda sneered, her disgust for Rourke clear on her face. Rourke ignored her, turning to walk toward the door. "You mingle with Others. You don't even have a haldis. What kind of Warden doesn't have a haldis?"

Rourke heard Sammy stop, and he looked at Sammy as he took a deep breath and turned toward Ozni and Neda. "You two have no idea what he's been through, what any of the refugees have been through. You sit here on your high horse and assume everyone should bow down to you! Rourke's a better man than you'll ever be, that's for sure."

"That's enough, Sammy, come on." Rourke tugged on Sammy's arm, dragging him a step or two until he turned, walking past Rourke out into the hall with Luna.

"Rourke of Olin," Ozni started, and Rourke turned slightly to face him. Ozni was seething with anger, his entire body rolling with his labored breaths. Neda had her arms crossed; a scowl etched deep across her mouth. "I want you out of my Sanctuary. You take that Other filth with you and get out!" Ozni pointed behind him toward where Rourke knew the entrance to the Sanctuary was.

Rourke frowned at Ozni insulting Sammy but nodded sharply. "That's all I really wanted anyway." Stepping out into the hall, Rourke closed the door behind him, able to hear Ozni push everything off his desk in a fit of rage.

Luna tucked her tail between her legs and ran for the front door at the loud crash, while Sammy was staring at the wall, as if he was trying to see back into the room at what was going on. As Rourke walked by, Sammy turned to follow. "R-Rourke," he started, stumbling over his words. "Are you okay?"

"Yeah, why wouldn't I be?" Rourke opened the front door, watching as Luna ran from the house out into the large lawn in front of Ozni's house. She turned around, and took a deep breath, huffing it out through her nose as she watched them both. "He said he wanted us out of the Sanctuary, which is what I wanted."

"Yeah, but." Sammy stopped at the bottom of the stairs, rubbing his arm as he looked over his shoulder. "That didn't exactly go well."

"That's what I have been worried about, Sammy." Rourke turned back to Sammy, noticing both Ozni and Neda glaring at them from the window. Reaching out, Rourke took Sammy's hand. "Come on, we aren't welcome here. Let's go get our things and go find the Illuminari."

"Yeah, okay." Sammy tightened his grip on Rourke's hand, numbly following Rourke across the lawn toward their lodging. Luna walked up to them, calmer now that they were out of Ozni's house. Rourke had known deep down that his want to leave wouldn't go over very well, but he had never thought that it would hinge on the fact that he had committed to Sammy. Sammy's presence wouldn't have affected how Rourke worked with the haldis at all, and if anything, Sammy could have become Rourke's new Guardian.

Rourke took a deep breath and closed his eyes for a moment. Despite how it sounded, Rourke knew that wasn't really what he wanted. Yes, he wanted to be with Sammy, but he didn't want to be tied to this Sanctuary, especially if Ozni was the one in charge.

Next to him, Sammy was quiet, and Rourke looked over at him to see a pained look on his face. "What's wrong," Rourke asked, sure it had something to do with Ozni.

"What am I to you," Sammy asked suddenly, stopping and pulling on Rourke's arm.

Rourke let himself get tugged to a stop and turned to face Sammy. "What is that supposed to mean? You're my committed."

"What else?"

Rourke shook his head. "I don't understand, Sammy, what else is there for you to be?" Reaching up, Rourke pushed Sammy's bangs back behind his ear.

Sammy was frowning, looking over his shoulder back toward Ozni's house. "What about being an Other? It's really clear to everyone I don't belong here."

Rourke took a deep breath and rested both hands on Sammy's shoulders. "You're letting what Ozni said get to you. I have never cared that you're an Other, you know that." Rourke pressed a hand to Sammy's cheek, watching as Sammy leaned into his touch and closed his eyes. "I think it will do both of us some good to go to the Illuminari."

"Maybe," Sammy shrugged. "I'm just trying to fit in, is all, and it seems like every time I turn around, someone else has to point out that I don't belong here."

"Sammy, we have been here for three cycles," Rourke stated flatly. "Bhaskara is a big city, and Ozni is one man. Come on, let's go gather our things before Ozni and his committed come after us."

Sammy chuckled, taking Rourke's hand. "Yeah, okay. I'm sorry, I guess I'm just overreacting. Alina, Lor, and Lao seem to like me."

"That's because they don't care where you came from, they care about what kind of person you are."

Sammy leaned over and pressed a kiss to Rourke's cheek. "How can you always be so damned insightful at the perfect times?"

Rourke shrugged. "I don't know, I'm just being honest." Sammy hummed in answer and the two started toward their lodging.

They were just passing Lor and Alina's house when they heard Lao yell at them from the front porch. "So," he started, jumping down the few steps to the grass and startling Luna. "How did it go?"

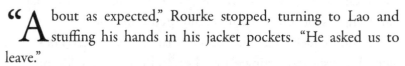

10

"About as expected," Rourke stopped, turning to Lao and stuffing his hands in his jacket pockets. "He asked us to leave."

"Wasn't exactly what he said," Sammy grumbled by Rourke's side. He was still upset about the entire meeting, and Sammy couldn't seem to get Ozni's words out of his head. *Just an Other*, that's all Sammy would ever be.

"Still sounds like him," Lor commented from the porch, leaning forward in his chair to rest his arms on the railing. "That's what you wanted though, wasn't it? To leave the Order so you could go to the Illuminari?"

"Yeah." Lao leaned down to pet Luna, who eagerly accepted the attention once she recognized him. "I already told Asha that I thought you would come this cycle."

"That's great!" Rourke seemed happy about leaving the Sanctuary, and while Sammy was happy for him, he was still worried about what would happen once they got there. Rourke closed the small gap to where Lor was sitting and leaned against the railing post. Sammy hadn't seen him this calm since they had met, spending most of their time in that small cave. "Don't worry, we will still come around to see you."

"I'll see you two at the barracks, but I am sure Alina would love to see you again. Sammy, you especially. She hasn't been able to stop talking about you, and well, I haven't seen her this happy before."

Sammy grinned; he couldn't help it. "I would really like that, Lor. I have greatly enjoyed getting to know her! Where is she anyway?"

Lor pointed toward the entrance. "She and a couple of the others you haven't met went to the market. I will let her know you would like to see her, but I think it's best if you left for now. If you don't hurry along, Ozni will send Neda after you."

"She's like his watchdog." Sammy threw his hands in the air. "I half expected her to start growling."

Lao laughed while Rourke and Lor just looked at Sammy in confusion. "What," Sammy asked. "She is!"

"Don't worry, I understand." Lao stood and threw his arm around Sammy's shoulders. "And I agree, she is! It really fits her! Puts a whole new meaning to the word *guard*-ian, doesn't it?" Lao was grinning from ear to ear, quite proud of his little joke.

Sammy chuckled and nodded in agreement. "It certainly does. We should go. If what Lor says is true, I don't want to cause any more trouble than I already seem to have caused."

"You didn't do anything." Rourke stood and looked over his shoulder toward Ozni's house. "Sammy, there is nothing wrong with being an Other. You're no different than the rest of us."

"For the love of the light! He didn't!" Lao frowned and shook his head. "Did he really attack you for being an Other? I can't stand people like him."

"He did." Sammy nodded before he took a step toward the little lodging Rourke and he had been staying in. "Come on, let's go pack our things. I don't want to be here any longer than I have to be." Sammy started walking, and Luna trotted along beside him. Rourke caught up, falling into step at Sammy's side. "We'll come back once we've packed, okay, Lao?"

"Okay!" Sammy watched Lao walk up the stairs to sit in the chair next to his brother. "And don't worry about it, Sammy! The barracks are full of Inducted Illume and Others! No one is going to say a thing to you about it!"

Sammy waved sheepishly. "Thanks, Lao. See you in a bit!" Turning back to see where he was going, Sammy and Rourke made their way across the open lawn to where they had been staying. They were quiet, and Sammy didn't mind, he was sure Rourke had a lot on his mind right now. Sammy knew he did.

Just as they were getting to the small building, Rourke stopped suddenly, looking over to the pond. "What is it," Sammy asked, pausing to see if he could figure out what Rourke was looking at.

"Nothing. I thought I saw that small haldis, but now I can't find it." Shrugging, Rourke brushed past Sammy into the building. "Shouldn't take long to pack since most of our things are still packed."

Sammy walked up onto the porch, and carefully pushed aside the curtain that was covering the doorway. "What do you think is going to happen once we get there?"

"I'm sure it will be fine, Sammy." Rourke walked across the small space into the bedroom. "You worry too much."

"Maybe you don't worry enough, Rourke." Sammy placed both hands on the back of a chair and frowned down at Luna. He had no idea how Rourke could be so calm about all of this. Once again, they were being uprooted before they had even been able to settle into a place. Sammy took a deep breath and sighed. Maybe that was partly why Rourke was so calm. He'd spent most of his life wandering from place to place that this most likely still felt natural to him.

"Hey," Rourke started, brushing his fingers against Sammy's cheek. Sammy blinked at him, startled by his presence. "It will be okay, Sammy." Pulling him forward, Rourke pressed their foreheads together. "Gather your things."

"Where are you going?"

Rourke leaned around Sammy and picked up the last apple from the bowl on the table. "The porch. I'm going to sit and just —" he paused, suddenly looking a little forworn. "And just watch the haldis before we leave," he finished quietly.

"You may not want to do the Warden thing, but you still love the animals, don't you?"

"Yeah," Rourke nodded. "I do. They are really special." Leaning over, Rourke pressed a kiss to Sammy's cheek. "Whenever you are ready to leave, we will go." Then he pulled away and took a bite of his apple.

"Okay." Sammy nodded and moved toward the bedroom to gather his clothing and his backpack while Rourke went out to sit on the porch. Luna followed Sammy, jumping up on the bed and purring while Sammy folded his few clothes and put them away. He wondered if they would be able to buy more clothes at some point, figuring that like most jobs, money of some sort would be involved. No one had mentioned money though, and Lao had said that most of the Illuminari lived in the barracks, so maybe pay was compensation in room and board. He would have to ask Rourke about it once they arrived there.

Scratching Luna on the head, Sammy tied his rolled pelt to his backpack — Rourke must have rolled it up beforehand — and slung it over one shoulder. "Are you ready to go," he asked Luna, who seemed more than happy to have Sammy rubbing her ears. Chuckling, Sammy ran his fingers under her collar to see how tight it was before he turned and made his way out of the small bedroom. Luna followed along quietly. "Okay," Sammy started as he stepped out onto the porch. "I'm ready to — Rourke?"

At Sammy's feet was Rourke's pack, and his half-eaten apple was sitting on the railing of the porch, but Rourke was nowhere to be seen. "Yeah?" He sat up, and Sammy turned to where he was on the far side of the porch in the grass. He stuck his hand through the slats on the porch rail. "Can you hand me my apple?"

"What on earth are you doing?" Sammy picked up the apple and walked over to where Rourke was, handing it to him as he leaned on the railing. "I thought we were leaving."

"We are." Rourke took a bite of the apple for himself, then a second bite that he took back into his free hand as he handed Sammy the apple. "I need to do this first."

"Do what? Don't talk with your mouth full." Sammy rolled his eyes and watched as Rourke climbed under the edge of the porch. Sammy raised an eyebrow as he watched Rourke work his upper body underneath the porch. "Again: what on earth are you doing?"

"That little haldis was chased under here. I want to get it out. Come on," he started, and Sammy knew Rourke was no longer speaking to him. "That's it, just a little closer. It's a good apple, I promise."

Sammy smirked as he watched Rourke try to get even farther under the porch. Resting his arms on the railing, Sammy shook his head. Rourke really was something else. A moment later there was a loud squeak and Rourke was pushing himself back out from under the porch, rolling over onto his back in the grass once he was completely out. In his hand was the small haldis, legs clawing madly at the air as its tail tried to smack Rourke in the face.

Carefully, Rourke set the haldis on his chest and gave it back the apple chunk. Immediately, the haldis settled down on Rourke's chest, happily munching away at the piece of fruit as its tail curled around its feet. "There, see." Rourke raised both hands to run down its sides and back. "Much better."

"Well, is he okay," Sammy asked, amazed at just how good Rourke was with the little thing. He'd never seen an animal calm down as quickly as this haldis did with Rourke. And Rourke was gentle, his voice low, and his movements slow. Sammy was getting used to seeing the many different sides of Rourke, and he especially liked this gentler side of him.

"She, and yes. This is an old scar. And she has bits of moss growing on her scales. You can see it here, and here." Rourke pointed to different purple spots on the little animal's body, but Sammy wasn't sure what Rourke was talking about. "She's healthy, just small."

Sammy nodded. "That's good. Are you going to keep her?"

Rourke snapped his head up to look at Sammy with wide eyes, his expression a combination of shock and horror. Sammy felt guilt twist in his gut as Rourke shook his head. "No."

"Why not? Everyone else has one, why can't you?"

Rourke took a deep breath and closed his eyes. "It's a bond that's made when young, Sammy. It's not something that can easily be created or replaced. I just wanted to help her, that was all. I more than likely won't be getting another haldis."

"But you could," Sammy asked, although he knew from the tone of Rourke's voice, and the little bit he'd managed to gather over the last few days — cycles, whatever — that Rourke's chances of bonding with a second haldis were very slim. "It has happened?"

"Yes." Rourke raised his hands as the haldis finished eating, chomping loudly on her last mouthful of apple before she slid off Rourke's chest and scurried away. "It has happened, but not to people like me. I've lost that connection, Sammy."

Sammy watched the small haldis waddle off as Rourke sat up. "Could have fooled me."

"I was just helping." Rourke's voice was quiet as he raised a hand to rub at the back of his neck. "Come on, let's go before Ozni figures out I was interacting with the herd." Standing, Rourke wiped his hands on his pants and reached out for the rest of his apple.

Sammy picked up Rourke's backpack and handed it to him as they walked back across to Lor's house where Lao was waiting for them. With a grin, he jumped off the porch steps again, and the three of them started across Bhaskara back toward the entrance to the city. On the way, Lao explained how the barracks of the Illuminari used to be one big pasture for umbra, but once the darkness fell, and refugees began to pour into the city, structures were built to house everyone. For the most part, the refugees integrated themselves into places within the city, but a few remained at the barracks and began the Illuminari.

Sammy recognized things as they drew closer to the entrance of the barracks and was able to spot the large city gate with the city banners waving in the breeze. As Lao pointed them in a new direction, Sammy was able to see the steps of the city council hall, and it helped piece together a little more of the city's layout. The area of the barracks had a high stonewall made from smaller dark stones. Lao explained that the wall had once been a fence for the umbra and was built as an afterthought when the city was first constructed, which was why it was built out of dark field and lake stone.

Walking under the archway into the Illuminari barracks was like walking into a completely different world. Sammy could see how this once may have been a large open area for the umbra, but it had clearly been converted into a courtyard with buildings that lined the edge of it. A large dark stone building stood to their left and next to that was a barn built out of more dark stone and wood. There were several smaller wooden buildings that completed the semicircle of buildings. Between two of the buildings, Sammy caught a glimpse of what looked like a pasture with several umbra ranging in color from black to light gray.

Despite what Sammy thought would have been the main building — the large, four-story stone building next to the barn — Lao turned them toward a small two-story wooden building just to the right of the entrance. There was no porch, but a staircase that led right up and into the side of the mostly windowless building. Lao knocked on the doorframe as he pushed aside the curtain. "Asha, you in here?"

"Lao," called a female's voice. "Just the man I wanted to see. I have been considering your scouting — oh." The woman stopped as Sammy and Rourke followed Lao into the room. The open area looked to be an office of sorts with a large desk, two tables littered with papers and maps, and several benches. In the center of each table was a large chuck of bhasvah stone that lit up the entire room. "The light shines upon you. You must be Rourke and Sammy. I'm Asha." Asha paused as she stood from behind one of the tables. "Head of the Illuminari."

"And guide your steps," Rourke said with a nod.

"I'm going to go." Lao pointed at the door. "I'll come by later, okay? I would like to talk to you about my proposal."

"Okay, good." Asha nodded sharply and Lao ducked out of the room. "Lao tells me you want to join our ranks. I have to be honest; I was a bit surprised when he told me you were turning away from the Sanctuary."

Rourke nodded. "There really isn't anything there for me anymore."

Asha sat down on the bench by the table and motioned for Rourke and Sammy to sit. They both sat at spots on different benches, and Sammy pulled Luna to him to keep her from causing trouble. Asha looked over at Sammy and Luna before she nodded. "I still can't believe this, even though I see it myself. You two really did train a shadow cat."

"Sammy mostly." Rourke nodded.

"So, tell me." Asha placed her hands on the tabletop and laced her fingers together. "Why does a former Warden — and forgive me, Lao said you hated the word — want to join the Illuminari? I thought your entire life's existence was dedicated to the haldis."

Rourke frowned, but Sammy watched quietly as he took a deep breath. "I'm sure you've heard I'm from Olin; it seems most of the city knows that. As I said, there really isn't much for me at the Sanctuary anymore, and Aetius —"

"Aetius," Asha interrupted. "Aetius of Amshu?"

"Yes, I know him. He said this would be perfect for me given all that he taught me, and I have taught myself while in the darkness."

Asha was quiet for a moment as she mulled over what it was Rourke had said, then she nodded sharply and stood. "Yes, I do remember him mentioning a young man he hoped was still alive. That must have been you. If you know half the things that Aetius does, I would be lucky to have you. Sammy, you, too."

"Oh, no." Sammy shook his head. "Not me. I'm not really the fighting type."

Asha shrugged and walked over to her desk. "I have some paperwork for you to fill out and sign, Rourke; pay, room and board, skill sets, that sort of thing. Then I will show you to your room, as well as the bathhouse, the blacksmith, butcher, bowyer, and the barn, though it is hard to miss the barn when you walk in."

"I think we saw it," Sammy spoke up. "Or well, I did. Can we go see the umbra?"

"Of course, you can. Even if you don't join, Sammy, you are Rourke's committed, you get all the same things he does, except the pay, of course, unless you join."

"Not going to happen."

Asha shrugged. "Worth a shot." They fell quiet while Asha shuffled through some papers before she picked up a small pile of paper. Walking over to Rourke, she handed him the stack. "You can go over these later if you want. Let's get you two settled in."

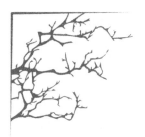

11

Asha pointed out smaller buildings before leading them to the large stone building. This was the actual barracks of the Illuminari, and where those who lived within the barracks slept. Sammy followed along behind Rourke with Luna between them and Asha leading the way. Neither of them said much as they first went down into what Sammy would call the basement so Asha could show them where the bathhouse was — several smaller more personalized tubs with a crude form of running water and drainage system — before taking them up the stairs to the third floor. She turned right off the stairs and walked about halfway down the hall before stopping in front of a door on the inside wall.

Light from the occasional window filled the hall with what Sammy thought was an afternoon sun; bright but not overbearing as little specks of dust floated about. Some things were the same even with everything being so very different. Asha turned the handle and pushed open a wooden door, letting light pour into the dark room. "It's not much," Asha started. "But it should be perfect for the two of you. Most of the Illuminari are on the second floor, so it's fairly quiet on this floor. Although there are a few who choose to live on the fourth floor above you." Asha pointed toward the ceiling. "You do have a few neighbors a couple rooms down, though. I will inform everyone to refrain from calling you 'Warden,' Rourke. Nari suits you just fine."

"Thank you." Rourke nodded and took a step past Asha into the room.

"If you need anything, let us know, Rourke, Sammy, and we will do our best to get it. The Illuminari takes care of their own. See you at dinner." With a wave of her hand, Asha turned and left, disappearing back down the stairs.

Sammy watched her go before looking down the hallway. It went on for several feet before turning right down a corner. At his feet, Luna was sniffing the doorframe to the room, and inside Sammy could hear Rourke drop his backpack to the floor with a heavy sigh. "What is it," Sammy asked, finally taking a step into the room. Luna followed and Sammy closed the door behind himself.

Rourke was holding his bhasvah in his hand and the small stone flared to life as Sammy closed the door. It cast strange shadows around the room, highlighting Rourke's face from where he sat in the single chair by a desk pushed against the wall. Sammy looked around, noticing a large bed, two bureaus, and a rug in addition to the chair and desk. There were also two small nightstands on each side of the bed, near the headboard. "This isn't so bad, I guess." Sammy took his pack off, setting it down against the bureau closest to him. It was clear that this room was meant more for sleep than for spending large amounts of time in, but if this building was built for the people who worked with the umbra — and Sammy thought it was since it was made of the same stone as the barn, unlike the other wooden buildings — than it made perfect sense that this room was meant mostly for sleeping.

Rourke took another deep breath, resting his arms on his knees and holding his stone tightly in both his hands. "I'm sorry," he started, his voice quiet. "I know you were expecting things to be different."

"What are you talking about?" Sammy walked over to Rourke, rolling his eyes as Luna jumped up on the bed, already making herself comfortable. Kneeling, Sammy rested his hands on Rourke's hands. "Different how?"

"Maybe I expected things to be different." Rourke didn't look up, and Sammy could see his eyes trained on the piece of bhasvah, the bright light reflected in the gray and gold of his eyes. "I wasn't expecting to have to put you through all of this. I never wanted — The Last City was supposed to —" Rourke cut himself off and shook his head.

Sammy frowned. He was sure Rourke was blaming himself for everything that had happened since they arrived here. The confusion, the moving, the marginalization, and the low level of hate that Sammy had dealt with. "Whatever you are thinking, stop. I don't blame you for anything that has happened. You needed to do this. For you. Things will get better now, you'll see."

"I just wanted to show you the city," Rourke murmured, still not looking at Sammy. "And all I have done is make things worse."

"How is this worse?" Sammy looked around the room. "Yeah, there are no windows, but we have this to ourselves. True, the last few days have been crazy, but you've been steadfast through all of it. You haven't wavered from what you wanted and look at where we are. This is our space, Rourke. Yours and mine and Luna's."

Rourke huffed what could have been a laugh. "Can't forget Luna," he grumbled, but he looked up. Taking a deep breath, he met Sammy's eyes. "Thank you."

Sammy reached up, pressing his hand to Rourke's cheek and rubbing his thumb over Rourke's cheekbone. The light of the bhasvah still reflected in Rourke's eyes, giving his eyes the illusion that they glowed ever so slightly. "For?"

Rourke shook his head. "Nothing, I guess."

Sammy leaned up for a chaste kiss, staying just far enough away to speak, and kept his voice low. "Then you're welcome for nothing, I guess."

Sammy could sense Rourke's hesitation before he closed the small gap for a kiss. It wasn't much more than a simple kiss, but an urgency quickly seemed to grow as Rourke deepened the kiss. Scooting forward in the chair, Rourke placed the bhasvah behind him on the seat as his other hand moved to rest against Sammy's shoulder.

Rourke pushed Sammy back by his shoulder as he slid from the chair, kneeling over Sammy's legs, and never broke the kiss. Sammy let Rourke push him to the floor, wrapping his arms around Rourke's shoulders and keeping him close. He moved his legs, one leg remaining between Rourke's knees while he bent his other leg to place his foot flat on the floor and adjust how he was laying.

Want flared through Sammy, and the sudden realization that there was nothing stopping them from kissing, or taking things further, only caused him to try to pull Rourke closer to him. Over him, Rourke shifted his hand to brace himself, breaking the kiss just long enough to take a breath. "What are you doing," Sammy asked, taking advantage of the pause and running his fingers through Rourke's hair.

"Kissing you." Rourke's voice was low, and Sammy wasn't sure if he was actually hearing the arousal in his voice, or simply imagining it. "Thought I could do that."

"Oh, you can." Sammy grinned as he looked up to Rourke, moving both hands to press against his cheeks. "I was just caught a little off guard, that's all."

Rourke shrugged, before kissing Sammy again, slower and softer this time than previously. Rourke's free hand came up to play with Sammy's hair, and only then did Sammy realize it had come loose from the hair pick. Taking a deep breath through his nose, Sammy wrapped his arms tightly around Rourke's shoulders again, and pushed with his leg, rolling the two of them over. Rourke seemed a little shocked to be looking up at Sammy now, but his shock almost instantly melted into a smile as he reached up and pushed Sammy's hair behind his ear.

Sammy felt want and longing twist in his chest in a way he hadn't before, and he leaned down for a kiss. Rourke met him eagerly, moving one arm behind his head while the other came to rest on Sammy's shoulder. Wanting to take this further, Sammy opened his mouth, and licked Rourke's bottom lip with his tongue. Sammy fully expected Rourke to pull away like he had before, but instead Sammy heard a low gasp as Rourke opened his mouth. Without hesitating, Sammy pressed deeper, moaning lowly into the kiss as Rourke tightened his grip on Sammy's shoulder.

Fingers carding into Rourke's hair, Sammy tipped his head a little further to the side, long dormant arousal rolling through him when Rourke mimicked his movements and pressed their tongues together. "Shit, you're perfect," Sammy murmured as he pulled away, licking the corner of his mouth.

Rourke looked away, a faint blush coloring his cheeks. "How can you say something like that?"

Sammy leaned down, capturing Rourke's mouth in a slow and sensual kiss. After a moment, he felt Rourke's fingers in his hair in an attempt to keep Sammy close. Not that he planned on going anywhere. He was perfectly happy to be kneeling over Rourke kissing him. This time Rourke opened his mouth first, and when their tongues met, Sammy heard Rourke inhale sharply as his grip tightened in Sammy's hair.

Rourke didn't pull away, and so Sammy didn't break their kiss, instead pressing deeper into Rourke's mouth, and seeing just how far they could go. Rourke, though hesitant, pressed back, only breaking the kiss when Luna appeared and licked the side of his face. With a grimace, he turned his head away, and Sammy laughed as he pushed Luna away. "That is so gross."

"She just wants a kiss, too." Sammy sat up, looking down at Rourke as Luna tried to lick his face a second time. Pushing her away again, Rourke sat up on his elbows, seemingly content with everything. He wiped his cheek on his shoulder before looking up at Sammy.

"Want to go explore a little bit?"

"Yeah." Sammy nodded, pushing his hair behind his ear. Luna tried to climb into Rourke's lap, and Sammy grabbed her before she could. "I know you don't really care for umbra, but I want to go see them! They look amazing and seem like an awesome animal."

Rourke groaned and fell back onto the rug under him. Closing his eyes, he took a deep breath. "All right," he started, moving his hands to push at Sammy's knees. "You have to get off me, though. We can't go see the umbra with you sitting on me."

"You're no fun," Sammy pouted, but moved to stand, then helped Rourke to his feet. Leaning over, Sammy pressed a kiss to Rourke's cheek. "You're adorable when you do things you don't want to. Thanks." Still muttering under his breath, Rourke's cheeks flushed again, and he turned from Sammy toward the door.

ઈઉ

The barn was attached to the barracks, and Rourke and Sammy, after a little bit of wandering around, made their way into the stables. Rourke paused to investigate the field, seeing a large herd of umbra grazing, and beyond them, the fence, the waters of the lake, and the fields that rose to meet the edge of the darkness. Sammy kept walking, only stopping at the wide-open doors to the barn when he realized Rourke wasn't at his side. "What are you looking at," Sammy asked as he walked back to Rourke. "Wow, that's a view." Sammy rested his head on Rourke's shoulder, and Rourke reached out, wrapping his arm around Sammy's waist.

"Yeah, it really is," Rourke agreed.

"Look at all the umbra. Why are they different colors? I thought they were black."

"Wild ones are. The gray ones are domesticated."

Rourke looked over to the woman who had answered Sammy's question, a sheepish smile on her face. She had curly brown hair and bright brown eyes. "Sorry. I didn't mean to eavesdrop, just heard the question. Name's Miley. You two must be new, I haven't seen your faces around."

"Yeah, we are!" Sammy turned and reached out his hand, and Miley instantly reached for Sammy's hand with a huge grin. "I'm Sammy, and this is Rourke. You are clearly not from this place."

"Did my complexion give it away," Miley reached for her curls.

"Accent honestly," Sammy replied, as Miley and him let go of each other's hands. Rourke bobbed his head in a quick nod when Miley looked his way. Miley studied Rourke for a couple heartbeats before moving back to Sammy.

"Yeah, Texas, everyone seems to pick up on that." Miley grinned. "Though the longer I am here, the more it goes away." With a laugh, she shook her head. "Well, come on. If you want to see the umbra, come with me. I was just about to start chores."

"Oh, cool. Come on, Rourke." Sammy turned back to Rourke with a huge grin on his face, and as much as Rourke didn't want to spend the next phase with the umbra, he took a deep breath and reached out for the hand Sammy was offering. Seeing Sammy happy and excited was great, and Rourke didn't want to ruin that.

Miley led them into the barn, which was darker than outside, but still bright enough to see. Empty stalls lined the walls, and Rourke realized the building was much bigger than he first thought it had been. Overhead he could hear people walking around and could only assume that other stable hands had already started on the chores.

"So, what do you know about umbra, Sammy? When I first got here, I was so shocked to see such a creature. They are huge! And the fangs! I never thought I would see such a thing on a sweet creature that only eats plants!" Rourke snorted back a laugh and Miley turned to him. "What?"

"Never seen an umbra in the wild, have you? These things are anything but sweet, and they will purposely hit you with their antlers."

Miley inhaled to reply, but Sammy grabbed Rourke by the arm. "Rourke doesn't like umbra," he said, and Rourke could see Sammy was clearly trying to keep everyone civil. Rourke was calm, he was just simply stating a fact. Miley didn't have to like him for it.

"Maybe you've just never met a nice umbra before, Rourke." Miley turned and walked off, waving over her shoulder for them to follow.

"You don't have to be such a jerk, Rourke." Sammy bumped him in the shoulder. "Miley is clearly excited about the umbra, and so am I."

"Never liked them."

"So, you keep telling me."

"Oh! Did you know you could ride umbra?" Miley had stopped in front of a stall and was leaning on the wall.

"No."

"Yes." Rourke spoke at the same moment Sammy did. "Though I don't know why you would want to." Sammy clicked his tongue in annoyance, and Rourke chuckled. "Okay, I'll stop, but I still don't have to like this."

"I never asked you to like this, and you asked me to go exploring." Sammy started after Miley. "Come on, Rourke. I want to see the umbra."

"I'm coming." Rourke was a little slower to make his way down to where Miley was, but Sammy made his way to Miley's side quickly, resting his hands on the edge of the stall wall. Rourke simply listened to the conversation — Miley was explaining why the herd was outside — until he was able to stand next to Sammy.

Inside the stall was a large gray umbra with a wide and impressive set of antlers. "So, then, why is this one in here," Sammy asked, pointing.

"Lilith is about to calf, that's why she's inside. We have been keeping an eye on her."

"Calf," Sammy asked. "What's that mean?"

Miley grinned at Sammy as she reached over the top of the stall wall to Lilith as she plodded over to them. "She's gonna have a baby! We bred her to Snap, that's our big wild buck, and she should be having her calf anytime now."

"Oh, that's so cool! Rourke, isn't that cool?"

"I guess." Rourke frowned at Sammy. "Though I don't quite understand how her having a calf is cool."

"No, not cool as in —" Sammy cut himself off and shook his head ironically. "I mean, it's amazing she's having a baby."

"Yeah, that is good." Rourke had to agree. Even though he didn't like umbra, he knew they had their uses, and new life of any kind was always an exciting moment.

"Do you want to pet her?" Miley opened the latch on her stall door. "She's the sweetest one I have met. Go on, it's okay. Just watch the antlers."

"Really?" Sammy walked into the stall as Miley opened the door. Rourke took Sammy's place at the stall wall as the door closed. Placing his arms on the wall, Rourke then rested his chin on his arms. Sammy walked over to Lilith as she turned her head, sniffing and blowing at him as he reached out a hand.

"Hang on, let me get you a handful of the sweet grain we are giving her right now. She will eat it right out of your hand." Miley walked off and came back a moment later with a bucket in her hand. Taking a handful, she reached over the wall to pour it into Sammy's hand. "Keep your hand flat, like this." Miley showed Sammy as she spoke, opening her hand and keeping her fingers together to form a sort of plate with the grain in Sammy's palm. "Just keep your hand low so she can eat it, she'll lick it right off your palm."

Rourke watched Sammy through Lilith's antlers as he did what Miley asked. He had a huge smile on his face, and Rourke didn't think he'd seen Sammy this happy or excited since they'd met, and he couldn't keep the smile off his face either.

Reaching out, Sammy ran a hand down the length of Lilith's neck, coming to rest on her shoulder as he let her eat the rest of the grain from his hand. "Here." Miley lifted the bucket over the edge of the stall door. "This is for her, too. Just set it on the hook that's over by where Rourke is standing. She'll eat it."

Sammy took the bucket and did as he was asked, still grinning as Lilith moved aside so he could hang the bucket. Rourke took a step back from the stall to avoid getting hit with her antlers, but Sammy was still standing in the stall with her, petting her and rubbing her pregnant belly while she ate. "This is an amazing creature. How can you hate them, Rourke?"

Rourke nodded toward the antlers. "You get smacked in the head enough by those antlers and you'll understand."

Lilith picked her head up and swung it around to face Sammy, who had to lean back so he didn't get hit with her antlers. She snorted at him again, nibbling at his shirt and getting her fang caught on the string ties of his pants. Sammy kept calm as he got her loose, and Lilith went back to eating without a care in the world. "I don't know," Sammy started, moving down her body a little bit to pet her sides. Reaching out, he scratched behind her ear. "I kind of want one. They are really amazing."

Rourke rolled his eyes as Miley leaned over the stall door. "Every Nari gets their own umbra. Maybe you could have Lilith's calf."

"No." Rourke shook his head. "Absolutely not."

Sammy laughed and leaned down to rub both hands over Lilith's side. He stood back up with the biggest and happiest smile Rourke had ever seen on his face. Rourke felt his resolve breaking the longer Sammy laughed. Even when it came to umbra, it seemed he was unable to tell Sammy 'no.' As he calmed down, Sammy pushed a loose piece of his hair from his eyes, and Rourke knew Sammy was going to get an umbra despite Rourke's refusal. "You said the same thing about Luna, Rourke."

12

With the help of Lao, Rourke had been able to get the paperwork filled out and returned to Asha, but she and Lao were about to leave on a short scouting trip, and so nothing would become official until her return. In the few cycles that passed while Rourke waited, he and Sammy got settled into their new lives at the barracks, slowly making friends and unpacking. They found out several things about the barracks, including that they had their own leatherworker, so Rourke and Sammy were able to order Luna a proper collar. Sammy even asked to have her name etched into the leather, handing the primary leatherworker a slip of paper with Luna's name on it in Lor's handwriting.

Sammy had expressed an interest in learning to read and write in Rourke's language, and Rourke thought it was a great idea, but also knew he wouldn't be able to teach Sammy, needing to relearn himself. They found a tutor at the barracks, also. An older Illume woman who taught all the Others how to read and write. Rourke felt a little awkward about going to lessons as an adult, but she was willing to come to their room where it was quieter, and so far, both Sammy and he were learning very quickly. It made learning easier for Rourke, too, being able to be in their room where it was calm and quiet.

The best part of the last few cycles had to have been when Rourke came back to the room with the palu-tai plant. He'd been out with Lor, and Lor had bought them one as a gift for their room. Sammy had thought the blue flowered plant had been very pretty, and asked Rourke to put it on the desk so Sammy could look at it when he studied. Without giving Rourke a chance to explain, Sammy took it from him, set it down on the corner of the desk, and the two of them had gone to sleep with a peck on the cheek and a shirt thrown over Rourke's bhasvah.

Rourke woke at the beginning of the cycle to Sammy screaming and falling over him as he tried to get away from the palu-tai plant. Rourke looked over to see the plant climbing up the side of the end table as it searched out Rourke's bhasvah. Laughing, Rourke took the stone from the plant, and walked over to the desk. Sammy jumped back on the bed, horrified as the plant walked across the room to the desk, climbed up to the top, settled back into its planter, and pulled Rourke's stone to it. They'd gone right out and gotten a small piece of bhasvah for the plant to have for its own, and it hadn't moved since, except to occasionally snap up a stray moth that made it into their room. Sammy still wasn't over how a plant could move like that, claiming plants just didn't do that where he was from.

They were finally beginning to settle into their new lives in Bhaskara, Rourke thought, but something still didn't feel right. He didn't like the feeling of being closed in, besides the smells of the city were nothing like the open air of the darkness, and Rourke was having trouble relaxing. Needing to be by himself, Rourke told Sammy he was going to go for a walk down by the lake side, but not to worry, that he wouldn't leave the city or be gone too long. Rourke found himself on the far side of the umbra pasture, sitting on the low stone wall fence overlooking the lake. A slight breeze was blowing, bringing with it the smell of the forest in the darkness.

Taking a deep breath, Rourke closed his eyes, and just listened. Behind him, he could hear the umbra, bugling and pawing, clacking antlers together and running around. Birds sang in the city and moths flitted about by the water's edge. Occasionally, Rourke would hear some sort of fish jump out of the water, more than likely after a moth that went too close to the surface. In the far distance of the darkness, he could hear the distinct calls of a crow. It was all together peaceful and quiet. Rourke felt himself relax more than he had allowed himself to do since he'd been on his own. He knew things were going to be different in Bhaskara, but he thought he would be able to adapt to the changes better than he seemed to have been able to so far. Having his eyes closed wasn't the same as being out in the darkness, but it helped to make him feel as if he was out there, and it was more comforting that Rourke thought possible.

"It is quite nice, is it not?"

Rourke jumped forward at the sound of the new voice right by his ear, and tripped on a rock, almost falling into the water at the edge of the lake. He stood back up, and turned to ask what the person's problem was, when his breath caught in his throat. Standing on the other side of the stone wall, leaning over it to make sure he was all right was a shaman. "Lysha," he asked, although he knew deep down it was her. He would never forget her short, lithe frame, or the thick braid of long black hair that was littered with beads, haldis scales, and random feathers. She had more marks than when he'd seen her last, but that wasn't important. She was family, and now, the only blood family he had left.

Lysha grinned, showing all her teeth. "Look at how big you've grown, Rourke!"

"Don't scare me like that."

"How else should I speak to you?"

"I don't know." Rourke shook his head as he climbed back up the small hill to sit on the wall. "How about by letting me know you are there before you just speak into my ear."

"I knew I was there. You should have, too. Our Aetius taught you better."

Rourke rolled his eyes at Lysha. "Yeah, I know he did. I've let my guard down since being here. I shouldn't."

"There is nothing to fear within the city, Rourke. It is outside the city that you must be guarded." Lysha climbed over the wall to sit next to Rourke, pulling her satchel into her lap. She swung her short legs as she looked over to Rourke. "Tell me how you have been. Last I saw you; you were nothing but a memory in the darkness."

"Yeah." Rourke reached up and rubbed the back of his neck. "Sorry for leaving like that. I knew Aetius was going to try and make me stay, and I knew I just couldn't —" Rourke broke off with a heavy sigh.

"You were never meant to be caged, Rourke. I told your parents so when you were born. Then you had the idea that you would be High Warden!" Lysha laughed, the light bubbly sound drifting off over the water. "I knew the moment I took you into my arms as a newborn, you were going to be doing something none of us knew about yet. And look!" Lysha spread her arms wide. "Here we are!"

Rourke looked out over the water and shook his head. Shamans were known for their greater understanding of the lands around them, but Lysha seemed more connected than most. Rourke could remember Asha telling him people thought it was because they came from a long line of shamans and Wardens. Their bloodline had lived and thrived in Olin for many generations. "Just as crazy as you've always been." He grinned as Lysha smacked him in the arm. "Thank you," he paused. "For saving me. I never did thank you for that."

"How did those scars heal?" Reaching over, Lysha grabbed Rourke's shirt, pulling it up toward his chin and running her fingers over the faded scars of his stomach.

Rourke pulled his shirt back down as he leaned away from her. "Stop it! I'm not a child anymore."

"No," Lysha laughed. "You certainly are not." Taking a deep breath, she continued with a sigh. "And yet."

"Yeah, I know." Rourke looked over to Lysha with all her marks and knew exactly what she was referring to: the fact that Rourke didn't have his rite of passage mark to show he had truly become an adult. A way for others to know that he was truly an adult within their culture.

While all adults had their rite of passage mark — a mark that represented the family in some way — and later most their committed mark, shamans were different. Shamans constantly added new marks to their skin until it was more covered than not. Each mark represented a part of training the shaman had gone through and ultimately mastered. The more marks a shaman had, the more they knew.

Unlike most Illume, shamans weren't limited to the number of marks they could have, but because of that, they weren't able to get their family marks, either. Because of their positions within Illume culture, they weren't allowed to be connected to one family or another; they belonged to the Illume people as a whole, so marks that connected them to one family weren't allowed for them.

Rourke couldn't remember what their family marks looked like, though he was sure Lysha knew. "But who am I going to get to give me a mark? Aetius said he would, but I've thought about it, and I don't know how I feel about that. Asha didn't have the family mark, she had the —" Rourke raised his fingers to his chin, looking over to Lysha's mark in the same spot. The Haldis Spheres, a mark given to those of Olin who had done something great within the city, had been the only mark Asha had ever gotten. "I don't even remember what my parents' marks looked like. Do you remember the family mark?" Rourke closed his eyes as he lowered his voice. "I barely remember them at all."

"Your parents would be proud of you. Your Asha," Lysha continued after a moment of silence. She reached out and placed her hand on Rourke's knee, squeezing gently. "She would be proud of you. You have grown into a fine adult."

Rourke leaned back on his hands on the wall. "I don't know what she'd think of me, Lysha. I would like to think she'd be proud of me, but I don't know. I've walked away from everything that I've ever known, and I don't know where this will lead me."

"You walk your own path, same as you have always done. Your Asha would be proud of you for staying true to yourself. She was proud of you for doing that, even when you were little."

"I guess so." Rourke shrugged. He looked out over the water, letting his eyes scan the terrain idly. "I just miss her."

"She is with you. Here." Lysha reached up and touched Rourke on the chest over his heart before reaching up and touching his temple. "And here. Your Asha will always be with you."

"I think I saw her Last Light. I really do believe she's attached to my bhasvah. I wouldn't be here if not for her guidance."

Lysha nodded, moving her arm to her lap. "I am sure she is. I would not doubt that, Rourke. And keep your bhasvah safe." Jumping off the wall, Lysha walked down to the water's edge, wading around in the shallow water in her bare feet. "How are you settling in?"

Rourke shrugged. "Okay, I guess. I'm struggling with adjusting, but I think it's been harder on Sammy —"

"Sammy? Who is this Sammy?" Lysha turned to face Rourke; eyes wide in curiosity. Her braid swung over her shoulder to her back with how fast her movements were.

Rourke felt his entire person flush with embarrassment as well as excitement at being able to talk about Sammy. "Sammy is my committed," he said with a grin. "He's an Other I rescued in the darkness from some Wolves."

Lysha narrowed her eyes for a moment before she threw both arms in the air and laughed. "Committed! This is wonderful! Truly, Rourke, you have grown! You make our great city proud."

"Are there others from Olin," Rourke asked as Lysha lowered her arms.

She shook her head. "I have not seen or heard of anyone other than myself and you making it through the darkness to Bhaskara. I fear that Olin and Amshu were caught so unawares by the attacks of the Wolves that very few of us survived. I have an even greater fear that you and I are all that remains of Olin blood."

Rourke nodded, feeling his chest tighten in pain. He thought a part of him knew that no one else survived the attacks on Olin, but to hear Lysha confirm it seemed to hurt more than he thought it would. "Oh," he said quietly.

"I know." Lysha came to stand in front of Rourke, resting her hands on his shoulders. "It is a hard thing to learn, Rourke of Olin, and a harder thing to accept. But there is still hope. You said you have committed, then that means there is a third of Olin now!"

Rourke took a deep breath, looking down to his hands in his lap as he spoke. "Yes, I guess you're right. Sammy is, well, Sammy is great. I don't know where else to start. He's adapted much better than I ever thought he could, and he makes me — I don't know. I don't mind him being around. In fact, I enjoy his company much more than I thought I would have."

Lysha pressed her hand to Rourke's cheek, and Rourke looked up, seeing the small and content smile on her face. "You really have grown up."

"I guess." Rourke shrugged but didn't pull away. Lysha's hand was warm against his cheek, and her dark gray eyes seemed to be searching for something Rourke didn't know the answer to.

After a moment, Lysha pulled away and walked back toward the water. "It is settled then."

"What is?"

"I want to meet your Sammy."

"Oh, no. I want him to settle in a little more first before you scare him." Rourke shook his head.

Lysha grinned, and Rourke felt a shiver run down his spine. He didn't like the mischievous look in her eyes. "I will meet your Sammy because I have also decided on something else. Something much more important than meeting your committed." Lysha bent over, dragging her fingers across the top of the water before cupping her hand and splashing water in Rourke's direction. She didn't hit him, but Rourke picked up his feet anyway so he didn't get wet.

"What's that," Rourke asked through a chuckle. There was a simplicity in being around Lysha that he had forgotten about, and now that it was back, Rourke realized he had greatly missed being with his cousin.

Lysha didn't answer right away, busying herself with coming back out of the lake, wringing the water from her skirt and tying it up near her hip so the longer part folded back near her knees. She was clearly stalling, but it was something that Lysha had always done, and so Rourke just sat and waited, watching the water and the moths, while listening to the umbra and the birds. He knew when she was ready, Lysha would continue. "It is the middle of the Season of the Haldis," she started quietly.

"Is it that late," Rourke answered, swinging his feet slowly against the wall.

Lysha frowned and crossed her arms. "Do not act like you do not know what I speak of."

Rourke grinned. "I honestly didn't realize it was that late, but yeah, I know what you are referring to." He looked down and picked at the stone under his fingers. "It sounds ridiculous when I say it out loud, Lysha, but I don't even know how old I am anymore. Sammy asked me, and I told him I didn't know and that it didn't matter, but —" he paused and took a deep breath. "It does matter; it matters a whole lot."

"You just turned nineteen, though I can hardly believe it myself. It doesn't feel like it has been that long, not when I can still picture how small you were on the cycle of your birth." Lysha sighed as she looked off across the water. It looked like she was thinking though, and after a moment she came back up to stand next to Rourke at the stone wall. Taking a deep breath, she looked behind Rourke into the field and Rourke was sure she was watching the herd of umbra. "Come with me to the market, there is something I must get, and I want you to accompany me there."

Rourke groaned, but followed Lysha's lead when she climbed over the wall into the umbra pasture. Hooking her arm in his, Lysha led the two of them across the field and through the barracks into the city without another word. Rourke didn't completely mind, but he did pause her long enough to pull his hood up over his hair, so he didn't get stopped by every person that passed them by, and even though he didn't have his sword, his smaller knife at his back gave him a sense of comfort. "Where are we going," he asked as Lysha turned onto the main market street which was crowded and very loud.

"I have some things I need to gather from the reagents shop."

"And you couldn't have done this yourself?"

"No, I could have." Lysha looked up to Rourke, running her free hand along the length of her braid. "But if I am going to be buying ink supplies for your mark, I thought you would like to join me."

"My mark?" Rourke stopped in the middle of the street, pulling Lysha to a stop, also. "What do you mean, my mark?"

"Just what I said." Lysha shrugged, as if getting a mark was no big deal. It probably wasn't to her, between her own, and her giving marks to other Illume, this was something Lysha was very used to doing. "I have decided what to give you for a mark — the Haldis Spheres — and since I am not only an Olin shaman, but your closest family besides your Sammy right now, I can decide for you. Do you not agree with me?"

"I didn't say that." Rourke felt his heart beating madly in his chest as fear and longing rushed up his throat. To finally be getting his mark, something he thought for sure he would never get, especially after Asha's death. And such a mark, no less. The Haldis Spheres were an honor to get, and not something given to just anyone. "Why the Haldis Spheres?"

"Why not? Have you not earned them?"

"I haven't. What have I done to earn then?"

Lysha turned to Rourke and glared up at him, her dark eyes reflecting her anger and rage at Rourke's refusal. "You have *survived*. On your own, in the darkness. You have brought Olin to Bhaskara, the same as I have. Between us, our culture will not die. You will teach your Sammy, I know you will, and I will pass on my ways to the next shamans."

"I just didn't think you could decide that, with us only being cousins." Rourke frowned. "But here you are, deciding to give me a mark, and right now! I don't think I'm quite ready yet."

"Silly boy, I do not plan to mark you right here in the middle of the road. You will take me back to your room where I will meet your Sammy and he will help us. When an Illume receives their mark, they are supposed to be surrounded by their family, Rourke. Where else would we do something that is so important?"

Rourke nodded, feeling tears of joy prick the corners of his eyes. He never hoped to get his mark, even with Aetius saying he would be willing to be a fill in for family he no longer had. "I didn't know your cousin could decide for you."

"Rourke, I am old enough to be your mother, and I am a shaman." Tugging on his arm, Lysha started toward the reagents shop. "Our home may be gone, Rourke, but we are not. You and I are the last, I fear, of very old blood. We cannot let our traditions die."

"I know." Rourke nodded, letting Lysha pull him along. Normally, Lysha talked in strange and cryptic ways, asking new questions instead of answering the one she was asked. More often than not, Rourke was more confused by their conversations than anything else. So, to see her so serious made Rourke rather somber as they entered the small store run by a man who appeared to be an Other. Noticing the wall with short swords, knives, daggers, and leatherwork, Rourke let go of Lysha to stop and look. In the background, he could hear Lysha ask for the ingredients to make ink for marks.

Lysha was right though, and Rourke knew it. They were the last of a very old family, one of the first families from the first city, but none of that seemed to matter anymore. Mindlessly, Rourke raised his hand to his chin. Was getting such a mark really worth it?

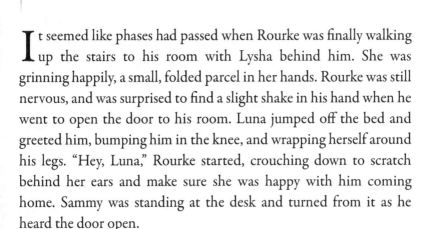

13

It seemed like phases had passed when Rourke was finally walking up the stairs to his room with Lysha behind him. She was grinning happily, a small, folded parcel in her hands. Rourke was still nervous, and was surprised to find a slight shake in his hand when he went to open the door to his room. Luna jumped off the bed and greeted him, bumping him in the knee, and wrapping herself around his legs. "Hey, Luna," Rourke started, crouching down to scratch behind her ears and make sure she was happy with him coming home. Sammy was standing at the desk and turned from it as he heard the door open.

"Where have you been?" Sammy crossed his arms over his chest and leaned back against the desk. Behind him, Rourke could see the palu-tai with five of the six blue flowers open. When he'd left, only one had been open. "I was worried something happened."

"Sorry." Rourke stood. "I know I said I was just going to go out for a walk. Did I miss our lesson?"

"Yes, and I had time to run over and spend part of the day — cycle with Alina at the Sanctuary. She says 'hi,' invited us to dinner, and baked us some cookies, I think. She said they were cookies, but I'm not sure what they are made of." Sammy turned back to the basket sitting on the edge of the desk as Lysha stepped into the room.

Rourke had no idea what she had been doing out in the hall, and he rolled his eyes at her as she quietly closed the door behind herself. "Sammy," Rourke started, walking over to him and placing his hand against Sammy's lower back. "I want you to meet someone."

"Oh?" Sammy turned in Rourke's arms before moving to rest his wrists on Rourke's shoulders. "I was really worried about you."

"I know." Rourke nodded, moving his hands to rest on Sammy's hips. He looked over to Lysha who was crouched down petting Luna, and thankfully ignoring them. "I'm sorry, but I didn't have a chance to stop and tell you about the change in plans." Stepping back from Sammy, Rourke raised a hand. "I want you to meet Lysha of Olin. Not only is she the shaman who healed me, but she's also my cousin."

Sammy turned toward Lysha as she stood. Luna stayed on the floor by Lysha's feet, purring loudly. Sammy bowed his head in a small nod. "It's nice to meet you, Lysha." Sammy looked back to Rourke and reached for his hand. "Thank you for saving him when he was little, I owe him my life."

Lysha looked at Rourke, her dark eyes not giving away one hint of what she was thinking. Walking over to Sammy, she stood on her toes to be eye level with him. She didn't say a word, and Rourke could tell Sammy didn't quite know what to do under Lysha's piercing gaze, especially when she reached up and pressed her fingertips to Sammy's chin. The two locked eyes for an instant before Lysha nodded and took a step back. "Your Sammy has a good soul," Lysha started, looking over to Rourke. "You have done well."

"Um, thanks." Rourke raised his hand to scratch the back of his neck.

Lysha raised the small package in her other hand. "I must get started making this if we are going to give you your mark."

"Wait, what?" Sammy moved aside as Lysha pushed between Rourke and Sammy, making space for herself on the desk before climbing into the chair. Rourke ignored her, surprising even himself at how used he was to her weird ways, even after not seeing her for so long. Sammy, though, looked overly confused. "Your mark? Like, your *mark*. You're getting a tattoo?"

"I don't know what that is, but yes. Lysha has decided on a mark for me." Rourke nodded, unable to keep the smile off his face. Sammy seemed just as excited, even though Rourke could tell that he didn't fully understand how important this was. Crouched in the chair, Lysha was ignoring them both, busy with mixing the ingredients she bought to make ink.

Sammy stepped in close to Rourke, and Rourke could see the playful glint in Sammy's eyes. "So, what are you getting?"

"The Haldis Spheres." Lysha pointed over to the bed. "Hush for a moment, Sammy of Olin, and I will explain. Rourke, take off your shirt and lie on the bed."

"Why do I need to take my shirt off?"

Lysha turned in the chair. "Do you want to get ink on your clothing? Just do as I tell you."

Rourke took a deep breath and sighed heavily as he pulled his shirt off over his head. "Fine." Dropping it on the floor by the edge of the bed, Rourke climbed onto what had become his side of the bed and got comfortable on his back. Sammy walked around to the other side and sat down cross-legged facing Rourke. Luna, finally having had enough of being on the floor, jumped up by Rourke's feet and walked across the bed to curl up at the bottom of the bed by Sammy.

Sammy reached out and buried one hand in Luna's fur. "So, does this mean you will be considered an adult in your culture now? No more weird looks from people."

"He is a Warden. Your Rourke will always get weird looks; it is a part of him."

"Lysha." Rourke turned to glare at her. "You of all people know not to call me that."

"I was not calling you 'Warden.' I was stating a fact."

Rourke rolled his eyes, unimpressed with Lysha's answer. "Now you sound like Aetius."

"I can see the family resemblance," Sammy snickered by Rourke's side. "Seriously, though, this is good for you, right?"

"Very." Rourke nodded and looked over to Lysha as she stood from the desk. Coming over to the bed, she handed Sammy a bowl, which Rourke knew was the ink for his mark. Rourke wasn't exactly sure how she mixed it all together, but he'd seen her buy bhasvah dust, charcoal powder, and ask for water from the kitchen downstairs. Lysha placed her hand on Rourke's stomach, taking a moment to trace her fingers along the faded scars of Rourke's wounds before she turned to bring the chair to the edge of the bed. Rourke rubbed his hand over the spot Lysha had touched, able to feel the lingering touch of her fingers. He wondered what she was thinking, knowing she had been the one to tend to him and bring him back from near death. Though Rourke didn't remember most of it himself, he'd been told about what Lysha had assumed had happened. His sister and himself had been attacked by Wolves, and though Rourke did get injured, Asha had managed to fight them all off, though it cost Asha her life in the end.

Sitting down in the chair, Lysha rested her satchel in her lap. "I need you to remain very still during this process, Rourke. Understand?"

"Yes, Lysha." Rourke nodded, shifting his shoulders on the bed a little more and looking over to Sammy, who was still looking at the ink, swirling it around gently in the small bowl.

With a sharp nod, Lysha opened her satchel and took out a long, thin, worn wooden box. Setting that aside, she also took out a small glass container. She opened the container and set it down on the edge of the bedside table. Lastly, she took out a charcoal writing stick and carefully traced out the three circles of the Haldis Spheres mark on Rourke's chin. Rourke tried his best not to move, but the sensation tickled slightly, and Rourke almost pulled his lower lip into his mouth. Putting that away, Lysha picked up the box and opened it, taking out several stick-like items. The thin rods were each tipped with several needles grouped together in the shape of a miniature comb and tied in place by a thin cord that wrapped around both parts until they were completely secured to one another. Each tool had a different number and arrangement of needles, and Rourke felt more than a little relieved when all but the smallest two went back into the box.

Carefully, Lysha set the box on the bedside table and then set the two rods on the box before picking up the glass jar. "I need you to lie flat, Rourke." Rourke shifted to do as she asked, making sure he kept his head tipped up a bit more so Lysha could easily get to his face. His heart was still beating madly in his chest, and his palms felt sweaty as he watched Lysha swipe some of the green goop out of the glass jar and smear it across his chin. "It is a healing ointment," she explained, clearly able to see the question Rourke must have been showing on his face. "I will leave this with you once we are done."

"Okay." Rourke nodded, glancing down to the jar as she rested it on his chest.

"Sammy, hold that bowl a bit closer for me." Lysha motioned for Sammy to move closer, and Rourke watched him scoot closer until his knees touched Rourke's side. Resting his forearms on his knees, Sammy held the bowl of ink out over Rourke's chest so Lysha could easily have access to it. Nodding in approval, Lysha picked up one of the two rods and grinned down at Rourke. "You must hold still while I do this. Understand?"

"Yes," Rourke breathed out. Taking a deep breath, he closed his eyes. Fear and excitement surged through him, but Rourke was trying to remain calm. Twisting his wrist, he brushed his fingers against Sammy's knee, and found himself relieved when Sammy took his hand. With a sharp nod, Lysha dipped the needles into the ink in the bowl. She pressed her other hand against Rourke's face, stretching the skin of his chin tight so she was able to work. Rourke could barely see her rest the rod between her thumb and pointer fingers.

"Be patient; this will hurt," Lysha said in warning before she started.

The needles digging into Rourke's skin felt like being burned by fire, and he barely resisted jerking away from the touch. Lysha paused, looking down at Rourke, and their eyes met. "Breathe," she said quietly, and Rourke exhaled the breath he didn't even know he had been holding. "It will not take long if you let me do this. I know it hurts." Lysha grinned, looking up to Sammy. "You would think your Rourke could take a little pain with all that he's been through."

"I can take the pain, Lysha." Rourke rolled his eyes, unimpressed with Sammy's snickering. "I just wasn't expecting it to be that intense."

"You will be fine. Your skin will go numb, and you will not feel a thing. Now, deep breath, in and out, and let us continue."

Rourke did as he was told, keeping his hand firmly linked with Sammy's while Lysha worked. It was quiet in the room, save for their breathing and Luna's snoring. Lysha continued with her work, falling into a steady pattern of cleaning the area with a piece of cloth, adding more ointment to Rourke's chin, and then continuing with his mark. It didn't take very long before the intense jab of the needles faded away into more of a throbbing burn, and Rourke kept his eyes closed, trying to focus more on Luna's snoring than the pain.

It must have been working because Rourke jumped when Sammy spoke — thankfully when Lysha wasn't working. "So, what is the significance of this mark? It looks really good, too, Rourke, against your skin."

Rourke opened his eyes and looked over to Sammy, who was looking down at him. "Thanks," he murmured, finding it hard to talk. His lip and jaw felt swollen. He squeezed Sammy's hand as Lysha took a deep breath.

"The Haldis Spheres have been a part of Olin culture since the first city rose from the darkness. It is a mark given to those who have overcome great peril or have given more of themselves than what was asked or needed to the city. I received mine," Lysha paused to touch her chin. "When I completed my shamanistic training. Your Asha received hers after your parents fell to the sickness that swept through the city." Lysha looked down at Rourke before looking up to Sammy. "And now, your Rourke is receiving his for surviving; for coming here and making it on his own. Traveling through the darkness has been hard on all of those who have survived, and your Rourke did it by himself."

Sammy nodded and squeezed Rourke's hand. "Pretty impressive I would say." Letting go of Rourke's hand, Sammy ran his fingers through Rourke's hair and leaned forward to press a kiss to his forehead. "I really like it."

"It does not matter if you like it." Lysha pushed Sammy back by the shoulder as Rourke felt heat creep over his cheeks. Sammy let Lysha move him but was still grinning down at Rourke. "This has become a family mark, a rite of passage into adulthood. The only one who must like it is your Rourke."

"Do you like it, Rourke," Sammy asked, once again finding his hand.

Rourke squeezed Sammy's fingers in his own. "Yeah, though I don't know what it looks like."

"It looks like mine. Hush now, I am almost finished." Lysha dipped the needle into the bowl of ink and rested it against her hand on Rourke's chin. "I will leave you alone after I am finished. It will take several cycles to heal. And it will itch, do not scratch it."

Rourke hummed in answer as Lysha went back to work, knowing that if he spoke, he could jar her movements. The longer he laid on the bed, the more he was resigning himself to accepting the mark Lysha had chosen for him. It was something to be proud of, a mark from a place that no longer existed, yet told everyone who saw him where he had come from. Rourke took a deep breath and exhaled through his nose as Lysha jabbed the needles into his skin again repeatedly. This would be over very soon, and he would finally have the right to call himself an adult, even though he'd been doing so for a while now. The mark would make it official, and no one would question where he got the mark since only shamans were able to give marks. He was suddenly much more excited about receiving his mark than he had been and couldn't wait for Lysha to finish so he could look at it for himself.

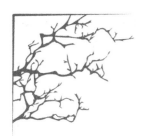

14

Sammy stepped into the room quietly, making sure not to disturb Rourke or Luna. After Lysha had left, Rourke had said he was tired, and so Sammy had gone downstairs to the first floor where the kitchen was to get food since Rourke was too drained to want to be around anyone. While they had eaten, they had talked, and Luna had gotten off the bed and had fallen asleep on the rug. Sammy's steps were light since he had left his boots upstairs when he'd gone back down to return their used dishes. He was slowly settling into how things were going to work while they lived at the Illuminari barracks and was simply glad to have their own space that didn't require them to have to look over their shoulders constantly for danger.

Rourke had moved to the middle of the bed while they ate, talking idly in low voices about everything and nothing, and he had remained there while Sammy had been gone. His eyes were closed, and his head was leaned back against the headboard. His arms were folded over his stomach, but despite Rourke's slow and steady breathing, Sammy could tell he wasn't asleep. He seemed too tense to be sleeping, even if Rourke was simply trying to relax. Sammy figured it was from his years of being on his own in the darkness that caused such a response even when there was no danger.

Closing the door with a soft click, Sammy took a moment to look at Rourke, appreciating not only his looks, and his new tattoo, but just the man in general. Rourke was a kind and gentle person, even though he had learned to do some not so kind things over the years, but Sammy could look past that — had to look past it — to the person Rourke really was. He quietly walked over to the bed, but instead of sitting down on the edge of the bed to give Rourke a kiss, Sammy climbed onto the bed, straddling Rourke's legs as he settled onto his knees. Raising his hands to rest on Rourke's shoulders, Sammy leaned in for a kiss, but before he could, Rourke opened his eyes. Their eyes met, and Sammy felt his breath catch in his throat. Rourke's eyes caught the light of his bhasvah, which was sitting on the bedside table against the wall as he lowered his head to look at Sammy better.

"What are you —" Rourke started, and Sammy felt want flare through him. He leaned down for a kiss, cutting Rourke off. Raising his hands, he carded his fingers into Rourke's hair, inhaling deeply through his nose as their lips met. "Sammy!" Rourke brought his hands up to Sammy's shoulders, pushing him back and holding him there. "That hurts."

"Sorry." Sammy slid his hand down to cup Rourke's cheek. "I'm not sure what came over me, I just really wanted to kiss you." Sammy leaned back in, Rourke narrowing his eyes at him in suspicion when he did. Sammy kept his voice low so that only Rourke could hear, despite the fact they were alone in their own room. "I just think your mark makes you look hot."

Gingerly, Rourke reached between them and touched his chin, still shiny with the healing ointment Lysha left for him. "Yeah, it does feel hot to the touch. It's really sore, too."

Sammy snorted back a laugh and shook his head. "That's not what I meant, but yes, I can understand that. I heard that getting a tattoo is like having a bad sunburn."

"Sunburn?"

"Ah, never mind." Sammy shook his head. "It will be sore for a few days — cycles. Eventually, I will get that right."

Rourke chuckled, moving his hands to rest on Sammy's hips. "I know you're trying, that's all I could ever ask."

Sammy smirked, feeling a bit flirtatious while sitting in Rourke's lap. "I am trying," he started, grinning as he leaned forward to close the gap between them, wanting to press the ghost of a kiss to Rourke's lips. "I want to make you proud of me."

"I am proud of you." Rourke turned his head away as Sammy leaned in for a kiss and instead Sammy kissed Rourke on the cheek. "Sammy, you're not being fair. I would like to kiss you, but talking hurts, let alone kissing you. My whole face hurts."

"So, don't talk," Sammy murmured, kissing his way up Rourke's jaw toward his ear. "Just let me fool around a bit." Taking a deep breath, Sammy spoke right against Rourke's ear, pressing their cheeks together. "And stop me if I do something you don't like."

Rourke hummed in answer, hands flexing on Sammy's hips as Sammy kissed just under his ear. Sammy moved slowly, working his way down the length of Rourke's neck with light and lingering kisses. Excitement coursed through Sammy at the fact that Rourke was willing to take things further. Sammy hadn't really thought about much more than simple kisses while out in the darkness, but now that they were safe in Bhaskara, he wanted to explore, and see just where their relationship would lead. He had always been physically attracted to Rourke, Sammy had resigned himself to that fact a long time ago, but as they had traveled and their relationship had grown stronger, and they had grown closer, Sammy knew he was falling for Rourke on a deeper level, as well.

Sammy softly kissed Rourke just above his collarbone, delighted when Rourke tipped his head away and gave Sammy more room to tease and explore. Moving his hand, Sammy slid his palm down Rourke's neck and shoulder to rest against his chest as he continued to kiss him, each kiss lingering just a little longer than the last as Sammy moved back up toward Rourke's jaw. Rourke shivered under Sammy's fingers as he gasped, and Sammy moved his hand down toward Rourke's pants as he bit gently at the juncture of Rourke's neck and jaw.

Inhaling against Rourke's skin, Sammy moved his hand to tug at the strings tying Rourke's pants. Sammy could feel his heart beating madly in his chest, excited to be trying something new with Rourke. He shifted on his knees a little, adjusting his position, as well as his growing arousal. He hadn't had time or energy to think about sex out in the darkness, but now he was, and he was hoping that sooner or later him and Rourke would be able to get to that point; preferably sooner. "You don't realize what you do to me, Rourke," Sammy murmured against Rourke's skin. Sammy could feel Rourke shudder against his lips. "I want you in the worst possible way."

"Wh-what do you mean," Rourke asked, voice broken as he spoke. He shifted slightly under Sammy, and his fingers dug into Sammy's hips. Sammy couldn't help but smirk against Rourke's neck.

Taking a deep breath, Sammy kissed Rourke's jaw, lingering close as he spoke, making sure his lips brushed against Rourke's skin. "You turn me on, get me riled up, so that all I can think about is you. I want to do things to you, with you, teach you, and have you do them to me, too." As he spoke, Sammy dipped his hand into Rourke's pants, brushing the backs of his fingers against the base of Rourke's length.

Rourke inhaled sharply, grabbing Sammy's wrist and pulling his hand free of his pants. Sammy blinked as he sat back, a little shocked by Rourke's reaction until he saw the wide-eyed look Rourke was giving him. There was something akin to fear in Rourke's gray eyes, and Sammy felt his heart drop into the pit of his stomach as he realized what had just happened.

Moving off Rourke, Sammy sat next to him, leaning against the headboard before taking a deep and calming breath. "I'm sorry, Rourke." Reaching out, Sammy hesitantly took Rourke's hand in his. "I shouldn't have —"

"I shouldn't have stopped you," Rourke cut in, leaning over to rest his head on Sammy's shoulder. "I just wasn't expecting you to do that."

"What? No. You are not in the wrong here. I told you to stop me if I did something you didn't like, and you did. I should have asked."

"You said that you didn't have to ask because we were committed." Rourke moved their hands back toward his groin. "And if that's what you want, th-then that's what —"

"Oh, no." Sammy pulled away from Rourke and turned to face him, raising both hands to cup Rourke's cheeks so they were looking at one another and Rourke couldn't look away. "You listen to me, and you listen well. I was wrong here, not you. Yes, I said that with us dating you don't need to ask for you to kiss me, Rourke. Kiss. I was working my way toward something way beyond kissing you, and I should have asked. Just telling you to stop me wasn't fair."

"But you were kissing me," Rourke protested, and Sammy could see the fight in his eyes.

Sammy sighed and shook his head. "Yes, I know I was kissing you, but my intention was to do something else, to do more than kiss you, and I didn't give you a warning, or a say in that. I'm sorry. That wasn't fair, and I shouldn't have done it." Sammy ran his thumb over Rourke's cheekbone. "You were right to stop me when I tried to get in your pants."

"You were in my pants." Rourke frowned at Sammy, raising his hands to press against Sammy's hands on his cheeks. "You're not making any sense."

Sammy sighed. "Do you at least understand that I was wrong, here? And that you were not?"

"Yes, I understand that. And I want you to explain what you were trying to do, and what you were expecting of me. I want to learn, Sammy, even if it makes me feel weird."

"Good weird," Sammy asked, hoping that maybe Rourke was feeling arousal, and just not realizing it. "O-or bad weird," he added, knowing it was also quite possible that Rourke had been truly scared and uncertain of what was happening. Sammy felt guilt twist in his chest when Rourke nodded at 'bad weird.'

Taking a deep breath, Sammy pressed his forehead against Rourke's and closed his eyes. "I am so sorry, Rourke. I didn't mean to put you into a situation you didn't want to be in. That was never my intention."

"You're my committed," Rourke murmured, his hands moving to thread into Sammy's hair. Sammy felt his heart break at the tone of Rourke's voice, knowing that somewhere along the way, Rourke must have thought that he didn't get the choice to say 'no' if he was uncomfortable. "I want what you want."

"That's bullshit," Sammy scoffed. "If I wanted to jump off a bridge, would you seriously let me? Come on, Rourke, you're smarter than this. You're your own person, you can tell me to fuck off or something if I do something you don't like. I would do the same." Sammy took a deep breath and tried to keep his voice calm. "From now on, I will try to explain my intentions better if you let me know if you don't want to do something. I am not here to force you, Rourke. I'm supposed to be your equal, your partner. Don't ever think your wants or needs come second to mine."

Rourke dipped his head in a small nod. "Okay, I'll try. I just want you to be happy, Sammy."

"I am happy, Rourke. I'll be unhappy if you start forcing yourself to do things you aren't comfortable with." Sammy leaned back in and kissed the end of Rourke's nose. "We can start slow, I promise. I will take this with you one step at a time, and we can work up to sex." Rourke swallowed thickly but nodded. Sammy could see the uncertainty in his eyes, but figured it was because Rourke had no experience in anything other than what Sammy had shown him so far. Sammy ran a hand up into Rourke's hair. "Don't worry, I'll be here with you every step of the way."

"I'm sorry I don't know what to do."

Sammy stifled a laugh, moving to sit back against the headboard. "Don't be sorry, it's fine." Wrapping an arm around Rourke's shoulders, Sammy pulled Rourke against him and pressed a kiss into his hair. Rourke relaxed against Sammy as he settled and rested his head on Sammy's shoulder. "Honestly, I was being a jerk. I know you don't have the same type of experience I do when it comes to this sort of thing. I didn't think. I just got caught up in the moment, and your mark doesn't help and —"

"My mark? What about it?" Rourke picked his head up to look at Sammy, lightly touching the smallest circle at the bottom of his chin. "Does it look bad?"

"No." Sammy shook his head, feeling that low stirring of want deep in his gut again. He swallowed, forcing himself to push those thoughts aside and concentrate on Rourke and his question. "It looks perfect, and it contrasts with your skin nicely. And for me, that's the issue. It does look good, and it makes you look good, and I can't help myself but want to be with you."

Rourke inhaled deeply, held his breath for a moment, and exhaled calmly. "You know I like being with you, too. I don't see how getting my mark changes that."

"It doesn't, not really." Sammy looked down to their hands, linking their fingers together. He kept his eyes on their joined hands as he spoke. "I just really like you; you know that. I think your body is attractive, and I want to act on that." Sammy huffed a laugh. "I am not explaining myself very well."

"No, I think I get it. You want to have sex because you think I'm physically attractive."

Sammy looked over at Rourke, seeing the blush on his cheeks as well as the slightly mortified look on his face. Sammy couldn't tell if

Rourke was happy about learning about Sammy's attraction to him, or not. Sammy didn't think Rourke was sure he knew how to feel about it himself. "Yes," he admitted. "But I like you more than just for looks, you know that."

Rourke nodded, but Sammy could tell he wasn't really paying attention to what Sammy was saying. He had his head tipped forward, staring off at nothing somewhere near their feet. Rourke was quiet a moment before he spoke. "I really enjoy being with you, Sammy, and I enjoy your company, but I don't think I understand what you mean about being attracted to me physically."

"I want to have sex with you because I like the way you look," Sammy replied, unsure if it was a question or an explanation to Rourke.

"No, I understand that." Rourke shook his head. "I just don't think I am there yet."

"Yet?" Sammy raised an eyebrow as he studied Rourke's face. He was clearly concentrating on whatever it was he was thinking about. "It's not a 'yet' thing, Rourke. Either you do." Sammy paused to take a deep breath. He could feel a slight rejection twist in his chest at Rourke not finding him attractive enough to want to take things further. "Or you don't. There is no 'yet.'"

"But I feel like there is a 'yet.' Sammy." Rourke looked up to him, twisting slightly so his knees bumped into Sammy's thigh. "I want to be with you. I know that. I don't like being around people, I never have, but I like being with you. I enjoy being near you, and I'm glad we decided to commit to one another. Yet," Rourke paused, and Sammy met his eyes, seeing some sort of hesitation there. Rourke raised his hand, cupping Sammy's cheek and running his thumb over Sammy's cheekbone. "I don't think I feel attracted to you. I don't know how to explain it. I really enjoy your company, kissing you, touching you, but I don't feel that enjoyment because of how your body looks."

Sammy nodded, unsure of how to answer that. He did know that even though Rourke's words stung a little, Rourke was telling the truth. "Do you find anyone attractive? If I'm not your type, who is?"

"I don't know." Rourke shook his head. "I don't know if I have one. Don't misinterpret what I am saying, Sammy. I do like you, and I want to be with you. I just — I just don't look at you like that."

Sammy took a deep breath and sighed. "Okay." He wasn't quite sure how to take what Rourke was saying. He was a little confused and upset at the entire conversation, but Rourke seemed just as confused himself about what he was saying as Sammy felt. "Don't worry about it right now." Sammy pulled Rourke against him, wrapping his arms around him in a hug. "We will figure it out. I'm not going anywhere, not unless you make me."

"I would never make you leave, Sammy." Rourke leaned into Sammy, and Sammy felt himself relax. Rourke still wanted to be near him, and for now, that was enough.

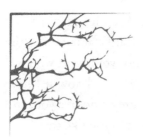

15

"**S**o, how are you fitting in?"

"What? Okay, I guess. It's been a bit hard honestly. I'm just getting used to everything." Sammy took a step back from Lao as they returned to their original positions. Lao had knocked on the door to Sammy and Rourke's room wanting to know if he wanted to spar for a bit before lunch. Sammy couldn't say 'no' to learning more about how to defend himself in any situation. Plus, learning from other people besides Rourke gave Sammy an advantage when it came to fighting Rourke.

Lao nodded, raising his hands and sliding his foot back into a defensive stance. "Just hadn't seen much of you, was all."

"Yeah, sorry about that." Sammy raised his arm to block a punch from Lao, before dropping down to try and sweep his legs out from under him. Using his hands for balance, Sammy pushed himself back to his feet. "I've kind of been overwhelmed since Rourke received his mark. I have a lot on my mind."

Lao ducked a punch from Sammy and snuck in close under it, grabbing Sammy by the shoulder and arm before tossing him to the floor by his hip. "If you want to talk," Lao started, pausing to take a deep breath. "I'm here. What's been bothering you? Do you not like Rourke's mark?"

"No," Sammy shook his head, feeling his hair stick press into the back of his head from lying on the mats. "It's not that. I like the mark, *that* is the problem."

Lao laughed as he helped pull Sammy back to his feet. "How is that a problem? Can't kiss him?" Lao smirked.

"That's not — it's none of your — yes, okay, that's part of it." Sammy felt a blush rise over his cheeks, and he took a deep breath.

"Him being a Nari," Lao asked. Lao, Lor, and Alina knew Sammy didn't exactly like the idea of Rourke joining the Illuminari. Sammy knew it was what Rourke needed, but hearing Lao talk constantly of going back out into the darkness worried Sammy to no end.

Sammy shrugged. "I guess maybe that's part of it. I know he needs to do this, but I worry about him. He seems, I don't know how to explain it."

"He seems fairly happy to me, even if he is always complaining about being around people. Lor and him get along really well."

"They do." Sammy smiled, thinking about all the times Rourke came home from some sort of patrol with Lor, constantly babbling about what had happened that day. "I'm glad he's making even one friend, he seemed really hesitant to do so at first."

Lao nodded in agreement before crossing his arms over his chest. "What about you?"

"What about me," Sammy asked, meeting Lao's eyes. Lao was the more carefree of the two twins, and Sammy had quickly learned to tell the two of them apart, but when Lao grew serious, he looked exactly like Lor and it always threw him off a little bit, having to double guess on which twin he was talking to. "I'm okay, just overwhelmed, like I said."

"I just worry about you. No one sees that much of you here in the barracks. I know you go see Alina a lot, and that's great, but we are here, too."

"I know." Sammy nodded looking over Lao's shoulder to the small palu-tai plant in the corner of the room. He was still getting used to them, but was beginning to understand them, as well. He raised a hand and pointed. "Third flower is open."

"Well, that's it then." Reaching out, Lao grabbed Sammy by the shoulder. "Talk to us, Sammy. You're not alone here." With a grin,

Lao let go and turned toward the door. "You hungry? I am starving. Missed getting food earlier."

"What were you doing?" Sammy followed Lao out of the small training building toward the main barracks building. While sleeping rooms were on the second, third, and fourth floors, a kitchen was on the first. The room was wide open with several tables placed about so that everyone could eat after getting what was offered from the counter near the back of the room. The Illuminari served food buffet style which Sammy really liked. It allowed him to pick what he wanted from a couple different main dishes, with bread, fruits, cheeses, and some sort of sweet, usually in the form of what appeared to be a cookie.

Lao and Sammy each built themselves a plate and were just sitting down to a table when Lao elbowed Sammy in the ribs. Lao pointed toward the door, and Sammy looked over to see Lor and Rourke walk into the building. He felt his breath catch in his throat at the sight of Rourke standing across the room. He was wearing his black leather clothing with his sword belted to his side, and a large smile on his face. Rourke and Lor were clearly deep in conversation, walking right by their table without even noticing them, Isik plodding along behind them. Sammy watched them go before turning back to his food. "Should we wait for them?"

Lao swallowed the mouthful he'd been chewing. "I guess so, but I already started while you were staring."

"I wasn't..." Sammy trailed off, knowing damned well he had been staring. "Can't help it," he admitted.

"It's fine. I think it's great that you two have such a strong bond. That's really the whole point of committing anyway."

Sammy looked at Lao, thinking back to what had happened between Rourke and himself the day he got his mark. Inhaling to speak, Sammy was distracted when Rourke sat down across from him, and Lor sat down next to Rourke. Isik laid down at the edge of the table near Lor. "Hi." Rourke grinned as he met Sammy's eyes.

"Hey," Sammy breathed out, pushing a loose strand of hair behind his ear, and feeling the heat on his cheeks creep across his nose. "You seem happy."

"Yeah!" Rourke picked up the roll he had gotten and rested his arms on the edge of the table. "We were out by the bridge, and since nothing really happens out there, we were talking and sparing, and just enjoying ourselves."

"Lor, have fun, unheard of." Lao grinned at his brother. "He was always such a haldis stuck in the mud. Never wanted to play."

"You always wanted to go on some adventure that more than likely would get us killed," Lor defended. "And I was not."

"You were, too!" Lao pointed a finger at him. "And I never died, so clearly your accusations are untrue."

Lor rolled his eyes. "Here we go. So, Sammy." Lor turned to him. "How are you? I haven't seen you in a while. Rourke says you spend most of your cycle studying, either here or with Alina."

"Still a haldis stuck in the mud," Lao grumbled under his breath.

"Yeah, well one of us needs to know how to read, and since Rourke is out working, that leaves me."

"I go to the lessons when I can." Rourke frowned at Sammy.

Sammy reached across the table to take Rourke's hand. "It wasn't a criticism. I know you are coming when you can. Don't worry about it."

"You two are absolutely ridiculous." Lao laughed. "It's adorable."

"Don't mind, Lao." Lor smirked at his brother. "He is just jealous no one has committed to him yet."

"Like I want to." Lao scoffed. "I have better things to do than worry about committing. I am just picking on Sammy."

"Thanks, Lao, truly what a friend." Sammy stated flatly, even as Rourke squeezed his hand. "Tell me why I hang out with you again."

"Because I am the closest thing you have to having what you call a normal Other conversation."

Sammy shrugged. "Got me there." Taking a deep breath, Sammy picked at his food. "So, anything exciting happen while I was busy studying?"

"Alina would like you two to come to dinner soon. She wants to be able to cook for all of us again." Lor raised his head to look at Sammy before going back to what he was eating. "She enjoys making lunch for the two of you but wants to make a big meal again."

"Sounds good to me," Sammy started. "What do you think, Rourke?"

Rourke nodded, raising a forkful of mashed potatoes. "The food here is a lot better than what we were able to get in the darkness, but Alina's cooking is much better."

"I am going to tell the cooks you said that, Rourke." Lao snickered from his spot by Sammy.

"Go right ahead. I have told them that a herd of haldis could probably cook better food than they could." Rourke waved a hand toward the kitchen.

"Come on, I think they do a great job given what they have to work with." Lor pushed some of his food around on his plate as he shrugged.

"You're just saying that, Lor, because you get to go home to Alina's cooking every night." Sammy laughed, poking at the food left on his plate. "I don't blame you though. I would like to cook for once, too. Maybe I can go over and help her?"

"I think Alina would like that very much, Sammy." Lor smiled. "I'm glad you two get along so well."

"I am, too. So." Sammy set his fork down and stole the last bite of Rourke's bread, earning himself a decent glare. "Anything else happen?"

"Actually," Lao started, glancing at Lor then Rourke. "I didn't tell you while we were sparring, but there is a group of Nari planning to go back out into the darkness."

"Really?" Rourke jerked his head up, looking at Lao. "Is that because of the Wolves they found?"

Lao nodded. "We convinced Asha that it is a good idea to make sure it was only an isolated incident. That she doesn't want to risk Wolves getting closer. It was only a couple when we were out there before, but there could always be more."

"Always is more," Rourke agreed.

Sammy looked over at Rourke as dread twisted in his gut. He had a feeling about where this conversation was headed, and as much as he hated it, he wasn't surprised when Rourke asked, "How many are going?"

"You can't be thinking of going out there," Sammy blurted.

Rourke swallowed a bite of food. "Yes. Why wouldn't I go?"

"We just got here." Sammy was already getting frustrated with the conversation, and it had just started. "What if something happens?"

"We could use his tracking skills. Ow! Lor!" Lao jumped next to Sammy at the table.

"You're not helping, Lao." Lor glared at his brother. "Stay out of it."

"You didn't have to kick me."

"Then be quiet and eat."

"Nothing is going to happen, Sammy." Rourke tightened his grip on Sammy's hand. "I will be with everyone who is going."

"That's what worries me. You're the one who said that it was dangerous to be in a group when Wolves were around, and now you want to go with a group?"

"I may not have a choice." Rourke's voice was calm, hesitant even.

"Is that supposed to make me feel better, Rourke?" Sammy dropped his free hand to the table where it caused all the dishes to rattle.

"No, it's not, but it's still the truth." Rourke kept his voice low, and Sammy could see he was trying to remain calm about this. "I'm going to have to go if Asha says I need to go."

"He does have a point." Lao leaned over to Sammy.

Sammy turned and glared at Lao. Taking a deep breath, he pulled his hand from Rourke's and picked up his cup. Deep down Sammy knew this could happen, but right now, he didn't want to listen to that logical part of his brain. "Promise me we can talk about this later."

Rourke bobbed his head in a nod, making sure he was looking Sammy in the eyes. "Later, I promise."

Sammy nodded, but it still didn't make him feel any better. Taking a deep breath, he decided to try and push it from his thoughts for right now so he could eat. The table was quiet as everyone started eating, clearly able to feel the tension in the air between Rourke and Sammy.

Just as Sammy felt things were beginning to calm down, and he thought maybe he was ready to start up a conversation again, Miley entered the dining area. "Sammy! There you are! I have been looking all over for you." Walking over to the table, Miley placed her hands on the top and leaned on them. She looked tired and had pieces of hay sticking out of her curly hair.

"Everything okay?" Sammy started to stand up, a rush of panic washing over him. Lor, Lao, and Rourke all turned to her, as well.

"Better than okay!" Miley grinned. "I talked to Asha at the end of the last cycle. Lilith had her calf! And she said you could have him if you wanted him!"

"Him?" Sammy stood from the table, a rush of excitement replacing the panic of moments before. "She had a boy?"

"For the love of the light," Rourke groaned. He took a deep breath and sighed heavily as Sammy looked over at him. "You want to go see him, don't you?"

Sammy grinned; all his earlier anger washed away with the news of Lilith's new calf. "Thought you said I couldn't have an umbra?"

"We both know damned well you'll end up with one anyway, might as well just accept it." Rourke stood from the table, picking up his plate. "Same as with Luna. Where is she anyway?"

"She was sleeping, so I left her in our room." Sammy picked up his plate and walked with Rourke toward the kitchen to dispose of their dirty dishes. "Are you thinking of taking her with you for the afternoon?"

Rourke hesitated before nodding, and Sammy realized he'd been using words Rourke didn't understand again. "I think playing in the fields will be good for her. Let her hunt some mice or something while Lor and I watch the bridge."

"I think she will love that." Sammy took Rourke's hand as they walked back to meet Miley. Lor and Lao decided to stay and finish lunch and catch up with family things, so Sammy and Rourke said their farewells before going out to the stable.

People were milling about the stables, cleaning stalls and getting ready for chores later in the cycle. Miley was babbling about how long Lilith was in labor and how she didn't sleep because she wanted to stay up with her in case something went wrong. Nothing had gone wrong though, and Lilith gave birth to a beautiful black buck who had yet to be named.

Miley went right to Lilith's stall door and opened it, waving to Sammy to follow her inside the stall. Sammy let go of Rourke's hand as he went to stand by the stall wall, and Sammy followed Miley into the stall, closing the door behind himself.

Lilith was eating from a pile of hay in the corner of the stall, but she instantly turned toward Miley and Sammy. From where they were standing, the young umbra was nowhere to be seen. "What did you do with him, huh," Miley asked Lilith as she walked over to her and rubbed her neck. "He's probably nursing on her other side. It's okay, go over and see him."

Sammy nodded, resting a hand on Lilith's side as he walked around her hind end to the far side of the stall. Standing in the shadow of Lilith was a wobbly legged calf, neck bent as he suckled from his mother. "Hey," Sammy started, keeping one hand on Lilith as he crouched down, offering his other hand to the young buck. "Look at you! Rourke!" Sammy turned and looked through Lilith's legs to where Rourke was looking into the stall over the half wall. "You have to see him! He's adorable!"

"I've seen a baby umbra before," Rourke replied, crossing his arms on the top of the wall and resting his chin on his forearms. "I'm glad you like him though."

Sammy couldn't help but grin when the baby turned from nursing to Sammy, sniffing at his fingers. He seemed very friendly, and Sammy was really excited about the possibility of the young calf being his. "Are you sure Asha said I could have him?" Sammy stood up and looked at Miley over Lilith's back.

"Yeah! I went and asked her myself. She didn't see any harm in it, since you and Rourke are committed anyway." Miley moved over to Sammy's side before reaching out to pet the calf. "Any idea what you want to name him?"

"I don't know," Sammy admitted. "What do you think, Rourke?"

"Luna's name means 'moon,' right? That's what you told me." Rourke sounded thoughtful, even though Sammy knew Rourke had no love for umbra. "What about something that goes with Luna?"

"Hm." Sammy turned back to the calf, who was now more interested in him and Miley than his mother. Sammy reached out, running a hand over the top of his head, able to already feel the horn nubs under his fur. His bright red eyes reminded Sammy of Luna in a lot of ways, showing a sense of intelligence that was remarkable. "A name that goes with Luna? That's a good idea. I am going to have to think about it."

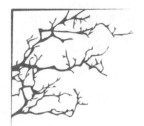

16

"I still can't seem to settle on a name for the little guy." Sammy sighed heavily and looked over to Rourke.

Rourke rolled his eyes at Sammy, pushing his hood back off his head as they turned onto the small street that led to the Sanctuary. On Sammy's right was the wall of the Sanctuary with its intricate carvings and crawling ivy vines. "The thing isn't even a handful of cycles old yet. I wouldn't worry too much about a name."

"Him, Rourke." Sammy frowned at his boyfriend and looked ahead of them to where Luna was sniffing at a crack in the stone street. "You did this with Luna, too."

"At least Luna is useful!" Rourke waved a hand at the shadow cat as she curled the front half of her body down to rub against the stones. "O-or she usually is. What is she doing?"

"Who knows, she's a cat. Cats are weird." Sammy shook his head, watching Luna as she rolled around on the street. "You're the only person I know who seems to hate umbra. Just help me think of a name. I know you said something that goes with Luna —" Sammy watched as Luna picked her head up and came back to them at the sound of her name. Rourke reached down and ruffled the fur between her ears. "But I want something that fits him, you know."

"I do not." Rourke frowned at Sammy and was quiet as they walked. Just as they were approaching the archway gate to the Sanctuary, Rourke chuckled darkly. "How about Roast? Or maybe Stew?"

"You're a monster, you know that!" Sammy smacked Rourke in the shoulder, but Rourke kept laughing. "That's horrible! Why would you think to name him that? Poor thing. I can just picture it now, standing in the middle of the pasture yelling for 'Roast.' I don't think so."

Rourke only laughed harder, and as much as Sammy didn't want to, he couldn't help but smile either, Rourke's good mood being highly infectious. "I don't have a clue how to name an umbra," Rourke managed between fits of laughter. "I've only ever named a haldis, and I don't even remember doing *that*."

"I'll ask Alina, she will actually be of some help to me." Sammy shook his head, but was still chuckling, quieting down his laughter as they approached the gate.

"Hey, what are you doing?" Rourke stopped laughing, bending down to scoop up one of the haldis that came running out of the Sanctuary. "Oh!" Rourke sounded shocked as he held the tiny animal up at arm's length. "It's you!"

Sammy watched the small haldis wave her tiny, clawed feet in the air excitedly as she tried to wrap her tail around Rourke's wrist. Even Sammy could recognize her as the small haldis Rourke had been slowly making friends with every time they came back to the Sanctuary. "You shouldn't be out here."

"Maybe she came to say 'hi' to you." Sammy grinned as Rourke cradled her close to his chest. She instantly snuggled into his arm, twisting her body so her stomach was upturned, and her tail wrapped protectively around Rourke's arm. She couldn't have been much bigger than a small cat, Sammy decided, with the entire length of her body, minus her tail, only being a little longer than Rourke's forearm.

"Doesn't that hurt," Sammy asked, tapping her tail with his fingers. "Don't her scales dig into your arm?"

"Naw, she's fine. I don't mind." Rourke started petting her belly with his other hand, head bent to pay attention to her. "I don't know why she came out though. From what Alina said, the haldis know to stay away from the archway."

"Maybe she came to see if you have more apples for her." Sammy reached out to pet her, hesitant of her tail, teeth, and claws.

"It's okay." Rourke looked up at Sammy. Sammy glanced up to Rourke, seeing the soft and content look on his face before looking back down to the haldis. Rourke seemed at peace with himself as they stood under the archway of the Sanctuary. Sammy felt himself fall for Rourke all over again. "She doesn't seem to mind you touching her. She's extremely docile now that I've managed to get my hands on her. I think she just doesn't like the others attacking her. Did you see that before? By the pond when we were still here? They came after her when she tried to get a drink!"

"I missed it, sorry." Sammy shook his head as they started across the yard toward Alina's house. Several other members of the Order were milling around, tending to the haldis, or headed toward their own homes since it was getting close to dinner time. No one paid any attention to them whatsoever. Sammy was really excited about being able to have dinner with Alina and Lor again and had been even more excited when somehow Rourke had managed to get the afternoon off, as well. Sammy had the suspicion that Rourke asked Asha if he could have it off.

"Rourke! Sammy!" Alina came running toward them from the pond. She was out of breath and clearly very worried. Sammy turned to face her as she came up to them, reaching out to help her stop herself since she was still moving too fast to do so on her own. "Have you seen any of the haldis? One of them is missing! The small one with the scarred — oh!" Alina gasped as Rourke raised his arms slightly in a gesture to show he had the missing animal in question. "How in the light did you get her?"

"She came running out of the Sanctuary, so I picked her up." Rourke shrugged before going back to scratching her stomach. The haldis stretched out in Rourke's arm, occasionally making little squeaking sounds that sounded greatly like enjoyment.

Alina seemed beside herself. "No one has ever been able to touch her. Her entire litter was in a stone den when it broke, we think the pups clawed through the side, but she was the only one scared enough to not let any of us near her. We've been watching her from afar to make sure she's okay."

"She seems okay. Look." Rourke wrapped his hand around her middle and turned her slightly as he raised his arm to show Alina. "She's growing moss, see the flecks of purple? And her shoulder has healed, even though she won't be able to grow new scales there." Through all of it, the haldis laid limp in Rourke's arm, not caring what he did to her in the slightest.

As soon as Alina reached out to try to touch her, she squeaked in alarm and curled into a ball in Rourke's arm. Alina instantly drew her hand back, and after a moment, the haldis uncurled and relaxed once more. Rourke was chuckling as he went right back to scratching her stomach. The three of them grew quiet as they watched Rourke cuddle with the small creature before Alina reached out and lightly touched Rourke on his upper arm. "Rourke," she started, voice low. Sammy looked up to her curiously. Alina had a look on her face that was mixed with awe, excitement, and hesitation. "Rourke, I think she may have chosen you."

Rourke snorted back a laugh. "That's silly. Why would —" He cut himself off and looked down to the small animal in his arms. His entire body went rigid before he shook his head and used both hands to push the haldis against Alina's chest. "That's not possible. I'm not — She isn't — We can't — I have to go."

Rourke turned on his heel and started back for the street. Sammy was too shocked to do anything, and simply stood there watching Rourke's back as he walked away from them. Luna ran after Rourke, and by the time Sammy was able to process what was happening, Rourke was disappearing around the edge of the archway. "Rourke," Sammy called, taking a step after him.

"Ouch!" Alina gasped next to Sammy, dropping the haldis who hit the ground in a ball, rolled back to her feet and started waddling after Rourke as fast as her little legs could take her. "She bit me! Sammy!" Alina wrapped her hand in her shirt, but Sammy could see blood. "You must catch her, Sammy! If she gets out into the city, she could get hurt!"

Sammy ran after the little haldis, easily scooping her up and holding her against his chest. She squeaked in protest and smacked Sammy with her tail, but she didn't bite him like she had Alina. Sammy placed his hand over her head in an attempt to calm her as he stepped out into the street to see if he could see any signs of Rourke or Luna. "He's gone," he said quietly, unsure if he was speaking to himself or the haldis, maybe both.

"Is she all right? I didn't mean to drop her! Where did Rourke go?" Alina peered out into the street, frowning at not seeing Rourke. "I'm sorry. I don't think I should have said that, but I think it's true."

"What do you mean she's chosen him?" Sammy looked down to the haldis in his arms. She was still hitting Sammy with her tail, but the fight was slowly leaving her. "It's okay," he murmured to her, rubbing behind her ears as he'd seen Rourke do one time. "Just calm down."

"Haldis pick who they want to spend their lives with. Unlike argi, it's the haldis that picks the Warden they want to be with. Most of them decide not to, and live their lives in the herd, but some will, like Izusa, and I'm sure Rourke's first haldis." Alina looked down to the haldis in Sammy's arms.

"So, are these haldis different somehow? The ones who pick people?"

"No." Alina shook her head. "They just seem to find a connection with a specific Warden. Come on, let's get her calmed down, and look at my hand." Turning, Alina started toward her home. Sammy followed along, still holding onto the haldis. "I don't think she bit too deep, she just wanted to go after Rourke. Another reason why I think she picked him, but I don't know for sure. His reaction is concerning."

"Not really if you know his history." Sammy took his hand off the haldis and looked down at her. She peered up at him with her beady little eyes. Sammy could see her ears shivering with her unease. Rourke had said he didn't think he would ever get another haldis, that for people like him — Sammy could only think that Rourke referred to when his haldis died when he was younger — they didn't get second chances. "But if she did, what does that mean?"

"It means Rourke isn't the failure he thinks he is. It means the haldis know he did what he could, and they don't blame him." Alina took a deep breath. "It means he's still truly a Warden, whether he's trying to run from that part of himself or not. The haldis don't care about that sort of thing. They see deep into our beings, they find one thing that connects them to a Warden, and then they stop at nothing to be with them. I'm honestly surprised she's being so calm with you."

"I smell like him." Sammy shrugged, plucking at his shirt. "This is his shirt."

Alina chuckled as they walked up the steps onto her front porch. "I do that with Lor's clothes, too." Opening the front door, Alina turned into the kitchen, greeting Izusa as she got up from a pillow she used for a bed in the corner. "Let's find her something to eat, Sammy. I don't want to let her out of my sight just yet."

Sammy sat down on one of the stools at the kitchen counter, settling the haldis into his lap. "Oh," he started, grinning as he thought back to Rourke laying on his back in the grass as the haldis ate her apple piece. Across from him, Alina was pouring some water from a pitcher over her hand to wash away the blood. "I know she likes apples."

ಭ

Rourke couldn't seem to catch his breath. He was afraid and nervous and joyful and prideful and sick all at once. Turning into a quiet side alley on the street, Rourke leaned back against the wall and slid down it until he was sitting on the ground. Knees in his chest, Rourke bent his head forward and rubbed his hand against the base of his skull. He could feel that little haldis lingering there, afraid and worried, yet comforted as well.

If he thought about it, Rourke knew she had been there for a while now, but he'd been so caught up with everything else that had been going on, he just hadn't been paying attention to her presence. With a heavy sigh, Rourke stretched his legs out and cradled his head in his hands.

His heart was pounding in his chest, and Rourke could feel his entire body shaking. He'd never prepared himself for something like this because he didn't think it would ever happen to him.

A second haldis.

Rourke had given up on that part of his life so long ago, it seemed that his life in Olin was a dream, something he'd only ever witnessed when sleeping. He couldn't picture himself with another haldis, especially not now. What would he even do with her?

He felt something sniffing his hair, and Rourke picked his head up to see Luna standing there. Without even hesitating, Rourke wrapped his arms around the shadow cat and pulled her into his lap, burying his head into her thick fur. Shakily, he took a deep breath, trying to calm himself down so he was able to think better.

Luna stood still, purring as she turned her head to try and lick his hair. Rourke ignored her, knowing it was just Luna's way of trying to comfort him. Taking another deep breath, Rourke tried to focus on the haldis' presence at the back of his mind. Orin had been loud, and Rourke had always known what he was thinking and feeling. Even when they weren't together, Rourke could remember simply knowing what Orin was doing. This was different. This was uncertain, and Rourke could feel the shakiness of the voice in the search to find and comfort Rourke, as well as find comfort for herself from their connection in the same moment.

He knew he needed to go back. Rourke knew deep down that he couldn't run from this, even if he wanted to. Even though he had walked away from that part of who he was, he knew he needed to do something about this haldis. Lysha's words struck him about how they were the last of Olin, the last of the old blood, and they had to uphold their history themselves. What type of Warden — as much as he loathed to consider himself as such — would he be if he turned his back on this honor? He had come to Bhaskara in hopes of starting his life over, and getting away from the Order, but Rourke could see now that it was, in part, just him trying to run away from what had happened at Olin.

While he didn't plan on going back to the Order, and honestly, he was really beginning to fit in with the Illuminari, Rourke knew this was something that needed to be done. With a groan, he pushed Luna off his lap, and stood. She looked up at him, her red eyes curious and insightful. Leaning down, Rourke slid his hands into the thick fur of her neck and rested his forehead on top of her head. "Come on, Luna," he started. "We have to go get the new remember of our family."

17

Rourke took a deep breath and exhaled as he knocked on the front door even though he knew he didn't have to. Both Lor and Alina had told Rourke and Sammy they were always welcome, but right now, Rourke felt that knocking was something he needed to do. He was a little taken aback when Lor opened the door because he hadn't expected him to be home so soon. "Welcome back." Lor grinned at him, and Rourke felt his face flush in embarrassment.

"Thanks," Rourke murmured, stepping into the house. Luna scooted by him and instantly went to what was quickly becoming her spot on Lor's couch. Rourke noticed a small stack of new books on the small living room table. "Did they tell you what I did?"

"Yeah." Lor nodded, closing the door behind them. He waved toward the kitchen. "They are in there. I was in my study when they came inside. She bit Alina, but Alina is okay. It was a shallow bite, just enough to get Alina to let her go."

"She tried to follow me?" Rourke was surprised, though he knew he shouldn't have been.

"Of course, she did." Lor laughed, reached up and rested a hand against Rourke's shoulder. His voice was soft as he spoke. "Sammy has her, go on."

Rourke nodded and sheepishly made his way into the kitchen. Sammy was sitting on a stool at the counter with his back to Rourke, and Alina was on the other side of the counter, a cutting board, a knife, and part of an apple in front of her. She looked up as Rourke and Lor reentered the room. "Rourke!"

Sammy looked over his shoulder to Rourke, a huge grin on his face. "You came back!"

"Had to." Rourke nodded, walking over to Sammy. With both hands, Rourke picked up the haldis from Sammy's lap, pulling her to his chest. The little haldis squeaked in delight, chomping loudly on the piece of apple she was finishing. Rourke could feel tears prick the corners of his eyes, and knew it was a combination of both his and the haldis' emotions. She was overjoyed as she settled against his chest, more than happy to be near him. Rourke didn't really know why he was on the verge of crying, but he knew he was. The swirl of emotions in his body was too many to count right now.

"Hey," Sammy started, getting up from his stool, and wrapping one arm around Rourke's waist. "Are you okay?"

"Yeah." Rourke nodded, wiping his face on his shoulder. "I can't explain it, so don't ask."

"It's her." Alina smiled, leaning back against Lor when he walked around the counter to wrap his arms around her waist. "She's so happy to see you, it's affecting you."

"That's part of it," Rourke admitted. "But not all of it. I need to process this. I wasn't — this wasn't supposed to happen." He looked down to the haldis in his arms as she finished her apple with a loud gulping swallow. Turning in Rourke's arms, she stood up on her back feet, resting her front feet near Rourke's collarbone and sniffing at his face. Shifting her weight to one hand, Rourke ran his other hand down the length of her scales, feeling them catch on his palm as he did.

He really wished he could better explain what he felt right now. The nervousness was still there, but also a sense of acceptance and relief. For this little one to want to bond with him, it must have meant that the haldis didn't consider his actions when younger as unworthy as he felt they were. The haldis still accepted him as he was, even if he struggled to do the same. He could also feel her unbridled joy at being with him humming in the back of his mind.

The haldis shifted her weight in his hand, and before Rourke could stop her, she jumped up toward his shoulder, clawing her way up there until she could find purchase. Rourke raised his arm to give her more room, chuckling as he looked over at her. "What are you doing," he asked, tipping his head against hers as she pressed her head to his cheek.

Sammy tightened his arm around Rourke's waist, and Rourke looked over at him, knowing he had a huge grin on his face. Sammy was smirking at him, a sense of amusement in his blue eyes that Rourke really enjoyed seeing. He could feel the haldis trying to steady herself on his shoulder before Rourke felt her tail wrap around his neck. "Oh, not so tight," he started, prying his fingers in between her tail and his neck. "I need to breathe."

"Yes, please don't kill him." Sammy reached out and scratched her under the chin. Rourke couldn't help but smile when she turned toward his touch. "I kind of like having him around."

"Only kind of," Rourke asked as he turned back to the haldis.

"Only kind of," Sammy confirmed, a playful smirk crossing his mouth.

"You need to name her." Alina moved from Lor's embrace to cut another piece of the apple, reaching across the counter to hand it to Rourke. He accepted it, offering it to the haldis, who eagerly took it, perfectly content to sit on Rourke's shoulder and eat.

"I know." Rourke nodded, still grinning as he watched her eat. "It has to be a good name."

"Oh." Sammy leaned over and pressed a kiss to Rourke's cheek. "I see how it is. You don't care to help me name the umbra, but the haldis has your undivided attention."

Rourke looked over at Sammy, a little stunned by his words. "I've explained to you what the bond between a — a Warden and their haldis would be like. This is so much more important than naming your umbra."

"Sammy, you got an umbra," Lor asked, leaning back against the far counter and moving out of Alina's way.

Sammy grinned happily. "I did! Lilith had her baby, and Asha said I could have him!" Sammy turned back to Rourke. "But yes, I do know how important this is. I am just picking on you."

Rourke frowned, the haldis' chomping loud in his ear. That was going to take some getting used to, especially if she decided his shoulder was her new place to sit. Carefully, he lowered his arm to his side, looking as best he could to the haldis, but she shuffled a little closer to his head and kept eating. "Just name your umbra."

"Name your haldis." Sammy laughed at him.

"Sounds weird to hear you say that," Rourke admitted, reaching up to scratch the haldis' stomach. "And I am thinking. I'm just not sure what I want to name her. Coming to Bhaskara was supposed to be a fresh start; a new —" Rourke stopped as he looked over to Sammy. "It was supposed to be a new beginning," Rourke finished, a name popping into his head. "I know what I am going to name her."

"Oh?" Sammy raised an eyebrow at him.

"Yeah." Rourke moved his hand to scratch behind the haldis' ears as he smiled. "I'm going to name her Nysa, it means 'a new beginning.' I think it fits."

"I think it's perfect," Sammy agreed, pressing another kiss to Rourke's cheek.

ॐ

Dinner with Lor and Alina had been great. Lao never arrived, and so it was just the four of them. They sat talking at the kitchen table long after they were done eating, and it was only when Alina noticed the flowers on the small palu-tai in the kitchen were all closed, did any of them realize how late it was.

After helping to clean up, which went quickly with all four of them helping, Rourke and Sammy left, casually walking through the quiet streets of Bhaskara toward the barracks. The streets were almost completely empty, and Rourke and Sammy were able to walk down the middle of the main market street, hand in hand, and not be bothered by anyone. Sammy said it was incredibly romantic, but Rourke just thought it was nice to be with Sammy alone somewhere besides their room.

Unsurprisingly, there were people awake and alert in the courtyard of the barracks, and Sammy idly waved to someone over his shoulder who called their names as they made their way toward the main building and their room to get a little sleep. Luna plodded along ahead of them, disappearing into the building, and more than likely up to their room where she would wait at the door to be let inside. On their walk, Nysa had curled up in the hood of Rourke's shirt, and he could feel her slight weight pulling on his shirt collar.

The person called their names again, and Rourke turned to see Isa waving at them as he made his way across the courtyard toward them. In one hand, he held a bow, a quiver slung over his shoulder. "A little late in the cycle for you two to be up. What are you two doing out so late," he asked as he walked up to Rourke and Sammy.

Rourke knew Isa was joking, but neither him nor Sammy were laughing. Next to him, Sammy crossed his arms over his chest. "Minding our own business. What are you doing here?"

Isa grinned at them, practically beaming with excitement as he held up his bow. "I'm working!"

"You're working here," Sammy asked, gesturing to the surrounding buildings.

"Where's your haldis?" Rourke felt a new weight come down on him as he asked that question. Nysa would more than likely want to go everywhere with Rourke, and he would probably have to make the same tough decision that Isa seemingly had already made.

"He's home, sleeping. I work patrol while most people are sleeping. Mother and Father don't know what I'm doing."

"So, sneaking around?" Sammy didn't sound impressed.

Rourke wasn't impressed either. "You don't even have your mark, Isa."

"You didn't either, Rourke, not until recently." Isa shouldered his bow and crossed his arms defensively.

"That's different," Rourke started, reaching up to touch the now healed mark on his chin. He hadn't been in a city where he had the availability to get his mark. Isa simply wasn't old enough yet. "I was already old —"

"I'm old enough to make my own decisions."

"You are not!" Rourke couldn't help but laugh at the irony of the situation. Isa reminded Rourke of himself when he was younger, and he suddenly understood why Aetius was usually so annoyed with him before he left to go off on his own into the darkness.

"Close! I talked to Asha about it anyway. She said it was fine."

Rourke groaned, but kept his mouth shut.

Next to him Sammy was rubbing at his temples in frustration. "Okay, okay, hang on. You asked Asha? So, did you join the Illuminari?"

"Yes." Isa nodded sharply. "I figured if Rourke was a Warden and could do it, so could I."

Rourke took a step back in shock. "My situation is anything but normal, Isa. You can't even compare them. I spent half my life in the darkness. Have you even ventured out of the city?"

"Yes. My parents don't care about what I do. I was born to carry on their blood. Father even told me so. They have never cared about what I do except when it comes to my role as his successor."

"Sounds familiar," Sammy grumbled next to Rourke as he looked over at him.

"Are you serious right now, Sammy?" Rourke choked back a bitter laugh. "Unbelievable. Isa shouldn't be here. If something happens, if the Wolves come here, it's the Nari who are the ones who are going to fight. Do you really think Isa is ready to fight Wolves?"

"I am!" Isa threw his arms in the air. "Rourke, why won't you listen to me?"

"Because I know what's going through your head. I understand that you want to help, but you're not like me. No one is like me. Isa, Bhaskara is still standing, you have a job —"

"You're right, Rourke. Bhaskara is still standing, and I want to help protect all the Bhaskarans who live here. I have heard the rumors of the fallen cities. I have heard the stories of Olin, and if the mightiest of our cities can fall — did fall — to the darkness, what's stopping the Wolves from coming to Bhaskara?" Isa balled his hands into fists. He was incredibly angry, but he was also very steadfast in his decision and reasoning for joining the Illuminari. As upset as he was, Rourke really couldn't blame him. Isa's reasons for joining may have even been better than Rourke's own. "I want to help make a difference. And I can do more here than I ever could in the Sanctuary. Aren't you the one who said you wouldn't stop anyone who felt they needed to leave because you knew what it was like to feel caged in?"

Rourke took a deep breath as Sammy placed a hand on his arm. "Isa is right, Rourke." Sammy kept his voice low. Rourke looked over at him. Sammy looked tired and ready for bed, but he had the same resolution in his eyes as Isa did. "He's right."

"I know." Rourke looked away and sighed heavily. "Isa, this is serious." He looked back to him, meeting his eyes. Isa nodded sharply but didn't waver. "It isn't some game. The Wolves could come here. There have been more of them in the darkness surrounding Bhaskara."

"I know. Lao told me."

"Lao's in on this, too." Sammy shook his head. "Shit."

"Lao actually said the same thing you two are." Isa looked away finally, a faint blush coloring his cheeks. "But, Rourke, listen to me, please. I am like you —"

"You're not."

"I am," Isa insisted. "I have never wanted to walk in my father's footsteps. I love the haldis, and I love being in the Sanctuary, but High Warden? I can't do that. I'm not cut out to run the lives of other people! Then you arrived, and you fought with my father on leaving, and it made me realize I didn't have to stay in the Sanctuary."

"Good job, Rourke," Sammy scoffed.

"Yes, because I did this on purpose," Rourke replied sarcastically. Rourke ran a hand through his hair and down to his neck, feeling Nysa's tail still wrapped around his throat. He ran his fingers along her tail before he dropped his arm to his side. "All right."

"Wait, is that a haldis?" Isa's eyes lit up and he laughed. "Rourke! When did you get a haldis? That's incredible! I have never met someone who got a second haldis, that's a great honor!"

"That's not important right now." Rourke shook his head. "How long have you been doing this? How long have I been doing this?" Rourke turned to Sammy.

Sammy shrugged. "A month? I don't know, I haven't been keeping track of the cycles."

"A month?" Rourke shook his head. "Never mind, that's not important. It took a lot longer than a *month* —" Rourke thought the word sounded weird when he said it. "— to master my sword skills. How long have you been using a bow?"

"Since I was little, honestly. I have been using it for target practice since I could hold it."

Rourke nodded, actually impressed. "Well, okay. I still don't like it."

"Good thing you're not my father then."

Sammy snorted back a laugh, turning to bury his face into Rourke's shoulder. "He's got your attitude for sure," Sammy said, voice muffled by Rourke's shirt.

"Yeah, yeah." Rourke pushed Sammy away from him. He turned back to Isa, who somehow seemed to grow older during the length of their conversation. "You stay in the city."

"You can't tell me what to do."

"You know what I mean. I don't want to see you get hurt."

"I know." Isa nodded; his voice somber. "I need to get going. I'm standing out at the bridge with some others." He took a step to the side toward the entrance to the barracks. "It was nice seeing you two. Congratulations on the new bond, Rourke. I'm sure I will see you around." With a small wave, Isa ran off, meeting up with a couple other people before all of them disappeared into the city.

Rourke sighed, reaching out for Sammy as they turned for the main building. "I don't like it," Rourke muttered as he followed Sammy inside and up the stairs.

"You don't have to like it," Sammy commented, looking back over his shoulder to Rourke. Rourke frowned as they topped the stairs to the third floor. "You just have to accept it."

"What if he gets hurt?" Rourke paused as Sammy opened the door to their room and Luna slipped inside. Yawning, Rourke followed Sammy in, and closed the door behind himself.

"That's not your problem. Rourke." Sammy pulled off his shirt, which Rourke was only now realizing was his, and turned to face him. "I know it's hard, and I know you want to help, but Isa isn't your problem. You have to worry about you." Sammy walked up to Rourke, resting his hands on Rourke's shoulders. "About us. What if the Wolves do attack, like you said to him? Are you going to be more concerned about saving Isa or keeping your own ass alive?"

"I could do both." Rourke reached up and carefully pried Nysa's tail from around his neck. "He's young."

"Rourke, *we're* young. Hell, I'm barely into my twenties, and you just turned nineteen. We are young, too. I know you want to help. I get it, it's one of the things I —" Sammy cut himself off before he looked away. He was quiet for a moment before he spoke, but he still didn't meet Rourke's eyes. Rourke reached out, resting his hands on Sammy's hips and feeling the warmth of his skin under his palms. "I don't want to see you get hurt, either, Rourke," Sammy murmured.

"I won't." Rourke's voice was firm. "There is nothing in the darkness that I can't kill."

"Doesn't mean it can't kill you." Sammy sounded defeated and tired. He shook his head and bit his lip. "Never mind. Turn around so I can get Nysa for you so we can go to bed."

Rourke turned around for Sammy, but something didn't feel right. Rourke felt a weight on his shoulders and something he couldn't name twisted in his chest. He could tell Sammy was worried and upset, but Rourke was, too. Isa was young, and Rourke knew he had been young when he'd been cast into the darkness, but that didn't mean he couldn't be worried. He knew what dangers were out there, and he didn't want to see anyone else get hurt because of the Wolves.

Turning to face Sammy again, Rourke took Nysa from him and cradled the still sleeping haldis in his arms. Sammy leaned in, resting his head on Rourke's shoulder. Raising his hands, Sammy gripped tightly to the hem of Rourke's pants. "Just please, Rourke, promise me that when it comes down to it, you will think of your life first."

Rourke felt his whole body go rigid. "Sammy, you know I won't do that. We are having this conversation because I won't do that."

Sammy's voice was barely audible against Rourke's shoulder. "I know."

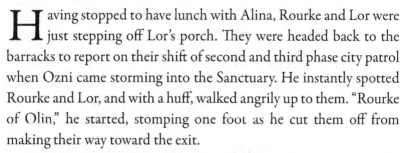

18

Having stopped to have lunch with Alina, Rourke and Lor were just stepping off Lor's porch. They were headed back to the barracks to report on their shift of second and third phase city patrol when Ozni came storming into the Sanctuary. He instantly spotted Rourke and Lor, and with a huff, walked angrily up to them. "Rourke of Olin," he started, stomping one foot as he cut them off from making their way toward the exit.

"I'm leaving." Rourke raised his hands in the air to show he meant no harm. He didn't want any trouble and there was always a little bit of concern that Rourke and Sammy would run into Ozni at some point. Ozni knew he had bonded with Nysa through word of mouth, but Rourke himself hadn't encountered the High Warden since they had argued and Sammy and him left. "Was just having lunch with Lor and Alina."

"I don't care about that!" Ozni waved a fat hand into the air in dismissal. "You will fix what you have done though!" He raised a shaking hand to point in Rourke's face. "This is your doing! And I will have none of it!"

"What in the light are you talking about?" Lor crossed his arms over his chest, clearly not impressed with Ozni. Next to Lor, Isik huffed a sigh, and Rourke couldn't have agreed more with the argi's reaction.

"You stay out of this, Lor!" Ozni turned on Lor. "This is between me and him!" Turning back to Rourke, Ozni squared his feet and tried to make himself as threatening as possible. Rourke wasn't impressed. "You will fix this," Ozni stammered again, and it took everything Rourke had to not smack Ozni's hand from his face.

"Fix what? I didn't do anything."

"You've poisoned him! Poisoned his mind, that's what you've done! I shouldn't have let you leave, even with that Other you insist on committing to!"

"You leave Sammy out of whatever problems you have with me!" Rourke took a step toward Ozni, and Ozni stumbled back, clearly afraid and flustered by Rourke's actions.

Next to Rourke, Lor grabbed his arm. "Easy, Rourke. He's not worth it."

Rourke knew Lor was right, but he wasn't going to just stand here and let Ozni insult Sammy again. Ozni regained his footing and threw his hands in the air, waving them around like it would somehow make him look more imposing. "Don't you forget who you are talking to, Rourke of Olin! I am the High Warden of this Sanctuary and I demand the respect I deserve."

"Oh, I know who you are." Rourke barely held back from rolling his eyes. He was getting annoyed and frustrated with Ozni. In his hood, he could feel Nysa stirring before she popped her head up to see what was going on, clearly reacting to Rourke's emotions. "Get to the point of what you want. I have things I need to be doing right now."

"The only thing you will be doing is fixing your mistake! I expect you to go straight to the head of the Illuminari from here and fix this immediately!" Ozni stomped his foot again, raising one fat finger into the air before quickly pointing it at the ground angrily. His face was flushed, and he was out of breath. Sweat began beading on his forehead with all the exertion he was doing with his flailing about.

Rourke stared dumbly at Ozni for a heartbeat. "You knew I wanted to be done with the Order. You have no control over what I do anymore."

"Not you!" Ozni yelled, balling his chubby hands into fists. "Not you! I could care less about what you do! Isa! You have poisoned his mind into thinking he can walk away from his birthright as you have done, and for the love of the light, Rourke of Olin, you will fix this!"

Next to Rourke, Lor gasped in shock. Rourke bit his lip to keep from laughing and wrapped his hand around the hilt of his sword. He wasn't doing it as a threat, he just needed something to ground himself, but Ozni glanced at his hand before taking another step away from Rourke and Lor. Despite how he felt about the situation, Rourke forced himself to say the words: "Isa isn't my problem."

Ozni sputtered, clearly disagreeing with Rourke despite not actually saying such. "He has turned his back on the Order, and it's all thanks to your treachery."

"Me? Maybe you should —" Rourke went to take a step forward, but Lor slammed a hand against his chest and stepped in front of Rourke.

"Ozni, let me take care of this. Isa will talk to me." Lor's voice was low and even, but Rourke could tell he was trying to figure out just exactly what was happening here. "We have to go, but we will return to the barracks to talk to Isa and Asha about this matter."

"Thank you, Lor." Ozni's entire demeanor changed, even as he glared at Rourke over Lor's shoulder. "At least one of you is sensible." Without giving Lor a chance to reply, Ozni stomped off across the yard toward his house, muttering under his breath.

As soon as he was out of earshot, Lor turned around to face Rourke. "Isa joined the Illuminari?"

"Lao knows!" Rourke threw his hands in the air out of frustration. Nysa squeaked at his sudden action.

"Of course, Lao knows." Lor rolled his eyes and rubbed his temples with his hand. "Why didn't you say something?"

"What do you want me to say, Lor? I don't want to see the kid hurt, but I'm not exactly the one to tell him to walk away from this.

I saw him at the barracks, and I did try to talk him out of it, but he made a really good point, and well, I can't argue with it."

"And what point is that?" Lor swore under his breath and turned for the entrance of the Sanctuary. "Come on, we have to get back."

Rourke nodded, moving to Lor's left as Isik moved to Lor's right side. "I'm not going to stop him. It's too late anyway. He's already joined, doing late patrols in the city." Rourke took a deep breath and sighed. "He's doing it because of me though. He saw that I was able to leave, decide for myself what I wanted to do, and he decided to follow in my steps."

"Isa has always been different, even when he was little." Lor rested a hand on Isik's head as they walked down the street. "I just never thought that he had plans to leave."

"To be honest," Rourke started, surprising himself with how quiet he sounded. "I'm not surprised. Isa reminds me a lot of myself, especially when I was little. I knew back then that I wasn't going to be satisfied with what it meant to be in the Order. My High Warden seemed to understand that, but Ozni, he doesn't understand. And he doesn't listen." Rourke took a deep breath, looking over to Lor before watching the street ahead of them. People were milling about and somewhere in the distance an umbra was bugling. "While I agree Isa is too young to leave the city, given what I did at a much younger age, I have no right to judge him. I forgot that for a moment when we spoke during the other cycle."

Lor nodded next to Rourke. His voice was also low as he spoke. "What's it going to mean for the Order though? Isa was supposed to be the next High Warden. What's going to happen now?"

"Find a new one." Rourke sighed, realizing that this must have been what Lysha meant when she said that he would have to help to keep Olin's traditions alive. He reached up and touched his chin rubbing over the mark that he knew was there. "In Olin, the High

Warden wasn't determined by blood, it was decided by dedication. Honestly, if I was in a position to choose, I would pick Alina."

"Alina!" Lor looked over at Rourke with wide eyes.

"Yeah, why not? She's always with the haldis and she seems very attentive to their needs. That's what a High Warden should be, not whatever Ozni thinks he is." Rourke reached up to pet Nysa, who was slowly beginning to climb up to perch on his shoulder as they walked around.

"I just never thought of it that way. Alina as the High Warden?" Lor chuckled as he shook his head. "Not in my wildest dreams."

"Don't get ahead of yourself, Lor." Rourke stuffed his hands in the pockets of his jacket. "I am just saying we did things differently in Olin than you seem to here."

Lor nodded as the two of them turned onto a larger and broader street. Rourke went to pull his hood up now that Nysa was on his shoulder, paused, but decided to do it anyway, only letting go of the fabric when it was pulled low over his forehead, and hunched his shoulders. The crowd was beginning to thicken the closer they walked toward the market street, and Rourke was already dreading the comments he knew were to come. Even though it seemed to have spread that he was a Nari, people still referred to him as 'Warden' when they saw him.

"You know that everyone can see Nysa, right," Lor commented dryly from Rourke's side.

"Makes me feel better." Rourke watched the people as they walked down the busy street. While people had begun to leave him alone since he was a familiar face within the city, with Nysa coming on patrols with him, people had begun to stop and talk to him again. Every interaction made him uneasy and looking for a way to leave the conversation. Thankfully, Lor noticed that quickly and often would comment on how they needed to keep moving.

"I still want to talk to Isa," Lor started, dragging the conversation back to the original topic. "I want to hear from him why he chose to leave."

"I'm telling you why." Pausing to let an umbra lumber passed pulling a cart at a crossroads, Rourke looked over at Lor. "He doesn't feel he belongs. It's a feeling I know too well."

"I understand that. Rourke, I'm on your side in this. I just said that to Ozni to get him to leave us alone. I have no love for him."

Rourke nodded sharply as they started walking again. If he looked between the buildings, Rourke could see the main building of the barracks, and felt his heart skip a beat. He'd be home soon, back to a place where he could be a bit more relaxed without having to worry about anything other than keeping Luna away from the umbra. They were quiet as they walked, simply letting the sounds of the city flow over them.

As they drew closer to the barracks, Lor took a deep breath. "I can only assume Isa is around the barracks somewhere since Ozni seemed to be returning to the Sanctuary. I need to find him then get back home. Something tells me he may try to speak to Alina, and I want to be there."

"Alina can take care of herself, but I understand. I won't keep you; I want to go speak with Asha anyway. Sammy and I still have to talk about this upcoming trip into the darkness, and I told him I would get details before we made a decision."

"Thanks, Rourke. I will keep you informed on what I find out."

"I will, too." Rourke nodded, moving to take Nysa off his shoulder so he could hold her. He couldn't explain why, he just felt like he needed to have her in his arms. She didn't seem to mind, instantly rolling over onto her back so he could rub her exposed stomach. He did so mindlessly as they walked along.

As they walked under the archway into the barracks, Lor turned off toward the main building with a small wave so he could complete their report before finding Isa and returning home. Rourke waved also before he turned and made his way up the steps into what he now knew was Asha's office. When Lao had first brought Sammy and him here, Rourke didn't exactly know where it was he was bringing them.

Knocking on the doorframe, he pushed aside the curtain when Asha called for him to come in. Sitting at one of the tables was Asha, her committed, Lao, and some of the other Nari Rourke had seen around the barracks. Asha stood from where she was bent over a map. "Rourke, I didn't expect to see you at this phase of the cycle."

Rourke pointed back over his shoulder with his free hand. "Lor and I just got back from patrol. I wanted to ask something, if I could."

"Of course. Come sit, we are just discussing plans for when we go out into the darkness." Asha waved him over as she went back to the maps littered across the tabletop. One of the Nari tapped one of the maps as Rourke walked over. "That's where they were spotted before," Asha asked in response to the map.

"Yes," the man nodded. "Juke and I killed them. They made easy targets with our bows."

Lao slid over a little bit on the bench to make room for Rourke, and as he sat down, Lao scratched Nysa's head. She squeaked and rolled over slightly away from Lao, and Rourke turned to half glare at him, hoping his unspoken message of *just leave her alone* was clear. Lao grinned but pulled his hand away anyway. Lao was always petting the animals, and while Rourke normally didn't care, Nysa didn't really like to be touched by anyone other than Rourke and Sammy. Thankfully, Lao respected that for the most part.

"So, who do we have going with us," Asha asked, moving around the maps to try to locate a piece of paper. "I know some of our more competent scouts, as well as the group who just returned from the darkness. Who does that leave out there?"

A woman at the far end of the table picked up a piece of paper that peeked out from under the corner of a large map. "Um, let's see," she started, picking up a charcoal stick and crossing out a line on the paper. "With our last group returning, there are three groups still out there, but Aetius and Molly should be returning shortly."

"Aetius and Molly," Rourke asked, looking over to the woman as she spoke their names.

"That's right." Asha nodded and picked up a different piece of paper with a much larger list of names on it. "You know them, don't you?"

"They are like family." Rourke nodded. "Aetius taught me the basics of what I know."

"Good, you're on my list of people who I still needed to get in touch with. You're going."

"But I — okay." Rourke nodded, looking down to Nysa and feeling unease twist in his gut.

"But what?" Asha set the paper down and scribbled something down by his name on her list. "You knew this would happen when you signed that paper."

"Yes." Rourke nodded. He did. He was expecting it. He wasn't the one worried about going back out into the darkness. "Just I told Sammy —"

"Sammy will get over it." Asha flicked her eyes up to meet Rourke's eyes, and only now did he realize they weren't gray but a deep, deep brown. The realization that Asha was an Other made Rourke pause. Not that it mattered, but he hadn't been expecting it either, not with her Illume complexion, plus how she acted and spoke. "Problem with that?"

"No." Rourke shook his head, holding onto Nysa a little tighter. Sammy would have a problem with this though. Nysa grabbed his hand and he looked down to her as Lao leaned across the table.

"Do you have the groups set up yet," Lao asked, taking the piece of paper Asha had written on. Rourke looked over at it, seeing a list of names, most of them ones he recognized as being members of the Nari. While he knew the names, most of them didn't mean anything to him. Unlike Sammy, who tried to make friends with everyone he could, Rourke tended to keep to himself.

"I'm still working on that. I do know I want Isa with me."

"Isa," Rourke asked, looking up to Asha. "Isa is going?"

"Volunteered actually." Asha nodded, only half paying attention to what Rourke was saying. She shifted the maps on the table, picking one up and handing it to one of the Nari at the table.

"And you're letting him," Rourke questioned. It occurred to him that this must have been what Ozni meant by Rourke needing to fix the problem with Isa.

"He understands what the Illuminari is about, Rourke. I'm starting to wonder if you don't." Asha flipped through the papers she was holding as she spoke, clearly not really listening to what it was Rourke was saying.

"I do." Rourke nodded, but the shock must have still been in his voice. "But letting Isa go into the darkness, that seems unreasonable."

"He will be with me." Asha looked offended, and Rourke couldn't blame her. He was basically saying he didn't think she could handle herself in the darkness. Which wasn't at all what he was trying to say, he just wasn't explaining what he meant correctly.

"I think what Rourke is trying to say." Lao looked over at Rourke then to Asha. "Is that maybe he isn't ready to go quite yet. I tend to agree, Asha, Isa is still young. He doesn't even have his marks, and he is the High Warden's only child."

"Yes." Rourke nodded, feeling a false sense of relief wash over him at Lao coming to his defense. "Thank you, Lao."

Asha was quiet as she looked between Rourke and Lao clearly in thought. Finally, after what seemed like too long, Asha took a deep breath. "Then you two will go with him. And me," she added. "If you are that concerned about his safety, and something happens, then I think between the three of us we should be able to protect one kid."

Rourke inhaled sharply as Lao nodded, answering Asha as he did. "As you say, Asha."

19

Sammy lifted the brush from Lilith's fur, resting his arms on her back as he looked over to where Miley was standing by the stall door. Even though Sammy still had no official place within the Illuminari other than a Nari's committed, he found he was spending a lot of his time in the stables. Miley kept trying to get him to join, but so far, he'd been reluctant to, even if it was just to work in the stables like Miley was suggesting. He had more important things to think about anyway, like naming the baby umbra. "Rourke said something that goes with Luna."

Miley looked up from where she was cleaning the stall. "Still on that, huh? Poor little guy needs a name, and you can't even think of one." Miley stood, and leaned on the wall, her shovel in hand. "How about Midnight?"

"Naw, doesn't feel right." Sammy shook his head and looked down to the baby umbra at Lilith's side. Standing, Sammy started brushing Lilith again, occasionally turning to run the brush down her baby's back to get him used to the sensation.

"Well, I'm out of ideas then." Laughing to herself, Miley went back to shoveling. "I have chores to finish unlike some lazy bums around here."

"Hey, I am here every day helping!" Sammy knew she was joking and couldn't keep the smile off his face. "You're just mad that I won't join."

"That's part of it, yes." Miley grinned at him as she picked up the wheelbarrow and moved it out of the way so she could close the stall door. "But I really do think it would be good for you. You spend most of your time cooped up in your room studying the Illume language. You love the animals, you could work here in the stables with me, and train the umbra. There is always one that needs training or something."

"I am not, I go see Alina, too," Sammy grumbled. "I'll think about it."

"You always say that, Sammy!" Miley shook her head, turned back to the wheelbarrow and picked it up. "All right, I will be back in a few. I have to go dump this and get some fresh sawdust for Lilith. I locked you in."

"Okay!" Sammy went back to brushing Lilith, trying in vain to think of a name for the young umbra. He didn't feel right calling the little one his without him having a proper name. While he was beginning to learn Sammy's voice, Sammy didn't want the calf to get used to coming to all the random things Sammy had been calling him.

Turning, Sammy crouched down in front of the young buck and ran his hand along the length of his neck. "Naming Luna was so easy. She reminded me of the moon in the night, but you're the exact opposite. You are the shadow of the moon in a land of light. You're —" Sammy stopped, laughing to himself and startling the calf with his sudden laughter.

"Oh, I'm sorry." Sammy shifted to his knees, pulling the calf to him and brushing down his flank. "I didn't mean to startle you. I just think I thought of a name for you, and I should have thought of it so much sooner!"

"Finally. I have a bet with Lor on when you will name him."

Sammy looked over his shoulder to see Lao leaning over the stall door petting Lilith's face. "So, what's the name? Something weird like 'Luna?'"

"Luna isn't weird." Sammy stood up and brushed the sawdust and hay from his knees. He walked over to Lao and leaned on the wall by the stall door. "I think I am going to name him Solar."

"Solar?" Lao scrunched up his nose. "Yeah, weird name. Ah, well, Lor wins. Sorry, Sammy, I bet on you naming him before now. Lor thought it would take you several cycles, and well, it did."

"You two are so baffling sometimes." Sammy rolled his eyes and pushed off the wall. "Let me out? Miley locked me in when she went to dump the wheelbarrow."

Lao nodded and unlocked the door, opening it so Sammy could step back out into the main hall of the stables. "When can Lilith rejoin the herd?"

"Not until the little — Solar. Not until *Solar* is a little older. I don't think she minds all the lavish attention I have been giving her though." Sammy turned and locked the stall door. Both Lilith and Solar ignored them as they walked away.

Lao laughed. "Probably not. I've always liked Lilith, she's a good girl. I think it was a bold move to breed her to Snap, but Solar looks like a fine young buck. I think with the right guidance, you'll have one exceptional mount on your hands."

"I'm sure I will." Sammy grinned. He was really excited to learn more about the umbra and the idea of being able to help train Solar was awesome. He looked up to the palu-tai plant that had made its home in the open rafters of the stables. Four of its yellow flowers were open, as well as both of its food catching maws. "Hey," Sammy started as Lao, and he walked toward the front of the stable and the courtyard. "Have you seen Rourke? I thought he would be back by now."

"Um, yeah, he is." Lao nodded, pointing across the courtyard. "He was talking to Asha."

"Oh, good. He told me he was going to do that." Sammy nodded. While they hadn't talked about it a lot, Rourke and Sammy had begun to talk about the newest expedition into the darkness. Rourke had told Sammy he would find out more information from Asha before they made a decision on Rourke going. Sammy knew deep down Rourke could do what he wanted without his approval, but Sammy also knew that Rourke knew Sammy was worried about him getting hurt, or worse, if he ventured back into the twilight.

"Oh, so then you have no problems with him going? That's great!"

"Going?" Sammy stopped and grabbed Lao by the arm. Where they were standing in the doorway of the stables spilled shadows across them both. "What do you mean: going?"

"Yeah." Lao looked confused as he answered, eyes darting across the courtyard to Asha's office before coming back to Sammy. "Rourke is going. I thought you had decided on that."

"No!" Sammy couldn't believe what he was hearing. "We hadn't talked about it yet. He was supposed to be getting more information on what was happening. He never told me he planned on going!"

"Well, I don't think — I mean, he found out that Isa was going and —"

"Isa is going?" Sammy could feel himself getting upset, and he took a deep breath to not yell at Lao. None of this was his fault. "Okay, look, sorry. Where is Rourke now?"

"I left him with Asha, but he was just about done, so he may be back in your room now." Lao pointed as he spoke. "I'm sorry, Sammy, I thought you two had decided on him going. He seemed very sure as he stepped into Asha's office. I just assumed you had already talked about it."

Sammy shook his head, biting his lip as he looked across the busy courtyard to Asha's office. "No, we hadn't, not completely." Sammy took a deep breath in an attempt to calm down, but he just couldn't seem to. He felt as if Rourke had gone behind his back and lied to him about trying to find out more before going. He knew

Rourke wanted to go, but he didn't think he wanted to go this badly. "All right. Thanks." Waving a hand, Sammy walked away from Lao headed for Asha's office.

Lao didn't say anything or follow Sammy, but he could feel Lao's eyes watching him as he made his way across the courtyard. Several people were coming down the stairs of Asha's office as Sammy approached, and they all smiled and said hi to him in passing. He forced himself to smile back, feeling anything but his usual self right now. As soon as the last person stepped off the stairs, Sammy started up them, knocking on the doorframe as he reached the top.

"Come in," a male voice responded, and Sammy pushed the curtain aside to see Asha's committed sitting at one of the long tables by himself. "Oh, hi, Sammy," he started, turning to face him. "If you're looking for Asha, she just ran upstairs, she will be right back."

Sammy looked up to the ceiling when he pointed, and Sammy remembered that the second floor of this building was Asha's private home. "No, thanks." He shook his head. "Looking for Rourke. Have you seen him?"

"You just missed him actually." The older Illume smiled. "He mentioned something about needing to find you."

Sammy bobbed his head in a nod and tried to keep from frowning. "Thank you," he tried to keep the anger out of his voice before he turned and trotted back down the steps.

The courtyard was beginning to thin out, and Sammy could see Lao, now with Lor, on the far side of the yard. Lor waved, and Sammy threw his hand up in acknowledgement, but he was too upset to be bothered to go over and talk to him. He took the steps into the main building two at a time and turned right up the stairs toward their bedroom.

Sammy couldn't believe Rourke had gone and done the one thing he had asked him not to do, and by the time he was opening the door to the bedroom, he was so frustrated that he slammed the door behind himself causing Rourke, Luna, and Nysa to all jump at his arrival. Rourke stood from where he was sitting in the chair at the desk, and Nysa, who was sitting at his feet, scrambled behind his leg. Luna, recognizing that it was Sammy, stood and padded over to him.

"You all right," Rourke asked as Sammy bent down to greet Luna.

"How can you say that?" Sammy stood back up, crossing his arms over his chest.

"You don't look all right." Rourke sat back down to finish taking off his other boot. "That's why I asked."

"Well, then, no, I'm not. I'm pretty pissed off actually." Sammy was growing angrier by the second. Rourke was so calm about this that it was just making Sammy even madder. Sammy scoffed and rolled his eyes. "When were you going to tell me about you going out into the darkness?"

Rourke snapped his head up, eyes wide. "As soon as I saw you."

"Well, I'm here now." Sammy swept his arms out to his sides. "What's stopping you?"

Rourke pulled off his boot and set it aside with the other one. "I'm concerned about why you're so upset."

"Oh!" Sammy threw his hands in the air before laughing bitterly as he let them fall back to his sides to smack loudly against his legs. "*Now* you're concerned about what I think?"

"That's not fair."

"Neither are you for not telling me that you are going!"

"How'd you find out?" Rourke picked Nysa up, holding her in his arms. Rourke was staying calm and speaking in short sentences which only upset Sammy further. He wasn't giving any form of explanation and Sammy was having to pry the little bit of information he was getting out of Rourke.

"Lao!" Sammy snarled the name. "I ran into Lao in the stables. He told me all about how you just had to go when you heard about Isa going."

"He is going, yes."

"You promised me we would talk about this, Rourke. And then you went behind my back and did it anyway."

"I can't just let Isa go out there alone." Rourke was beginning to get frustrated, too. Sammy could see the anger in his movements and the way he held his body stiffly. "What if something happens to him?"

"That's not your problem, Rourke. I am your problem. Nysa and Luna; they are your problems. Not Isa!" Sammy could feel his body shaking with rage and he moved to the bed to sit down on the edge of it. He scrubbed his face with his hands. His voice was muffled as he spoke. "I just can't believe you decided to do this without me. You promised me we were going to talk about you going."

The fight left Sammy suddenly, and he just felt tired and defeated. He thought Rourke and him had a level of trust that was unbeatable, but this just seemed to prove that Rourke still didn't consider his opinion when it came to matters that concerned them both. Taking a deep breath, Sammy leaned forward, resting his forearms on his knees and staring off at a spot on the rug that Luna had dug loose with her claws. "You promised," he murmured again, not caring how broken his voice sounded.

Rourke walked across the space to sit next to Sammy. He set Nysa down behind them, and Sammy could feel her moving around on the mattress. "I ran into Ozni earlier," Rourke started quietly. He didn't try to touch Sammy, and Sammy felt weirdly glad at the fact that Rourke was keeping his distance right now.

"So," Sammy snapped, not really caring.

"He thinks it's my fault that Isa joined the Illuminari."

"It is your fault he joined the Illuminari. He got the crazy idea from you."

"Thanks." Sammy could hear the frown in Rourke's voice without even turning to look at him. "I came back from my patrol to get information from Asha."

"Was this before or after you decided to go without talking to me about it? Do you care more about Isa's safety than your own? Is this some Warden thing I don't know about?"

Rourke inhaled sharply. "That wasn't called for. Why are you being so mean right now?"

Sammy shrugged. "I'm pissed off, and mad at you for just deciding to go without talking to me about it."

"I'm trying to explain what happened because what you seem to think happened, didn't."

"You didn't decide to go on this expedition without talking to me?" Sammy picked his head up, glaring at Rourke.

"No." Rourke shook his head, his eyes catching the low light of his bhasvah. "Can I just explain?"

"I guess, but you're still going, right? So, what's the point?"

Rourke huffed a sigh and rolled his eyes. "I have to," Rourke said quietly, shifting to rest his arms on his own knees. He dropped his head forward and ran his hand through his hair. "I mentioned how Aetius basically taught me the beginnings of what I know now, and Asha just told me I had to go. I didn't find out Isa was going until after that. I was just going in to get information so we could talk. I promise, Sammy." Rourke looked over to Sammy, and Sammy met his eyes. He could tell Rourke was telling the truth, but he was still too upset to really accept it.

"So, what, you just decide to keep Isa safe then?"

"I did tell Asha I thought he was too young to go. Lao agreed." Rourke shrugged his shoulders. "But Asha decided that if that was the case, Lao and I should be with her and Isa. That's what happened. Like she said, I signed that paper, Sammy. I have to go. I tried to explain that we needed to talk about it, but she told me, and her exact words were, you'd get over it."

Sammy sighed heavily and sat up just to fall backward on the bed with his arms over his head. Nysa waddled over to him and curled up in his armpit, completely unaware of his foul mood. Or maybe she was aware, which was why she was cuddling up to him. Rourke twisted to look back at Sammy. "I'm sorry." Rourke's voice was still quiet as he reached out and rested his hand on Sammy's knee.

Luna jumped up on the bed and curled up on Sammy's pillow, groaning as she made herself comfortable. Sammy tried to glare a hole in the ceiling. "I fucking hate this."

"I know." Rourke took a deep breath and shifted on the bed to face Sammy. "I thought you would be happy here. I was wrong."

"It's not that." Sammy shook his head. "I don't know what it is. I feel restless, like I have no purpose here. Everyone wants me to join the Illuminari, and I don't know if I want to, especially if it means going back out there." Sammy waved a hand at the wall but meant the darkness that lay beyond the city. "I'm not like you, Rourke. I was fucking terrified out there."

"I know you were, but you're safe now."

"And you're going back out there. Shit." Sammy sat up, disturbing Nysa as he did. Her squeak of alarm went unheard as she waddled her way to sleep up by Luna and the headboard. "What if something does happen? To you? To Isa, or Lao? I will be here, not knowing what happened."

"Nothing is going to happen."

"You don't know that!"

"I do, Sammy! I have lived out there. I know how to survive, and I'm going to come back. I've told you there is nothing in the darkness that I can't kill, and I'm not going to let a few Wolves keep me from coming back to you."

Sammy felt his breath hitch in his throat. Rourke's resolution was steadfast. He truly believed what he was saying, and Sammy felt shame well in his chest. He should have more faith in Rourke, and he let his anger and fear about the situation get the better of him. Sammy nodded, looking off to the side. "I'm sorry I yelled at you, Rourke."

"I'm sorry I got us into this mess, Sammy." Rourke took a deep breath. "Asha wants to leave in three cycles. It will be the beginning of the new season."

"Okay." Sammy nodded, reaching out to place his hand on Rourke's hand that was still resting on Sammy's knee. Rourke leaned over and kissed Sammy, bringing his hand up to thread into Sammy's hair. Melting into the kiss, Sammy let his eyes close, enjoying the feeling of Rourke being so close. "I'm going to miss you," Sammy said quietly when Rourke pulled away.

"I'm going to miss you, too." Rourke pressed their foreheads together.

Sammy could already feel that sense of loneliness rise in his body and he moved to kiss Rourke again, lingering passed the chaste kiss Rourke had started with. Rourke responded instantly and eagerly, deepening the kiss of his own accord as he opened his mouth and licked Sammy's lip. Sammy was overjoyed at the action, opening his mouth and encouraging Rourke to deepen the kiss even further.

Rourke pushed against Sammy's shoulder slightly and he leaned back until he was laying against the bed with Rourke leaning over him. Finally, Sammy broke the kiss, inhaling deeply when he did. "What's gotten into you?"

"I don't know." Rourke shrugged, bending down to kiss Sammy's chin.

"Do you want to keep going? Try again?"

Sammy saw the hesitation in Rourke's eyes. "I think so," he started. "But I'm not sure."

Sammy smiled softly. "Just tell me when you want to stop. We will get there eventually."

"And if we don't? I still don't know how I feel about..." Rourke trailed off as he looked away, but Sammy knew what he was thinking. Rourke was worried about doing anything beyond kissing.

Sammy took a deep breath. "You know, something Lao said to me got me thinking. Committing to you isn't about the physical stuff, it's about the bond we share."

"Of course," Rourke agreed, bobbing his head in a nod.

"So, I guess what I am saying is, if we don't get to the physical stuff, we just don't. Though I would like to try. Not going to lie, I would really enjoy sleeping with you, when you're ready."

Rourke frowned. "You already sleep with me."

"No." Sammy laughed. "Not sleep *next* to you, sleep *with* you. Have sex. It's just been a long time, and I would like to be with you in that way."

Sammy could see the uncertainty on Rourke's face. "All right. If that's what you want."

"Well, I want you to want it, too, Rourke. The whole point is for us both to enjoy sleeping together." Rourke didn't seem convinced, and Sammy reached up to pull Rourke close by the back of his neck. "Don't worry about it right now, just kiss me."

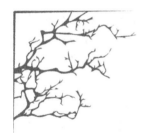

20

It was clear it was going to rain. The courtyard was crowded, flooded with umbra, Nari, and their families, as everyone was either saying goodbye to the people leaving, or finishing up the last of the packing in order to leave. Sammy and Rourke stood off to the side, near the smaller building where Sammy and Lao would spar. "Are you sure you don't want your jacket," Sammy asked again.

Rourke lifted the corner of his mouth in a faint smile. "I told you I will be fine. Stop worrying about me." Reaching up, Rourke pushed some loose hair behind Sammy's ear. In the rush of the morning, Sammy hadn't had the chance to pull it back, and he could feel the longer strands get caught under the weight of Rourke's jacket. "Besides, you wanted it."

"Because it's cold out here today. How are you not cold?" Sammy pulled Rourke's jacket a little tighter around his shoulders. "I always have my vest though, so if you want —" Sammy stopped as Nysa popped her head and front claws out of the partly buttoned front of the jacket.

With a chuckle, Rourke scratched behind Nysa's ears. "No, she likes it."

"Smells like you, that's why."

"Will you be okay with her? I don't want to take her into the darkness with me." Rourke kept his attention on the haldis. Sammy could feel her scales against his body through the thin shirt he was wearing. Her tail wrapped around his side and her back claws caught on the hem of his pants as she tried to climb higher up the front of the jacket to get to Rourke.

Sammy looked down to where Luna was laying at their feet. "You have Luna." Sammy reached out, placing his hand on the bend of Rourke's elbow as he stopped Nysa from climbing out to him. "Nysa and I will be okay."

Rourke nodded, finally looking up to Sammy. Behind Rourke, Sammy could see people beginning to line up in some sort of formation, and Asha was riding around on the big, black buck named Snap. Leaning forward, Rourke pressed their foreheads together, ran his hands into Sammy's hair, and took a deep breath. "I am really going to miss you."

Sammy squeezed Rourke's arm a bit tighter. "I am, too," he whispered, voice just loud enough for Rourke to hear. Sammy knew there were lots of people around them doing the same thing right now, but somehow Sammy felt all eyes were on the two of them.

Taking a step closer to Rourke, Sammy tipped his head to the side for a kiss, knowing it was the last one he was going to get until Rourke returned. Rourke instantly moved his hands to Sammy's hips, his fingers digging into the hem of his pants as if he never wanted to let go. Sammy inhaled through his nose and closed his eyes as he pressed his free hand to Rourke's chest and gripped his elbow a little tighter.

Asha's voice rang out for everyone to depart, and Sammy could hear several people giving their final goodbyes, but Rourke didn't move. If anything, he held Sammy tighter, and kissed him a little harder. Sammy knew this was just for a few days, but he felt like something was breaking inside his chest. This was going to be the first time he and Rourke had been apart since first meeting. Sammy could only imagine how Rourke felt if this was how he was reacting.

The umbra were beginning to grow anxious, Sammy could hear it in their short calls and stomping hooves. As much as he hated to, Sammy knew he needed to pull away, or Rourke would never leave. It took everything he had to make himself do it, and Sammy had to push against Rourke's chest with his hand when he did. Rourke blinked at Sammy as he took a step back, and Sammy could see the same pain in Rourke's eyes that he felt. "Sammy," Rourke started as Asha yelled again.

Rourke looked over his shoulder to Asha as he started to turn away. Sammy didn't know exactly how long it had been that he and Rourke had known each other, had been together, but he knew it had been several months at the least. He could tell by how long his hair was getting and from what other people in the barracks had told him about tracking the cycles as if they were days, as well as learning the Illume's equivalent of a calendar.

Rourke was walking away from him now, Luna at his side, and Sammy jerked into motion to follow so fast, he heard Nysa squeak in fear at his movements. Sammy had no idea what had come over him, but he knew he needed to do something before Rourke left. He didn't know what, but the feeling of loss at being apart was eating away at him so badly suddenly that Sammy felt he would regret not doing whatever it was he didn't know he was going to do.

Grabbing Rourke by the shoulder, Sammy spun him, crushing their mouths together in a brutal kiss. Sammy didn't think he'd ever kissed anyone with that amount of passion before, but he didn't care as he ran his hands into Rourke's hair and felt tears sting his eyes. Rourke's hands fisted into the jacket as he melted into the kiss. Asha yelled a third time and Rourke reluctantly pulled away. "I have to go," Rourke said quietly.

"I love you." Sammy blurted, and as soon as the words left his mouth, he knew that was the thing that was eating away at him. He gasped in shock at his own words, watching Rourke try to process what it was that Sammy had just said.

"Sammy, I —"

"All right, love birds. Let's break it up." Sammy and Rourke both had to step back as Asha guided Snap between them and tossed the reins of an older doe named Mosh to Rourke. "Get on the umbra, Rourke. We are leaving." Asha turned to Sammy. "I understand this is hard, Sammy, but we have a job to do. Stop distracting my Nari."

Behind Asha, Rourke clumsily climbed up into the saddle and as soon as Asha directed Snap to turn, Mosh chased after him, taking Rourke with her, and leaving Luna to follow along. Rourke turned and their eyes met. Sammy could see the apology in Rourke's eyes, along with something he couldn't identify.

Nysa squeaked in alarm and tried to climb out of Rourke's jacket to chase after him. Sammy looked down to catch her as she fell out of the opening, cradling her to his chest to try and calm her down. He didn't understand the connection between Rourke and Nysa, but he was beginning to understand that they both fed off one another's emotions, and something Rourke was feeling was strong enough for Nysa to want to go to him. "It's okay," Sammy started, petting her head. Around him, he could hear the group leaving the courtyard, the umbras' hooves loud on the cobblestone as they headed as a group toward the front gate of the city. Someone rode by trying to catch up. Sammy looked up, but he was unable to see Rourke in the crowd now, and he felt his heart drop into his stomach.

Sammy, along with several other families, stood in the empty courtyard until the last of the umbra couldn't be heard on the stones outside the barracks. Nysa had calmed down a little, but she was still occasionally thrashing about and smacking Sammy with her tail.

He wasn't sure how long he stood there, numb to everything around him, and trying to work through telling Rourke he loved him. Sammy figured he'd known for a while that he had, but he'd just never put it into conscious thought or words before. Pulling Nysa a little closer to his chest, Sammy finally forced himself to turn toward the barracks when he saw Lor and Isik walking across the courtyard.

"Have they left," he asked, looking up into the sky. "Looks like it may rain."

Sammy nodded. "Yeah, it does." Sammy looked up, searching the clouded skies over their heads. "Rourke left me his jacket because I said I was cold. It's damp, I can feel the chill seeping into my body."

Lor smiled, a small sympathetic lift at the corners of his mouth. "I was just about to return home when I saw you standing here. Do you want to come with me?"

Sammy shook his head. "No, I think I want to be alone right now." Turning from Lor, Sammy stopped. He didn't really want to be alone, he wanted to be with Rourke, but he knew that wasn't possible right now. Lor was still standing there, watching him when he turned around. "Actually, Lor, I think I do want to go with you."

"Great!" Lor's whole face lit up. "Alina would love to see you! And Nysa, as well. I see Rourke did decide to leave her with you."

"Probably for the better." Looking down, Sammy tucked Nysa back into his jacket and pulled it a little tighter across his shoulders. He could feel her moving around his stomach before she popped her head up out of the opening.

"Did their departure go smoothly," Lor asked.

Sammy didn't answer until they had started to walk back across the barracks courtyard toward the archway. "Yeah," he started, biting his lip. Overall, it had gone well, only for Sammy he felt he hadn't enough time to react to his confession before Rourke left. "Went fine."

Lor nodded. "It will be okay, Sammy. They will all be back before you know it."

Sammy looked over his shoulder as they stepped out onto the street. From where they stood, he could see the big archway of the main gate, and beyond that the grass hills that surrounded the city. "I hope so."

Sammy and Lor walked quietly along the streets, weaving in and out of the crowds and deciding to avoid the busier market street. Instead, Sammy and Lor went down to the docks where Lor bought a couple fish, beautiful blue ones that had what looked like spots of gold splattered across them. Lor said it was one of Alina's favorite things to eat, and she had asked him to pick up some on his way home. He also picked out a large yellow fish for Isik, who sniffed the package all the way back to the Sanctuary.

Sammy let himself inside with Alina's fish while Lor stayed on the porch to unwrap the fish he'd gotten for Isik. Closing the door behind himself, Sammy made his way into the kitchen, setting the package down before retrieving Nysa and taking off Rourke's jacket. It was hard to balance the two tasks, not used to maneuvering with Nysa like Rourke was, and he ultimately gave up trying to stop her from climbing up on his shoulder as he set the jacket over the back of one of the chairs at the table. He was just pulling Nysa off his shoulder to hold her when Lor and Alina came into the house.

Alina was all smiles and came right over to Sammy to give him a hug. "Lor said you might be lonely with Rourke being gone. You can stay here until he comes back if you'd like."

Sammy hugged Alina tightly, feeling something drain from his body in the hug. He hadn't realized how tense he had been until he wrapped his free arm around Alina, and he sighed heavily before he let go. "I wouldn't want to overstay my welcome."

"Nonsense. Oh! Is that my fish? Lor, you're simply amazing."

"I know." Lor smirked and pulled out one of the chairs at the table, sitting down and leaning back as he crossed his arms. "They are really nice looking, too."

Alina unwrapped the package they were in and grinned happily. "They are perfect! And you are more than welcome to stay, Sammy. I understand how lonely it can be. When Lor is gone most of the cycle, I find myself waiting at the door for him to return."

"I just — I don't know." Sammy pulled out a chair and sat down. Nysa twisted in Sammy's arms to rest her front claws on the table and tipped her head back to sniff at the air.

In the kitchen, Alina was moving around. "Let me start some tea, and let's talk about it."

"The tea sounds like a good idea." Sammy scratched behind Nysa's ears as he looked down at her. "I don't know about the talking part."

"What happened," Alina asked as she brought three stone cups to the table, setting them down in front of Lor, Sammy, and a third spot for herself. "Oh, Lor?"

"Yeah?"

"Would you go get that package I picked up? I placed it on the desk in your study when I brought you home that book."

"The package," Lor muttered under his breath as he stood. "I remember the book. What pack — oh! Yes. I'll be right back."

Alina smiled as she went back into the kitchen. Sammy turned to watch her as she opened a glass container full of dried tea leaves and scooped some out into a kettle that was heating over the small fire she had in the hearth. Alina hummed to herself as she worked, and Sammy found a comfort he didn't know he'd been missing. While this wasn't the same as being with Rourke, Lor and Alina had become good friends, and Sammy found he was able to relax and be comfortable around them both.

It was nice to just rest in the silence of the space, Sammy realized. There was no need for any of them to speak, and it was still comfortable. It reminded him of how Rourke and himself would just sort of settle down at night, sometimes with one, or both, of them going over what they had learned that day from their language lessons, or simply covering the bhasvah stones and being content to lay next to one another in the darkness of their room. It was simple, and felt like home, and Sammy realized it was the first time he'd really felt that way since he's been snatched from his apartment by his reflection.

Taking a deep breath, Sammy ran a hand through his hair, his fingers catching on a random knot. Wincing at the slight pull, Sammy worked the knot out of his hair as Lor came back into the room. He held up a small thin package and a book before offering it to Sammy. "What are these," Sammy asked as he took the items.

"It's a book on umbra that I was given when I was little. It's meant for children, but I think you will find a lot of useful information in there." Lor pointed to the book. "Keep it as long as you need it."

"Thanks!" Sammy flipped through the hardbound book quickly, able to pick out words he was learning in the Illume's native language. "And this?" He held up the small package.

"Something I found while out shopping, and it made me think of you." Alina slipped into the chair at the end of the table. "Open it."

"You got me a present? You didn't have to do that." Sammy chuckled. "I don't know what to say."

"Typically, people say 'thank you' when receiving a gift."

Sammy grinned at Lor's comment as he started to tear away the paper. "Thank you, I still wasn't expecting you to get me anything though. I don't have —"

"Sammy." Alina reached out and rested her hand on his arm. "I'm not asking for anything in return. I think you will like this though, so open it, and let's talk about what's bothering you."

Sammy nodded and looked back down to what he was doing, gently pushing Nysa aside as he could see. He took a deep breath as he finished tearing away the paper to reveal a bhasvah stone hair pick. It was squarish in shape and tapered off to a rounded end. On the very top of it was a chiseled animal that Sammy was easily able to identify as a haldis. He looked up to Alina as he held the hair pick tightly in his hand. "This is beautiful, thank you."

"I was hoping you would like it. I saw the haldis, and knowing how you've been worried about fitting in, I thought this would help.

Rourke's mark let's everyone know he's from Olin, what better way than a haldis for you to show that part of you, as well."

Sammy felt guilt twist in his chest. "I've never been to Olin though. I don't even know where it is." Looking back down at his gift, Sammy ran his thumb over the intricate scales of the stone haldis. The details on the hair pick really were incredible. The longer Sammy looked at the artistry, the more awed he became. Besides the scales, the claws on the feet were etched into the stone, and there were little round hollows for eyes. "How can I represent a city I know nothing about?"

"You've committed to Rourke, that's how. That's all that matters." Lor leaned forward and laced his hands together on the table. "You know it really means a lot to Rourke that you're trying, and that you're learning. Don't doubt yourself, Sammy, you're doing fine."

"Thanks." Sammy carefully set the hair pick on the table and pulled his hair back into a ponytail, twisting and holding his hair with one hand before he picked up the new hair pick and secured his hair. "How's it look?"

"It looks great." Alina smiled as the kettle began to whistle from the fire. She got up to tend to the kettle, and the room fell into a comfortable silence once more. She came back a moment later with the kettle, setting it between the three of them on the table. "I have to start the fish if we are going to eat it. You're staying to eat with us, right, Sammy?"

"I could never say 'no' to your cooking, Alina." Sammy nodded.

"I don't know what it is," Alina started, half talking to them, half talking to herself as she worked in the kitchen behind them. "I just woke up and wanted fish."

"So." Lor reached for the tea kettle and poured each of them a cup of tea. Sammy watched the steam rise from his cup as he listened to Lor ask his question. "Tell us how you're doing? This is the first you've been away from Rourke since arriving here, right?"

Sammy nodded, unable to pull his eyes away from the teacup as he thought back to that day they met in the woods. Even now when he thought about it, he could feel the chill on his skin and the fear crawling up his spine. "Yeah. I think I'm okay. I mean, I'm still trying to adjust to living here in Bhaskara, and now Rourke is gone, too. I know it's only for a few cycles, but I feel a little lost now."

"Well, that settles it. You can just stay here with us! We have the extra bedrooms, and it won't take long to make up one of the beds." Sammy turned to Alina, who was brandishing a knife in the kitchen, one of the two fish in front of her on a cutting board.

"Thank you, Alina, really, but I have a few things I really need to think about, and I just sort of want to do it in my own space. I am comfortable here, and I am forever grateful for what you and Lor do for Rourke and me, but it's not the same as being in the barracks."

"You've really made that room into your home." Lor nodded. "Don't worry about it, Sammy. We understand, but you still must stay and eat. Alina bakes these fish, and they are absolutely amazing."

Sammy nodded and reached out for his teacup, pulling it toward himself. Nysa sniffed at the cup as Sammy wrapped his hands around it. He would stay for lunch, and he was glad he'd come, but now he just wanted to go back to the barracks, curl up on Rourke's side of the bed, and figure out exactly what all these emotions swirling around his head meant. He'd told Rourke he loved him. Sammy knew Rourke would be thinking about that while he was out in the darkness, and he deserved an explanation when he returned.

21

Sammy woke to a weight pressing down on the other side of the bed. Brain foggy from sleep, he half rolled over to see who it was. "Rourke," he slurred, but he knew it couldn't have been him. He'd only left that morning.

Sammy heard a low chuckle, and he rubbed his eyes as he leaned his weight on one elbow. When he blinked his eyes open, Lysha was mere inches from his face. "Hello, Sammy."

"Lysha!" Sammy jumped away from her, not realizing just how close to the edge of the bed he was, and promptly fell on the floor, dragging the hides and blankets with him. Sitting up, he pulled the blanket off his head and glared at her over the bare mattress. "What the hell are you doing in my room?"

"I came to see how you were." Lysha leaned a little farther over the bed. "Are you all right?"

Sammy sighed heavily through his nose, glancing over to Nysa as she waddled her way over to sniff at him. "Yeah, I'm fine." Throwing the blankets off himself, Sammy stood before picking up the blankets and tossing them back on the bed. "What do you want?"

"Is that any way to talk to me?"

Sammy pinched the bridge of his nose. "No. I'm sorry. I'm just — You startled me. I didn't expect you to just barge into my room like this."

"I told you I came to see how you were. I knocked, but you did not answer."

"So, you just let yourself in? What if I wasn't here?" Dropping his arms to his sides, Sammy moved again, adjusting his shirt before he started untangling the sheets. "The hell time is it anyway," he muttered more to himself than Lysha. "Phase, what phase is it?"

Lysha stood and helped Sammy to smooth out the blankets. "It is just before the last phase. It is late, I know, but no one had seen you since you returned earlier, and they were worried about you."

"So, they sent you to find me?" Sammy felt a small lump of guilt crawl up his throat. He hadn't meant to worry anyone, but when he'd come back from having lunch with Lor and Alina, he'd gone straight to the bedroom, and must have eventually fallen asleep. Nysa waddled around the mess of blankets to come stand by Sammy, pawing at his leg to be picked up. Scooping her up with one hand, he set her down on the floor. "Hang on a sec, Nysa. Let me fix the bed first." Nysa huffed but wandered off toward her little bed in the corner by the desk.

Sammy looked over to the palu-tai sitting on the desk, seeing all six of the blue flowers open and bright. One of the two mouths were closed, and Sammy knew it had found something to eat at some point while he was asleep. Lysha tugged one of the blankets back into place on Rourke's side of the bed as Sammy smoothed out the shadow cat hide over his side. Taking a deep breath, he walked around the bed to get a drink from the pitcher on the desk in order to wash some of the bad taste in his mouth away.

"Are you hungry," Lysha asked, making herself right at home on the bed.

Sammy poured a glass of water and raised it to his mouth, pausing to push his hair from his face. "No," he answered, gulping down the water, which did little good to rinse away the taste. "Need to brush my teeth."

"Ah." Lysha nodded and dug into her satchel. Sammy wasn't even surprised at this point. He was convinced the thing was magic and probably held the secrets to the damned universe inside it. She produced what looked like a stick, then pulled out her small knife, and cut away a small strip of the bark at the top. She offered it to Sammy.

"What is it," he asked, taking the stick and looking down at it. It seemed like a typical stick, but at the part where the bark had been stripped away, the inside fibers sort of looked like a wet paintbrush.

"Strip the end apart." Lysha motioned with her fingers to demonstrate. "You can brush your teeth with that."

"What is it?"

"Li'kai berry root."

Sammy shrugged and did as he was told, moving to sit in the chair as he cleaned his teeth. There was a slightly sweet taste, but nothing overpowering, and Sammy had to admit, it worked fairly well. "Where did you get this?"

"Illume have used them for many generations. Have you not been cleaning your teeth?"

Sammy dropped his arm into his lap. "Not out in the darkness, no, and I hated it. But since arriving in Bhaskara, Rourke has had a constant supply of apples and that's helped."

Lysha nodded before she broke out into a grin. "Your Rourke really does enjoy apples, he always has."

"Yeah." Sammy chuckled, turning to place the stick on the desk, propping it up against a glass to keep the end clean. "He sure does." Turning back to Lysha, Sammy leaned back in the chair and crossed his arms. His hair was slowly falling back into his face, but he tried to ignore it. In her bed, Nysa inhaled deeply before falling into a sounder sleep. "So, again, why are you here?"

"I wanted to make sure you were all right."

"U-huh." Sammy nodded, but he wasn't buying it, not completely. He'd been around Lysha enough times to know she had another reason for showing up other than to simply check on him. She had a habit of just popping in to see how Rourke and he were doing. Sammy figured some of it was the fact that Rourke and Lysha were the only family they each had left, but Sammy knew there was more to it than that. "Tell me why you are really here."

Lysha leaned back on her hands on the bed, crossing her feet at the ankles and smirking at Sammy. "You are too smart for your own good."

"Rourke enjoys it," Sammy shot back, smirking himself.

Lysha grinned, showing her teeth. "Of course, your Rourke would." Lysha took a deep breath. "No, I really am here to see how you are. You cannot hide from me, Sammy of Olin."

Sammy flushed at Lysha calling him by his apparently new title. "I'm not hiding from anyone."

"Yet you are here; in your room, hiding."

Sammy rolled his eyes. "Well, when you put it that way, you make it seem like I am hiding." He shrugged. "I don't know, I just want to be alone right now. What's so wrong with that?"

"Nothing!" Lysha laughed and pulled her satchel across the bed to her side. "Come here and sit. Let us talk. Tell me what troubles you and I will listen."

Sammy was quiet for a moment as he thought about it. He did have a lot on his mind, and being able to talk about it would help, but Lysha was Rourke's cousin, and he didn't know what to think about that. Then again, Sammy reasoned, Lysha was a shaman, and she seemed to take her position within Illume society vastly seriously. Sammy was sure she would keep whatever they talked about between them.

Taking a deep breath, Sammy stood, moving to sit next to Lysha on the bed. She picked up her satchel, holding it in her lap as Sammy settled next to her. "I don't really know where to start," Sammy said, voice low. He laced his hands together in his lap and sighed heavily. "There's been so much that has happened since I got here, I don't feel like I can even wrap my head around it all."

"So, start there." Lysha nodded. "Start with being pulled through the mirror."

"How do you know it was my mirror?" Sammy looked over to Lysha, and Sammy swore he saw Rourke in the way she smirked.

"I am a shaman. I know many things you would not think I would know. Besides." Lysha waved a dismissive hand in the air. "It is known that Others arrive here through mirrors, pulled to these lands by the Mistwalkers."

Sammy nodded. "Ah, well, okay. I'm not sure what to tell you. I know if Rourke hadn't been there, I would have been killed. It's mostly the nightmares that I have to worry about now. I still get them from time to time."

Lysha flipped open her satchel, and Sammy frowned. She didn't look like she was paying attention, even though Sammy knew that she was. "I am sure they must be horrible. Your Rourke's Molly — you met her, yes — she had terrible dreams, too, for a long while after first coming here."

"Makes sense, it was pretty traumatic." Sammy looked down at his feet, curling his bare toes into the rug. "But honestly, it's mostly been since coming here. Out in the darkness, it was just Rourke and myself, and we didn't talk about things like my being an Other, or him being a Warden. Well, not a lot. I tell you what, that was quite a shock. I didn't — I mean, he has such a coveted position within your society, and he walks away from it? Who does that?"

"Are you upset with your Rourke over it?"

"What? No." Sammy shook his head. "I don't really have a reason to be, or say in the matter, I guess. It was something that Rourke had decided long before we met, and I wouldn't take that away from him. Besides, that Ozni guy, he's a real jerk. And he doesn't seem to approve of me, or Others in general."

Lysha hummed, pulling her hand from her bag. "The arrival of the Other Dwellers has caused a rift to settle into the Illume people.

There are those who wish to include them — like your Rourke — then there are those who wish to cast them out and forget they ever came."

"Ozni," Sammy asked, even though he already knew the answer to that. "Why does he hate Others so much?"

"You are different. While the people of Olin welcomed those that were different, the people of Bhaskara became afraid, and there are those that blame Others for the destruction the Wolves have caused."

"That's not true, is it?"

"I do not think so, no." Lysha shook her head. She moved her closed fist in front of Sammy and opened her hand, showing Sammy several beads that lay in her palm. One looked like it was made of bhasvah, but the others were colored glass. "These are for you."

"What do you expect me to do with beads?" Sammy looked up to Lysha, holding out his hand as she poured the beads into his palm. Lysha reached up and tugged on a strand of his hair. Sammy frowned. "You want to put beads in my hair?"

"Why not?"

"It's just not something I thought about doing before, I guess. But I never thought of having my hair this long before either." Sammy looked at his hair as he tugged on a strand of his bangs. "How are you going to do it?"

"Just small braids, you will not even notice them when you tie it back."

Sammy looked down to the beads in his hand. Besides the bhasvah, there were five others: red, blue, green, purple, and yellow. "What will," he started quietly, rolling the bhasvah bead around with his thumb. "What will Rourke think?"

Lysha reached up and cupped Sammy's far cheek with her hand, turning his head to look at her. Lysha's eyes were the same dark gray as Rourke's eyes, even though they lacked the gold flecks, and Sammy felt his breath hitch in his throat. "Your Rourke does not care about your looks, Sammy."

"Yeah." Sammy dropped his eyes back to the beads. "I know." He took a deep breath, their conversation about Rourke not knowing if he'd ever find Sammy physically attractive surfacing in his mind. He'd tried to not let it bother him, but Sammy knew deep down he was worried and concerned about what it would mean for their relationship. Sammy knew not everything was about looks, but at the same time, Sammy knew for himself that part of his attraction to Rourke was physical.

"I have a question." Sammy kept his voice low. Lysha stood to retrieve the brush from the desk, pausing to look at his new hair pick before returning to the bed. With her hand, she silently asked Sammy to turn, and he turned his back to Lysha as she sat back down. Sammy let his eyes close as he felt Lysha's fingers comb through his hair. "It's about Rourke though, so if you don't want to answer, you don't have to."

"Why would I not answer a question concerning your Rourke?" Lysha seemed slightly puzzled, and Sammy shrugged.

"I don't know, I guess because you're related. But maybe you are the person to ask because of that fact."

Lysha paused, resting her hand on Sammy's shoulder. "Just talk, and I will listen. Clearly there is a lot on your mind."

"Yeah," Sammy agreed. "And I talk to Rourke, but I don't know who to talk to when my concerns are about Rourke. It sounds stupid."

"It sounds normal."

Sammy nodded. "Okay, yeah, I guess. It's just —" He stopped and took a deep breath. "You said Rourke doesn't care about how I look. And at one point when we were fooling around, or, well, I was trying to fool around, Rourke said he didn't find me attractive. So, I guess I'm just a little worried."

Lysha pulled a small segment of Sammy's hair away from the rest near his temple, breaking it apart in order to braid it. "Are you worried your Rourke is not interested in being your committed?"

"No, I don't think that's it." Sammy tried very hard not to shake his head. He could feel Lysha pulling at his hair, the sting at his scalp somewhat uncomfortable. "He said he wanted to be with me. He just doesn't know how he feels about being intimate, you know?"

Lysha hummed in acknowledgement. "You kiss your Rourke; I have seen it."

"Yes, but that's about it." Sammy shut his eyes and closed his empty hand into a fist in his lap. "I am not explaining this right. I sound like I am upset that Rourke doesn't want to go beyond kissing, and it's not that. I am just trying to understand."

"What did your Rourke say about it?"

"He said he didn't think he was there yet, whatever that means. I don't know. I knew the first time I saw Rourke he was attractive, that's partly why I asked him out — asked him to commit to me — in the first place. I guess I just assumed Rourke thought I was attractive, too."

"That is s an unwise thing to assume."

"Yeah." Sammy frowned as Lysha paused and leaned around Sammy looking for the beads. He moved his hand, and she grabbed one at random — the blue one — before going back to what she was doing. "I can see that now. Also." Sammy tried to turn, but stopped, momentarily forgetting Lysha was braiding his hair. "Rourke doesn't seem to want to do anything on an intimate level. The time I tried, he seemed scared, and not scared in the 'I don't know what I am doing' aspect, but in the 'I am genuinely afraid of this' sense. I felt horrible, that wasn't my intention at all."

Lysha was quiet as she seemed to finish with the braid she was working on and moved a little higher up, pulling several small strands of Sammy's bangs from the top of his forehead to work with.

"Perhaps your Rourke just is not one to want to take those further steps. Committing to one another is not about the physical things, it is about the bond between two people."

"Lao said pretty much the same thing to me, and it got me thinking about it, and I said that to Rourke. I know that's true, and I don't mind if we don't do anything. Okay, well, that's a lie, I would really like to do more than just kiss, but it doesn't mean I am going to walk away from him if he doesn't want to have sex."

"And if your Rourke does not?" Lysha kept her voice even as she spoke. "Some people just do not desire to be physically intimate with their committed. You will find other ways to satisfy that want in your relationship."

"I've thought about that. I have been thinking about this a lot. It would be frustrating, but I don't think it would bother me." Sammy took a deep breath, focusing on the tug and pull of Lysha braiding his hair. "I know it wouldn't bother me. I did something stupid earlier and told Rourke I loved him."

"That is great!" Lysha laughed, patting Sammy on the shoulder before reaching around him for another bead. This time she took the bhasvah bead. "What did your Rourke say?"

"He didn't. He didn't have a chance. Asha got in between us, and he didn't get a chance to say anything to me about it. I don't know how he feels." Sammy felt sad, worried, and upset at the entire situation. "I just want to take it back."

"Why? Do you not actually love your Rourke? Why say it?"

"That's not it, Lysha." Sammy paused as Lysha picked another segment of his hair to braid. "I just wanted to do it differently, I suppose. I don't know what came over me. I do love him, or well, I think I do. I know I have never felt this way about someone before. I just got worried when he was leaving, and I felt the need to try to make him stay as long as I could. I just had to — I had to tell him, and I didn't even know what it was I was going to say until after I kissed him."

Lysha picked up another bead. "Sounds like love to me." Her voice was quiet as she kept speaking. "I think you are thinking too much, Sammy. I think you just need to let your relationship with your Rourke unfold as it will. I am sure you two will be happy no matter what happens. As long as you are together, that is what is important, yes?"

"Yes," Sammy agreed.

22

It was dark all-around Rourke, darker than he knew it should have been. Fear crept up his spine, and no matter how hard he tried, he couldn't make that feeling go away. In the distance, a light flared to life. It was flickering and hued orange in color instead of the steady bright white he was used to. He could see fire, smell smoke, and hear screams. Without thinking, he ran toward the chaos, hoping there was something he could do to help; knowing he needed to try and help, but it felt like every step forward he took, the source of the fire took two more away from him.

Stopping, and out of breath, Rourke realized he was going in circles. He looked up into the trees surrounding him, their large trunks blocking out the fire in great black pillars as their branches shook with the wind. They looked familiar, but Rourke couldn't place them. It was almost as if the trees were from a forgotten memory he couldn't quite recall. He was sure the leaves were laughing at him.

Heart still pounding in his chest, Rourke took a step toward the fires, then a second, and a third as he forced his body to keep moving. He was just nearing the tree line when someone grabbed his arm and tugged him down, throwing him into the hollowed-out trunk of a large tree. Rourke was just about to protest when he felt his stomach roll with nausea and sadness. He looked up as hands grabbed tightly to his shoulders to be met with the wild gray eyes of his sister, her long black hair falling in wet clumps into her face. Suddenly, Rourke realized it was raining. "Rourke," she was saying, and he felt a desperate need to run wash over him. The fear he had earlier pushed aside crawled back up his throat and his mouth tasted as if he'd thrown up, even though he was sure he hadn't. Asha looked over her shoulder, then back to Rourke, her grip on his shoulders tightening. "*Run.*"

Rourke woke with a start, inhaled sharply as he opened his eyes, and reached for his sword. The tree he was leaning against was sheltering him from the weather, but Rourke could hear the light pattering of rain on the underbrush around him. Closing his eyes, Rourke took a deep breath, and rested his head back against the trunk of the tree he'd been sleeping against. He raised a hand to press against his chest, feeling his heart pounding under his palm.

He wasn't sure when he'd last had a bad dream about his sister or the fall of Olin. Exhaling, Rourke stared unseeing up into the tree branches. The small fire Asha had insisted on lighting had burned down to a bed of glowing coals but was quickly being put out by the falling rain, the hiss and sputter of the water hitting the coals grounding in some way. Taking another deep breath, Rourke looked around their small camp.

After riding for what seemed like forever, Rourke had finally slid from the saddle, and walked along with Luna. He had been sore from riding and needed to stretch his legs. They made camp soon after in a small hollow created by the roots of three large trees, supplying them shelter while being large enough for them and all their umbra.

Everyone else was still asleep, and the umbra were calm as they nudged one another with their noses, antlers clacking together as they bumped into one another. Next to him, Luna groaned and stretched out, taking a deep breath before going back to sleep.

Despite everything being calm, the feeling of unease wouldn't leave, and Rourke carefully pushed his umbra hide aside before he got up. Climbing the small hill out of the hollow and around one of the large trees, Rourke took a moment to relieve himself before looking around. It was just as dark as it always was, even darker with the rain. The birds were quiet, which made Rourke nervous as he searched the woods. Something didn't feel right, and there was unease in the air. Not wanting to be unarmed in the woods, Rourke turned and made his way back into the hollow. Luna was up now, jumping up the far side of the bank to presumably go find something to eat. Rourke was just bending to pick up his sword when he heard a low grumble of thunder in the distance.

The rain suddenly became much heavier, pounding down through the tree branches and dropping off the needles-like leaves to fall onto Rourke's head, as well as the rest of the camp. Lao, Isa, and Asha stirred to life as Rourke buckled his sword to his side. "Where are you going," Asha asked, instantly sliding back into her role of being in charge. When they had been eating before sleep, she had relaxed a little bit, but apparently it wasn't meant to last.

"It's quiet." Rourke looked around them again, trying to listen for anything over the rain and low thunder. The rain was growing harder, and Rourke knew the moment they stepped out from under these three trees, they would all get soaked. He pulled Sammy's vest a little tighter against his neck, suddenly wishing he hadn't left his jacket back with his committed. Sammy's confession in the courtyard popped into Rourke's head, and he felt his entire body yearn for Sammy's touch, but Rourke pushed it aside as Isa stood and looked around.

"It's always quiet out here," Isa stated, raising his arms to emphasize his point.

"Not like this." Rourke shook his head. He looked up through the branches of the trees trying to see if he could see anything. This close to Bhaskara, the clouds took on a slightly purple hue, and he was able to see the large, heavy, and low clouds of a storm. "This is because of the storm."

"Could just be a storm." Asha waved a hand in dismissal. "It wouldn't be the first occurrence of rain when out here in the darkness."

"Maybe." Rourke shrugged his shoulders.

"But you don't think so." Lao looked over to Rourke from where he was standing by the umbra. One of them turned into him, making him move or get hit by the animal's antlers. Their eyes met and Lao nodded. They may not have known one another for long, but it was long enough for them to trust one another's instincts.

"No." Rourke kept his voice low.

"So, what's the plan then?" Isa sat back down and began digging through his backpack.

"Same as it was before Rourke woke up." Asha crossed her arms and looked over at Rourke. "We keep moving, keep scouting, and you get back on the umbra."

"I'm going to walk." Rourke looked from Asha to Mosh and back to Asha. "Something isn't right, and I don't want to be on the back of one of those umbra when it happens."

Asha rolled her eyes and watched as Luna came slinking back into the hollow, wet from the rain. "Suit yourself. I don't want to hear you complain if you fall behind."

"I've spent half my life in the darkness. I don't think I'm the one you need to be concerned with." Rourke crouched down to pat Luna as she walked over to him. From the looks of her, she hadn't eaten yet, and that was one of the things he wanted to take care of while they were scouting about. "I'm going to eat and start out. I don't like this rain, either. Something just doesn't feel right."

"The umbra are getting a little restless," Lao offered, looking over at Rourke. "What do you think is going on?"

"I don't know exactly." Rourke shook his head. "I just know to trust my instincts. They've gotten me this far."

"Eat something." Isa walked over to Rourke and handed him a small, wrapped package of food. Rourke knew from dinner, it was some type of granola: grains, dried fruit, and nuts all held together by honey. Rourke took the small bundle with a word of thanks, and opened it, picking at the food as Isa passed out the same thing to Asha and Lao. It wasn't Rourke's favorite thing in the lands to eat, but he knew it was only for a few cycles, and honestly it was better than some of the things he'd found on his own.

Asha sat down and pulled her pack toward herself. "Rourke, come here."

Rourke walked over, sitting down next to Asha as she pulled a folded piece of paper from her backpack. Rourke knew it was the map from seeing her with it previously. Asha set her breakfast in her lap as she opened the map. "We are about here." She pointed to a spot near the center of the map. "And are going to be traveling this way." Dragging her finger toward the right side of the map, Asha looked up to Rourke. "If you are going to be walking, I want you to stay within earshot of us."

Rourke nodded. "I can do that." He pointed to a spot on the map near the right-hand corner where the word "Bhaskara" was written in rough handwriting. "Then next cycle we head back toward the city."

"Assuming everything goes smoothly, yes." Asha folded up the map and put it away as to not let it get wet. "All of the groups are following a similar course of action."

Rourke hummed in answer and went back to finishing his food. When they had all left Bhaskara, Asha had stopped them in the fields surrounding the city. Breaking the one large group into smaller groups of four, Asha gave them each their own smaller assignments of scouting a segment of land surrounding the city looking for Wolves. One cycle of travel deep into the darkness surrounding the city, the next heading sideways across the land, and the last cycle was to turn around and head back into the city.

"If Rourke is going to go off on his own, what are the rest of us going to do?" Isa was once again sitting by his things, eagerly eating the food he held in his hand.

"We are going to stay together and continue on our way." Asha looked over to Isa then back to Rourke. "You're not going to go too far, are you? Get whatever nonsense it is out of your system, then get back to the rest of us. Lao, you take Mosh with you."

"Can do." Lao nodded.

Rourke opened his mouth to protest that what he was doing wasn't nonsense but decided to stay quiet. The truth of it was, he didn't want to be around the rest of them anyway. Not that he didn't mind their company — especially Lao — it was just, Rourke felt something was wrong, and he didn't want to be caught off guard if something did happen. Not that Rourke wanted anything to happen anyway, but if Wolves attacked, either they attacked him alone, which he could defend against, or they attacked the group, and then he could catch the Wolves unawares.

The group fell into silence as they ate. Around them the rain continued to pour down, growing heavier with each passing moment. The thunder grew louder the longer they sat in the hollow, and the longer they sat, the more anxious Rourke became. Once finished with his food, Rourke took a deep breath and stood. He whistled to Luna, who had once again slunk off on her own. When she returned to the group, she was licking blood from her muzzle. Rourke felt bad that he probably disturbed her while she was eating, but he was glad to see that she'd found something on her own.

Rourke rolled up his umbra hide, tied it to his backpack, and shouldered his pack. "I'm going to head out. I will stay within range of hearing, don't worry."

Lao stood and grabbed Rourke by the shoulder. "Stay safe out there. I don't want to have to explain to Sammy why you won't be coming home."

Rourke smirked. "Don't make me have to tell Lor the same thing."

Lao grinned and pulled Rourke into a half hug. Rourke easily returned the gesture quickly before pulling away. "Stay safe, Rourke."

"Yeah, you, too." Nodding, Rourke turned and climbed out of the hollow into the darkness and the rain. Luna stayed right by Rourke's side, her shoulder pressing into his leg with each step that they took. Looking down at her, Rourke could see that she was restless, and her ears flicked about trying to listen for sounds in the rain.

A raindrop managed to land on his neck, and Rourke could feel the cold water slide down his skin before it soaked into his shirt. It sent a shiver down his spine, but Rourke pushed it aside as he kept walking. The storm was growing worse, the rain getting heavier, and the grumbling thunder becoming louder. A wind began to blow, rustling the trees, throwing water drops and needle leaves to the forest floor.

Looking over his shoulder, Rourke realized he'd already lost sight of the hollow and where the others were. Part of him was thankful. Even after traveling with Lao, Rourke was finding he would still rather be alone in the woods. Pausing, Rourke took a deep breath. If he was honest with himself, he knew he would have rathered Sammy by his side, but Sammy was back in Bhaskara with Nysa, waiting for him to come back.

Sighing, Rourke adjusted the straps of his backpack against his shoulders and looked down to Luna. She looked up at him, and even in the darkness of the storm and the woods, Rourke could see how red her eyes were. "Come on," he started, jerking his head in a nod toward the direction he wanted to go. "The sooner we get this over with, the sooner we can go home to Sammy and Nysa."

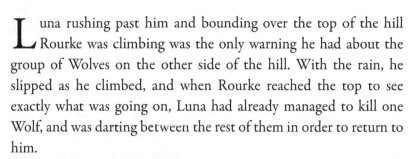

23

Luna rushing past him and bounding over the top of the hill Rourke was climbing was the only warning he had about the group of Wolves on the other side of the hill. With the rain, he slipped as he climbed, and when Rourke reached the top to see exactly what was going on, Luna had already managed to kill one Wolf, and was darting between the rest of them in order to return to him.

Rourke swore under his breath as he counted how many there were. With the dead one, he counted seven. He'd never seen a group of Wolves that large before. Several questions popped into his head, but he pushed them aside as lightning flashed overhead, quickly followed by a loud boom of thunder so close Rourke could feel it vibrate the air around him.

Luna jogged around him and came to stand by his side as Rourke crouched on the ground. He knew he only had a moment before the Wolves sniffed him out, and he was already trying to think of a plan on how to kill them all. Reaching out to Luna, Rourke felt a warmth coming from her shoulder, and when he pulled his hand away it was covered in blood. Below them, the Wolves had their noses turned toward the sky, but the pouring rain helped to keep Rourke's scent hidden from them as he pulled Luna to him and took a closer look at her shoulder. Sure enough, the blood was hers, and Rourke was able to see a large gash on her shoulder from where one of the Wolves must have struck her.

Rourke shrugged his backpack off and tossed it against the tree. Luna had her ears forward as she watched the Wolves, and Rourke could hear a low growl that he knew was coming from her. Carefully, Rourke drew his sword, feeling for his knife at his back just to reassure himself that it was still there. "Six to go, Luna," he muttered to the shadow cat as the Wolves finally spotted him. They began to climb the hill, and Rourke knew he needed to make a plan.

Behind him, the hill sloped down into a ditch that Rourke thought maybe had once been an old riverbed. The hill dropped off suddenly at the edge of the ditch. Rourke figured it could work to his advantage if he could manage to stay on his feet. In front of him, the Wolves stalked up the hill, a larger one breaking away from the group, and heading right for Rourke's spot under the tree.

Lightning flashed and thunder shook the trees, and with the bright flash, Rourke was able to know where they all stood. With a quick plan forming in his head, Rourke pushed against Luna's good shoulder to get her to move away from him and break up the group. "Go," he started, unsure of exactly how much the shadow cat would understand. He knew Luna was smart, had conceited that point to Sammy long ago, but this was completely different from her learning her name or how to sit on command. "Go; attack."

Luna flicked an ear back toward Rourke to let him know she heard him, then she bounded away, distracting two of the Wolves near the front of the group as she did. Rourke nodded, this put some distance between the first Wolf and the last three, which would allow him a long enough moment to kill this one and collect himself again.

Knowing he had the higher ground, and the better position, Rourke let the Wolves come to him. The rain made everything slick, and he settled into a defensive position as he made sure his footing was solid. The last thing he wanted to do was slip and fall in the middle of a fight.

The Wolf stalked closer, and even through the driving rain, Rourke could see the want to kill in the monster's eyes. He felt a rush of anticipation run through him, his body instantly reacting to the threat in front of him. Rourke didn't like to kill, never had, but he couldn't deny the excitement he felt at the rush of the fight and the thrill in his body as he moved without thought. Shifting the grip he had on his sword, he watched as the Wolf snarled, eyes gleaming with the intent to kill.

As the Wolf raised its arm to strike, Rourke swiped upward with his blade, cutting deep into the Wolf's upper arm. It wasn't a strike meant to kill, only maim and cause damage, but Rourke couldn't help but smirk as the Wolf yelped in pain and blood joined the rain as it fell to the ground. The Wolf stumbled back, clawed feet digging into the soft, wet ground to help steady itself, but Rourke wasn't about to let the beast have a chance to think about what had just happened. Moving forward, Rourke shifted his grip on his sword hilt, slamming the length of his blade through the base of the Wolf's throat, the soft spot right above the clavicle. Hot blood poured over his hands and the hilt of his sword as he pulled away from the Wolf, who fell to the ground with a gurgle before sliding back down the hill toward the others.

The more forward of the three remaining Wolves lunged at Rourke, mouth open in a snarl as it tried to bite him. Rourke ducked under the attack, kicking the Wolf's knee before stealing a move from Sammy and using his sword to slice through the back of the Wolf's leg. It howled in anger, shifting its weight as it twisted to try and strike Rourke again. Rourke barely ducked below the attack and could feel the very tips of the beast's claws rake through his hair.

Rourke slipped in the underbrush, reaching his right arm out to catch himself as he swung with his left, his sword cutting into the fleshy part of the Wolf's supporting leg. With a yelp of pain, the monster tumbled over backward down the hill, knocking one of the remaining two Wolves down as it went.

Panting for breath, Rourke made his way back up the hill. Lightning flashed and thunder boomed overhead as the rain seemed to start coming down even harder than it had been before. In the lightning's flash, Rourke was able to see a low fog beginning to wind around the tree trunks. Something twisted in Rourke's gut, and he felt like he'd seen this once before, but he couldn't place where or when. He shook his head to clear his thoughts, he couldn't afford to be distracted by things like fog right now, not with the Wolves trying to kill him.

Cresting the top of the hill, Rourke found his chest tightening with every breath he took. He knew it was the growing chill in the air, but it still made his chest hurt. Swallowing, he pressed his free hand against his chest, trying to calm his breathing in the one moment he knew he had. Twisting to see where the Wolves were, he stumbled in the slick underbrush, sliding down the other side of the hill toward the ditch he knew was behind him, and losing sight of the two Wolves still stalking toward him.

Looking over his shoulder as he steadied himself, Rourke looked up to see one of the remaining Wolves crest the top of the hill. Its red eyes shone in the darkness, and its claws flexed at its sides. Rourke knew he'd lost his advantage, and instead tried to secure his position before the Wolf came to him like he knew it would. They always did.

The lightning flashed again, and the thunder sounded almost instantly afterward. Rourke could feel the vibration in his bones as the Wolf started down the hill. Snapping its jaws, it lunged at Rourke, and all he could think to do was brace for the impact he knew was coming. Turning his body slightly, Rourke raised his weapon, aiming to impale the beast as it tried to strike him, and deciding to use the momentum that the Wolf built as it ran to his advantage.

The Wolf didn't seem to care that Rourke was ready and waiting for him to attack. They never seemed to care. They just came rushing in blindly looking for the kill. Rourke had learned to use that to his advantage, just like he was doing now.

The Wolf jumped at him, and Rourke lowered his body, preparing to strike as the monster landed. Raising his sword higher, Rourke let the situation do the work for him, and as the Wolf came down toward him, Rourke felt his blade sink up to the hilt into the Wolf's chest. Ducking lower, Rourke used the Wolf's weight to help himself throw the beast over his shoulder, hoping to pull his blade free before the Wolf could slide down into the ditch to die.

Lightning flashed again, and the Wolf reached out, grabbed Rourke by the shoulder, and pulled him off his feet as thunder boomed above them. He let go of his weapon as both he and the Wolf tumbled down the hill. Landing hard on his back, Rourke felt his breath leave him and a searing pain burned down his spine. He could do nothing more than gasp for air as he stared up into the sky. The rain poured down around him, raindrops stung his face, and his heart was pounding in his chest. Next to him, he could hear the Wolf moving, but if the monster was getting up, or just spasming in its death throes, he couldn't tell.

Fear took hold of Rourke as he lay in the muddy water in the bottom of the ditch, unable to do anything. Then, as quickly as his breath left him, he was able to inhale deeply, and he forced his body to move as he did. Rolling to the side, he pulled his knife from the sheath at the small of his back and looked over to the Wolf. The beast was still twitching, but it was clear to Rourke that it was dead, his sword blade sticking up through the middle of its chest with bloody water pooling around the corpse.

Shifting to his knees, Rourke sat back on his heels, and returned his knife to its place at the small of his back as he tried to catch his breath. Leaning his head back, Rourke closed his eyes and just let the rain wash over him a moment before he closed his mouth, feeling grit between his teeth and tasting blood. Spitting to the side, he struggled to his feet, the mud making each footstep harder than the last as he walked over to the dead Wolf. Rolling the corpse over, Rourke was able to pull his sword free with a sickening squelch, stumbling back a step as he slipped in the mud. Returning his weapon to its sheath, Rourke wiped water from his face — though it did little good — and turned from the Wolf.

Every part of Rourke's body hurt, and he groaned as he climbed his way out of the ditch toward the top of the hill to kill the last Wolf and look for Luna. He thought about calling her, but with so many Wolves, as well as the rain, he was uncertain if she would hear him. He fully expected to be attacked by the last Wolf that remained, but it was nowhere to be seen, and Rourke could only figure it had fled upon seeing Rourke kill the others. That was a strange thing for a Wolf to do, run away, but Rourke had seen the Wolves do a lot of strange things this cycle, so he didn't dwell on the one escaping him.

As Rourke reached the top of the hill, he could see the injured Wolf crawling its way toward him. He half walked, half slid his way down to the Wolf. The beast was snarling at him, trying its best to rise back to its feet, but with the damage Rourke had done earlier, there was no way it could stand. He thought about just leaving the Wolf here to die, to bleed out alone and scared as the Wolves had let his sister do, and he hesitated to draw his sword. He easily took a step to the side as the Wolf tried to attack him, and Rourke shook his head. If he left this Wolf to die here, he was no better than the monsters themselves.

Rourke took a deep breath, and as he pulled his sword from his sheath, he felt a stinging pain in his shoulder. He ignored it as he gripped his sword hilt tightly and plunged the blade straight through the Wolf's neck, near the base of the skull. The monster cried out before dropping to the ground, body going limp. Pulling his sword free, Rourke took a step back, moving to the Wolf's side to wipe his blade as clean as he could before returning it to his side.

Looking at his shoulder, Rourke could see tears in his shirt, as well as Sammy's vest, and blood against his skin. The wounds didn't look too deep, but they were deep enough to bleed. Pressing his hand against his wound, Rourke turned, and took a deep breath. "Luna," he called into the rain. Stepping around the dead Wolves, Rourke kept on his path, wondering if the others had encountered anything, or if his fight was isolated.

"Luna," he yelled again as lightning flashed and thunder answered. From the corner of his eye, Rourke thought he saw something move, and he turned, seeing Luna slink toward him. Against her light fur, a spot on her shoulder was dark with her own blood. Rourke nodded to himself, seeing her alive was all he really needed. "Good girl," he said as she walked up to him. "Come on, let's get my backpack."

Turning, and with Luna by his side, Rourke made his way back up the hill, slipping occasionally until he was underneath the tree he'd dropped his pack under. Sitting down with his back against the trunk, Rourke tried to get Luna to come closer to him. Sammy would be upset they had both gotten hurt, but there was nothing Rourke could have done to prevent the injuries. While he knew his own injury wasn't that bad, he couldn't say the same for Luna. She was keeping her distance from Rourke, clearly favoring that leg as she moved.

"We should keep moving." Rourke sighed as he spoke. He was tired, and his body was sore. "We need to find the others and tell them what happened." He forced himself to get to his feet and pick up his pack. "I've never seen a group of Wolves that big before, usually only two or three, maybe four, but seven? Something isn't —" Rourke stopped, interrupted by the long and low howl of a Wolf, followed by a scream.

24

S ammy hated the rain. He stood in the doorway to the main barracks building, grumbling under his breath as lightning flashed and the rain started pouring down even harder. In the distance, thunder rumbled. Taking a deep breath, he pulled Rourke's jacket a little tighter against his shoulders and pushed Nysa's head back into the jacket. "Sorry, Nysa," he apologized as she squeaked in protest. "Not with the rain. It's only until we meet up with Alina, I promise."

The haldis shifted in the jacket, and Sammy could feel her settle down, her small body curled into a ball against his side. With a heavy sigh, Sammy stepped into the rain, and crossed the courtyard, keeping his head low as he moved to keep the rain from striking his face. While it had rained while he and Rourke had traveled to Bhaskara, it had never rained like this before, and Sammy wasn't sure when the last time he'd seen rain like this was, or if he ever had. It never rained a lot where he grew up.

The city was eerily quiet as Sammy made his way toward the market street where he told Alina they would meet, and he was suddenly glad he'd decided to bring his knife with him. While he didn't think he would need it, something had tugged at him to bring it with him, and he felt better knowing he was armed, even though he was only going shopping with Alina. When they were done, the two of them would return to her house to make lunch for themselves and Lor, and start planning a dinner for when Lao, Rourke, and Isa returned from the darkness.

Jumping over a puddle, Sammy turned onto the market street, and stopped short when he realized how few people were wandering the street. Even the vendors, normally loud as they tried to sell their wares, were subdued by the rain. Nysa, nosing her way out of the jacket, sniffed at the air in confusion. "I agree," Sammy responded idly, not even bothering to try to push her back inside the jacket. Stuffing his hands in his pockets, Sammy started down the street, making mental notes of which shops and stalls he wanted to stop back by once he'd met up with Alina. He knew of a small bakery that made the best bread, and he'd been told about a small herb shop by one of the Others at the barracks who said they had spices that reminded them of being on Earth. Sammy wanted to check them out at some point.

"Sammy!" Alina called his name, waving to him from where she stood in the doorway to the butcher she always went to. Sammy jogged across the street to her, narrowly missing being hit by an umbra that suddenly appeared from a side street. "Are you all right," Alina asked, laughter in her voice.

"Yeah." Sammy nodded, catching his breath. He ran a hand over his hair, feeling how wet it was, even with it pulled back. "The umbra missed me."

"That's good." Alina smiled, not even arguing with Sammy as he offered to take her basket. The two of them shopping had sort of become something they did together regularly now, and Sammy always offered to hold the groceries while they walked. Alina protested at first, but now she just handed over her basket, knowing Sammy wouldn't quit until she did. "What do you want for lunch?"

"I passed that new bakery." Sammy pointed back the way he'd just come. "The small one near the top of the street."

Lightning flashed again, and the thunder that followed seemed closer now. Alina reached out, placing her hand on Sammy's arm. "I don't like this storm, Sammy. This isn't normal."

Sammy shrugged, trying his best to convince both himself and Alina that there was nothing to fear. "It's just some heavy rain. I agree, it's really bad, but it's just some thunder and lightning."

Alina shook her head. "I've heard rumors about storms like this."

"About thunderstorms?" Sammy laughed but reached out with his free hand to cover Alina's hand. "It's all right, you'll see."

Alina nodded, but Sammy could see she didn't seem convinced. He wasn't either, but he pushed it from his mind to focus on shopping. They stepped out into the rain, carefully making their way back up the street toward the small bakery to see what they had to offer. Lightning flashed again, and when the thunder came, it boomed loudly right overhead. Alina gasped in alarm, stepping closer to Sammy. He shifted the basket to his other hand and wrapped his arm around her shoulders. "It's all right, Alina, I got you."

Nysa squeaked in fear, ducking back into Sammy's jacket. He could feel her body shaking against his stomach. "No," Alina shook her head. "Something is wrong. Let's hurry, I want to go back home."

"Okay." Sammy nodded, and they hurried along to the bakery to get a loaf of bread for lunch. The woman running the bakery was just as concerned about the storm as Alina was, and Sammy began to think about what this could mean. While he was worried, to him it was just a bad storm, but the Illume people were showing signs of actual fear, and Sammy didn't know what to think.

The storm was getting worse, too. The lightning and thunder continued, growing louder as the storm seemed to stall over the city. The rain became heavier, pelting their faces as a strong wind blew off the top of the hills and down into the crater. By the time Sammy and Alina reached the Sanctuary, they could hardly see several paces in front of them.

Crossing the yard to Alina's house, they stood on the porch, listening to the pounding rain. The herd of haldis were hunkered down against the wall, curled upon themselves to shelter their faces from the storm. Nysa popped back out of Rourke's jacket, sniffing the air. Sammy pulled her from the jacket and set her down in the chair before pulling his stone hair pick from his hair. Shaking out his hair, he sighed heavily and bent forward to pull the wet strands together and pull it back again.

"I'm worried about Lor." Alina's voice was quiet at Sammy's side.

Sammy didn't answer right away, taking a moment to get his hair pulled back and held in place before standing and looking out over the yard. The rain was falling in sheets, shimmering in the light of the city as it fell. So much rain had fallen, it was beginning to pool in the dips of the lawn. "He'll be here soon for lunch, right? Besides, he has Isik with him."

"Isik can't save him from this." Alina's voice sounded hollow as she spoke.

Sammy looked over to Alina with wide eyes. "What is that supposed to mean?"

"I-I don't know." Reaching up, Alina touched the back of her neck, similarly to how Rourke would when he would talk about knowing what Nysa was saying. "The haldis are afraid, though."

Sammy looked over his shoulder to Nysa, who was still perched in the chair. She was sitting on her haunches, front feet held close to her body as she watched the rain. She was shivering, Sammy could tell from how her little ears shook, but he didn't think it was from the cold. Even though Rourke and him hadn't had Nysa long, Sammy knew to trust what Alina was sensing, what a Warden was sensing, as he'd seen Rourke do the same thing Alina was doing now. "What do they say?"

Alina shook her head, hugging herself. "I don't know," she whispered. "They are just afraid."

Sammy reached down and felt his knife against his thigh. Somehow, the knowledge of it being there was more reassuring than he thought it would have been. He was glad he'd listened to his instincts, even if he didn't fully understand what was happening. "If Lor doesn't come soon, I will go find him."

Alina looked over to Sammy. "No, please. I am worried about Lor, but I don't want to be alone, either. Something is coming, Sammy, I just don't know what."

Sammy crossed his arms over his chest and nodded. He had no idea what could be so worrisome about a thunderstorm, but he wasn't going to belittle Alina for being afraid either. "Let's go inside, make lunch, and start planning dinner for when everyone comes home. I'm sure they are going to want a home cooked meal after being out in the woods for a few cycles."

"Yes," Alina nodded. "You're right. Thank you, Sammy." Turning, she went into the house, and Sammy followed, picking up Nysa as he went.

Alina's home was always warm and welcoming, and even with the storm outside, Sammy felt right at home as he took off Rourke's jacket and set Nysa down in the chair at the counter. Walking around into the kitchen part of the room, Sammy took the basket from Alina, and started unpacking as she stoked the kitchen fire in the cookstove. She idly spoke to Izusa, who was now huddled at her feet.

Just as Sammy was reaching up to hang the basket back on its hook over the counter, the front door opened, and Sammy heard Lor swear under his breath. "Lor!" Alina practically dropped the cutting board she had been holding onto the counter as she ran for him. He was still standing in the front entrance, eyes wide as she just about jumped into his arms. "I was so worried about you!"

"I'm all right, Alina." Lor pulled her close, wrapping his arms around her and kissing the top of her head. "The storm is bad though. The few people remaining at the barracks are nervous."

"I'm worried, too." Alina pulled away from Lor enough to look up at him. "The haldis are afraid."

Lor nodded. "Something isn't right, that much we know."

"What are the people in the barracks saying," Sammy asked, resting his hands on the counter. He was suddenly much more nervous about Rourke being out in the darkness with Luna.

Lor took a deep breath, and finally let go of Alina to finish taking off his jacket. "Some are restless, others are afraid. One of the Inducted Illume said they were told this was how the fall of the other cities began."

"The fall of the other cities?" Sammy met Lor's eyes over the top of Alina's head. "You mean like Olin?"

Lor hesitated before he nodded. "Most of the people who arrived in Bhaskara and joined the Illuminari are in the darkness right now, the ones who didn't go, they are Others like you, Sammy, committed of those who did venture into the woods."

"So, in other words, no one really knows for sure if this is a thunderstorm or a fucking attack on the city?" Sammy gripped the edge of the counter so tightly he could feel it in his fingers as frustration swept through him. "Rourke's out there."

"So is Lao." Alina took a step back from Lor to look at Sammy before looking back at Lor. She was clearly scared, so worried that her words were barely audible as she spoke. "What do we do?"

"We fight." Sammy didn't even realize he'd spoken until Lor agreed with him. His knife suddenly felt heavy against his thigh, and he could see the same resolve in Lor's gray eyes. Shifting on his feet, Sammy took a deep breath. "Did they say anything else about what happened during the attacks? All Rourke has ever told me is that the Wolves did attack, he won't go into it. I don't think he remembers it all honestly, but that's not what is important. How do we protect the city from the Wolves?"

Lor shook his head. "I don't know. I could head back to —"

"No!" Alina cut Lor off. "Lor, please don't leave!"

"Alina, I have —"

"No, Lor, she's right, you stay here." Sammy walked around the counter and up to the two of them as Lor pulled Alina to him again. "I will go. Watch Nysa for me. I don't want her to get hurt, and I think she will be safest with you two."

Alina nodded but refused to let go of Lor. Sammy couldn't blame her. He was worried about Rourke and wanted nothing more than to know he was safe from harm. He could sympathize with Alina's want to keep Lor close. Turning, Sammy picked up Rourke's jacket, reaching out to pet Nysa before he turned to leave.

Lor grabbed his arm. "Go straight to the barracks, find out what's going on, and come straight back."

Sammy nodded. "Don't worry, I don't want to fight as much as the next person." Lor nodded and let go of his arm. Sammy pulled on Rourke's jacket, buttoning it up to help keep out the rain. "But I will if I have to."

"Sammy, please be safe!" Alina reached for him for a hug, and Sammy gave her one before he pulled away.

"I will, don't worry. I won't be gone long." Turning, Sammy opened the front door and stepped out onto the porch. The sky was dark, darker than he thought it was when they had gone inside. The rain was still pouring down, drowning out all other sound. Overhead lightning flashed and thunder boomed in answer, vibrating the very air. From where he stood on the porch, Sammy could barely see the edge of the wall of the Sanctuary, let alone the rest of the city, or the crater beyond, and he hoped Rourke was okay. Nodding sharply to himself, Sammy pulled Rourke's jacket collar a bit tighter to his neck and stepped into the rain.

The walk back toward the barracks was quiet, even less people were out than before, and a chill now hung in the air. Sammy could feel it in his fingers and the end of his nose. He was just rounding the corner to the main street, and was able to see the main archway with the banners being whipped about by the wind, when someone called his name. Turning toward the sound, Sammy was surprised to see Lysha running toward him from the bridge, her bare feet splashing in the puddles. "Sammy, come with me!"

"Lysha, what's wrong?" Sammy could see the panic in her eyes. Lysha was always calm and collected, even if she was a bit crazy, but there was pure fear he saw in her eyes.

"The bridge," she started. "We must go to the bridge."

"I was going to the barracks to find out what was going on."

"Go to the bridge and you will know." Lysha pointed, the raindrops splattering off her bare skin. She grabbed him by the arm and pulled. Sammy could sense the urgency in her voice, and followed along, not that he had much of a choice since she refused to let go of his arm.

"Lysha, what's going on," Sammy asked as they crossed under the archway and onto the bridge. She let go of his arm and pointed toward the lip of the crater where the darkness met the light of the city, and Sammy turned to look. Pouring over the edge and into the light was a thick fog. Over the pounding of the rain, Sammy could hear what he thought were the howls of Wolves. He felt fear twist in his gut as he turned back to Lysha, but she was looking straight ahead. "Lysha," he started. "What happened when the cities fell? When Olin fell?"

"From what I have been told," she started slowly, and Sammy strained to hear her over the rain. With each breath they took, the fog grew closer, silently gliding through the grass and over the ground like a quiet river. Sammy had never felt so afraid of something that seemed so harmless. "The rains brought the Mistwalkers, and then the Wolves attacked."

As if the Wolves had heard Lysha, one howled, the low sound much closer than it had been before. Sammy thought he saw something move on the lip of the crater, teetering on whether to step out of the darkness or not, and raised his hand to shield his eyes from the driving rain. A chorus of howls answered the first Wolf.

"If the Wolves are here, then Rourke —" Sammy felt sick. If the Wolves were at the edge of the crater, then they must have met up with the Illuminari in the woods. "If the Wolves," he started, but trailed off, unable to finish the thought out loud. If the Wolves were here at Bhaskara, then it was possible that Rourke was dead.

Sammy felt his body move before he was even aware of what he was doing. He heard Lysha call his name and didn't even realize other people were on the bridge until two men from the barracks grabbed him and stopped him. He tried to push against them, but between the slick stones of the bridge and Sammy's own slight weight, they were easily overpowering him. "Let me go," Sammy growled, trying to grab a hold of one of them.

"You can't go, Sammy," one of them said.

"We have committeds out there, too," the second reminded him.

Sammy knew them both, but right now their names escaped him as he struggled to get out of their grasp. He needed to get to the darkness. He needed to know that Rourke was alive. "Let me go," he started, but he felt all the fight leave him as his knees gave out, and he sagged against one of the men. "Rourke's out there."

"We know." Lysha placed a hand on Sammy's back, and he looked over his shoulder to her as he tried to find his footing again. Lightning flashed and thunder shook the air when it rumbled overhead. Wolf howls filled the silence that followed as the fog began to creep over the water and across the bridge toward where they were standing. "But right now, you are needed here."

Standing, Sammy watched the fog slip quietly past them and enter the city. There was nothing they could do to stop it, and Sammy turned back toward the city to watch it spread deeper as it covered the streets. "What do we do?"

Behind him, one of the two men drew his sword. "We fight." Sammy turned back toward the darkness at the sound of resolve in his voice. Pouring over the edge of the crater into the fields were more Wolves than Sammy had ever seen before; too many to count. From within the city, someone screamed, and smoke began to curl into the sky.

Sammy drew his knife and squared his stance between the others as he waited for the Wolves to approach. Around him other people from the barracks began to arrive, as well as random citizens from the city. Everyone was clearly scared and nervous. Sammy could only concentrate on one thing, though.

The one thing that he had never dared to think about before.

Bhaskara was under attack.